PATRICIA WENTWORTH
FOOL ERRANT

PATRICIA WENTWORTH was born Dora Amy Elles in India in 1877 (not 1878 as has sometimes been stated). She was first educated privately in India, and later at Blackheath School for Girls. Her first husband was George Dillon, with whom she had her only child, a daughter. She also had two stepsons from her first marriage, one of whom died in the Somme during World War I.

Her first novel was published in 1910, but it wasn't until the 1920's that she embarked on her long career as a writer of mysteries. Her most famous creation was Miss Maud Silver, who appeared in 32 novels, though there were a further 33 full-length mysteries not featuring Miss Silver—the entire run of these is now reissued by Dean Street Press.

Patricia Wentworth died in 1961. She is recognized today as one of the pre-eminent exponents of the classic British golden age mystery novel.

By Patricia Wentworth

PATRICIA WENTWORTH

FOOL ERRANT

With an introduction by
Curtis Evans

DEAN STREET PRESS

Introduction

BRITISH AUTHOR Patricia Wentworth published her first novel, a gripping tale of desperate love during the French Revolution entitled *A Marriage under the Terror*, a little over a century ago, in 1910. The book won first prize in the Melrose Novel Competition and was a popular success in both the United States and the United Kingdom. Over the next five years Wentworth published five additional novels, the majority of them historical fiction, the best-known of which today is *The Devil's Wind* (1912), another sweeping period romance, this one set during the Sepoy Mutiny (1857-58) in India, a region with which the author, as we shall see, had extensive familiarity. Like *A Marriage under the Terror*, *The Devil's Wind* received much praise from reviewers for its sheer storytelling élan. One notice, for example, pronounced the novel "an achievement of some magnitude" on account of "the extraordinary vividness...the reality of the atmosphere...the scenes that shift and move with the swiftness of a moving picture...." (*The Bookman*, August 1912) With her knack for spinning a yarn, it perhaps should come as no surprise that Patricia Wentworth during the early years of the Golden Age of mystery fiction (roughly from 1920 into the 1940s) launched upon her own mystery-writing career, a course charted most successfully for nearly four decades by the prolific author, right up to the year of her death in 1961.

Considering that Patricia Wentworth belongs to the select company of Golden Age mystery writers with books which have remained in print in every decade for nearly a century now (the centenary of Agatha Christie's first mystery, *The Mysterious Affair at Styles*, is in 2020; the centenary of Wentworth's first mystery, *The Astonishing Adventure of Jane Smith*, follows merely three years later, in 2023), relatively little is known about the author herself. It appears, for example, that even the widely given year of Wentworth's birth, 1878, is incorrect. Yet it is sufficiently clear that Wentworth lived a varied and intriguing life that provided her ample inspiration for a writing career devoted to imaginative fiction.

It is usually stated that Patricia Wentworth was born Dora Amy Elles on 10 November 1878 in Mussoorie, India, during the heyday of the British Raj; however, her Indian birth and baptismal record states that she in fact was born on 15 October 1877 and was baptized on 26 November of that same year in Gwalior. Whatever doubts surround her actual birth year, however, unquestionably the future author came from a prominent Anglo-Indian military family. Her father, Edmond Roche Elles, a son of Malcolm Jamieson Elles, a Porto, Portugal wine merchant originally from Ardrossan, Scotland, entered the British Royal Artillery in 1867, a decade before Wentworth's birth, and first saw service in India during the Lushai Expedition of 1871-72. The next year Elles in India wed Clara Gertrude Rothney, daughter of Brigadier-General Octavius Edward Rothney, commander of the Gwalior District, and Maria (Dempster) Rothney, daughter of a surgeon in the Bengal Medical Service. Four children were born of the union of Edmond and Clara Elles, Wentworth being the only daughter.

Before his retirement from the army in 1908, Edmond Elles rose to the rank of lieutenant-general and was awarded the KCB (Knight Commander of the Order of Bath), as was the case with his elder brother, Wentworth's uncle, Lieutenant-General Sir William Kidston Elles, of the Bengal Command. Edmond Elles also served as Military Member to the Council of the Governor-General of India from 1901 to 1905. Two of Wentworth's brothers, Malcolm Rothney Elles and Edmond Claude Elles, served in the Indian Army as well, though both of them died young (Malcolm in 1906 drowned in the Ganges Canal while attempting to rescue his orderly, who had fallen into the water), while her youngest brother, Hugh Jamieson Elles, achieved great distinction in the British Army. During the First World War he catapulted, at the relatively youthful age of 37, to the rank of brigadier-general and the command of the British Tank Corps, at the Battle of Cambrai personally leading the advance of more than 350 tanks against the German line. Years later Hugh Elles also played a major role in British civil defense during the Second World War. In the event of a German invasion of Great Britain, something which seemed all too possible in 1940, he was tasked with leading the defense of southwestern England. Like Sir Edmond and Sir William, Hugh Elles attained the rank of lieutenant-general and was awarded the KCB.

Although she was born in India, Patricia Wentworth spent much of her childhood in England. In 1881 she with her mother and two younger brothers was at Tunbridge Wells, Kent, on what appears to have been a rather extended visit in her ancestral country; while a decade later the same family group resided at Blackheath, London at Lennox House, domicile of Wentworth's widowed maternal grandmother, Maria Rothney. (Her eldest brother, Malcolm, was in Bristol attending Clifton College.) During her years at Lennox House, Wentworth attended Blackheath High School for Girls, then only recently founded as "one of the first schools in the country to give girls a proper education" (*The London Encyclopaedia*, 3rd ed., p. 74). Lennox House was an ample Victorian villa with a great glassed-in conservatory running all along the back and a substantial garden--most happily, one presumes, for Wentworth, who resided there not only with her grandmother, mother and two brothers, but also five aunts (Maria Rothney's unmarried daughters, aged 26 to 42), one adult first cousin once removed and nine first cousins, adolescents like Wentworth herself, from no less than three different families (one Barrow, three Masons and five Dempsters); their parents, like Wentworth's father, presumably were living many miles away in various far-flung British dominions. Three servants--a cook, parlourmaid and housemaid--were tasked with serving this full score of individuals.

Sometime after graduating from Blackheath High School in the mid-1890s, Wentworth returned to India, where in a local British newspaper she is said to have published her first fiction. In 1901 the 23-year-old Wentworth married widower George Fredrick Horace Dillon, a 41-year-old lieutenant-colonel in the Indian Army with three sons from his prior marriage. Two years later Wentworth gave birth to her only child, a daughter named Clare Roche Dillon. (In some sources it is erroneously stated that Clare was the offspring of Wentworth's second marriage.) However in 1906, after just five years of marriage, George Dillon died suddenly on a sea voyage, leaving Wentworth with sole responsibly for her three teenaged stepsons and baby daughter. A very short span of years, 1904 to 1907, saw the deaths of Wentworth's husband, mother, grandmother and brothers Malcolm and Edmond, removing much of her support network. In 1908, however, her father, who was now sixty years old, retired from the army and returned to England, settling at Guildford, Surrey with an older unmarried sister named Dora (for whom his daughter presumably had been named). Wentworth joined this household as well, along with her daughter and her youngest stepson. Here in Surrey Wentworth, presumably with the goal of making herself financially independent for the first time in her life (she was now in her early thirties), wrote the novel that changed the course of her life, *A Marriage under the Terror*, for the first time we know of utilizing her famous *nom de plume*.

The burst of creative energy that resulted in Wentworth's publication of six novels in six years suddenly halted after the appearance of *Queen Anne Is Dead* in 1915. It seems not unlikely that the Great War impinged in various ways on her writing. One tragic episode was the death on the western front of one of her stepsons, George Charles Tracey Dillon. Mining in Colorado when war was declared, young Dillon worked his passage from Galveston, Texas to Bristol, England as a shipboard muleteer (mule-tender) and joined the Gloucestershire Regiment. In 1916 he died at the Somme at the age of 29 (about the age of Wentworth's two brothers when they had passed away in India).

A couple of years after the conflict's cessation in 1918, a happy event occurred in Wentworth's life when at Frimley, Surrey she wed George Oliver Turnbull, up to this time a lifelong bachelor who like the author's first husband was a lieutenant-colonel in the Indian Army. Like his bride now forty-two years old, George Turnbull as a younger man had distinguished himself for his athletic prowess, playing forward for eight years for the Scottish rugby team and while a student at the Royal Military Academy winning the medal awarded the best athlete of his term. It seems not unlikely that Turnbull played a role in his wife's turn toward writing mystery fiction, for he is said to have strongly supported Wentworth's career, even assisting her in preparing manuscripts for publication. In 1936 the couple in Camberley, Surrey built Heatherglade House, a large two-story structure on substantial grounds, where they resided until Wentworth's death a quarter of a century later. (George Turnbull survived his wife by nearly a decade, passing away in 1970 at the age of 92.) This highly successful middle-aged companionate marriage contrasts sharply with the more youthful yet rocky union of Agatha and Archie Christie, which was three years away from sundering when Wentworth published *The Astonishing Adventure of Jane Smith* (1923), the first of her sixty-five mystery novels.

Although Patricia Wentworth became best-known for her cozy tales of the criminal investigations of consulting detective Miss Maud Silver, one of the mystery genre's most prominent spinster sleuths, in truth the Miss Silver tales account for just under half of Wentworth's 65 mystery novels. Miss Silver did not make her debut until 1928 and she did not come to predominate in Wentworth's fictional criminous output until the 1940s. Between 1923 and 1945 Wentworth published 33 mystery novels without Miss Silver, a handsome and substantial legacy in and of itself to vintage crime fiction fans. Many of these books are standalone tales of mystery, but nine of them have series characters. Debuting in the novel *Fool Errant* in 1929, a year after Miss Silver first appeared in print, was the enigmatic, nautically-named *eminence grise* Benbow Collingwood Horatio Smith, owner of a most expressively opinionated parrot named Ananias (and quite a colorful character in his own right). Benbow Smith went on to appear in three additional Wentworth mysteries: *Danger Calling* (1931), *Walk with Care* (1933) and *Down Under* (1937). Working in tandem with Smith in the investigation of sinister affairs threatening the security of Great Britain in *Danger Calling* and *Walk with Care* is Frank Garrett, Head of Intelligence for the Foreign Office, who also appears solo in *Dead or Alive* (1936) and *Rolling Stone* (1940) and collaborates with additional series characters, Scotland Yard's Inspector Ernest Lamb and Sergeant Frank Abbott, in *Pursuit of a Parcel* (1942). Inspector Lamb and Sergeant Abbott headlined a further pair of mysteries, *The Blind Side* (1939) and *Who Pays the Piper?* (1940), before they became absorbed, beginning with *Miss Silver Deals with Death* (1943), into the burgeoning Miss Silver canon. Lamb would make his farewell appearance in 1955 in *The Listening Eye*, while Abbott would take his final bow in mystery fiction with Wentworth's last published novel, *The Girl in the Cellar* (1961), which went into print the year of the author's death at the age of 83.

The remaining two dozen Wentworth mysteries, from the fantastical *The Astonishing Adventure of Jane Smith* in 1923 to the intense legal drama *Silence in Court* in 1945, are, like the author's series novels, highly imaginative and entertaining tales of mystery and adventure, told by a writer gifted with a consummate flair for storytelling. As one confirmed Patricia Wentworth mystery fiction addict, American Golden Age mystery writer Todd Downing, admiringly declared in the 1930s, "There's something about Miss Wentworth's yarns that is contagious." This attractive new series of Patricia Wentworth reissues by Dean Street Press provides modern fans of vintage mystery a splendid opportunity to catch the Wentworth fever.

Curtis Evans

Chapter One

THE LANE WAS very dark; it was difficult to see where the tall hedgerow ended and the heavily clouded sky began. It was six hours since the sun had set, and during those six hours the darkness had deepened steadily until the cold, heavy air was saturated with gloom. An hour ago it had begun to freeze.

Hugo Ross stood for a moment by the Meade House entrance gates. The white posts just showed; the dark gate was invisible. Hugo leaned on it, staring into the impenetrable blackness of the drive. The trees on either side were moving a little, though he could feel no wind. The stripped branches and bare twigs that over-arched the drive were moving. They made small restless sounds hardly to be heard, sounds that would not have been heard at all if there had been anything else to hear.

Hugo turned from the gate and walked a little farther along the lane. The hedge on his left skirted the grounds of Meade House, and suddenly out of the darkness there sprang to view one lighted window—just one, high up in the black wall of the house. The window looked at Hugo with a square, bright eye; and then down came a blind like the dropping of a lid.

He walked another hundred yards, and then turned back again. It was rather odd to think that perhaps he was going to live in the house that had looked at him for a moment with that yellow staring eye. He wondered what the house was like. He could see it only as a black, blank wall running up into a black, blank sky. It had no substance nor content; it was just length and breadth, and a yellow staring eye. It reminded him of something that he couldn't quite get hold of—something in a dream. He passed the gate with a glance over his shoulder and a faint thrill of the old "let's pretend" feeling that had made the nursery a place of high adventure to Susan and himself.

He began to feel sure that he would get the job. Up to this moment he had been almost sure that he would not get it. Manning had said, "Why not have a shot at it?" But even Manning—very good fellow Manning—had certainly not been hopeful.

"Of course, my dear chap, you can but try. He'd be a jolly good man to get in with. And of course, as I say, if you can get in before the crowd who are sure to answer his advertisement—you see what I mean. Hacker told me about the advertisement, and I thought I'd give you the tip. It comes out first thing in the morning, and if you're on the spot before anyone else, it might give you a bit of a pull, though of course, as I said, he may want someone..." He proceeded to enumerate the qualifications which Ambrose Minstrel might reasonably require in a secretary.

Hugo possessed none of them. He had no degree. He knew nothing about mechanics, engineering, electricity, or chemistry. He supposed vaguely that an eminent inventor like Minstrel might require such knowledge in a secretary. Manning seemed sure of it.

"Still, I should have a stab at it, you know."

Hugo was having a stab at it; and quite suddenly and irrationally he began to feel that the job was his. To-morrow at nine-thirty—he had fixed on nine-thirty as the earliest hour at which he could decently present himself—well, at nine-thirty he would pass between the white gate-posts, walk briskly up the drive under those over-arching trees, and in the house that he had not seen, he would presently find himself Ambrose Minstrel's secretary. He had not the slightest idea how this was going to happen; he had stopped bothering about it.

He turned his mind to the question of how to spend the next eleven hours. There is a lot of time in eleven hours, especially at night. He thought hopefully of haystacks. The proverbial needle in a bundle of hay would be easier to find than half a dozen haystacks in a pitch black field. It made him wild to think that there might be a perfectly good dry, warm haystack within a stone's throw of him at this very moment. It tickled him to think of feeling for haystacks in unknown and frozen fields; it didn't somehow seem rational. Like a great many people of strong and keen imagination, Hugo prided himself on being rational. He decided not to feel for haystacks but to go on walking.

It was growing steadily colder. The fog, which had been rising from the fields ever since the frost set in, had topped the hedges and came drifting down between them like the flow of some sluggish, impalpable stream.

Hugo turned back towards Meade House and began to run. The lane was quite straight here for three or four hundred yards, rising slightly and then sloping until it reached the gate. He ran up the rise and down the slope—and half-way down the slope he ran into the girl. It was very startling, because, somehow, it had never occurred to him that there might be anyone else afoot—the lane was his; and then not his, because he bumped heavily into someone and heard the girl's faint scream. It was his shoulder that struck her, and she screamed just once, with a faint breathless sound; it was as if she had begun to scream and then her breath had failed.

Hugo swung round, groped, touched a shoulder, and said,

"I'm frightfully sorry! Did I hurt you? I'm most *frightfully* sorry!"

She had sprung away when he touched her. He could hear her breathing quickly with a little sobbing catch between the breaths.

He spoke again:

"I say, I'm afraid I did hurt you. Is there anything I can do?"

The answer was the most unexpected thing. She laughed, a long, pretty, shaken ripple of a laugh.

"No—it's all right."

"Are you sure? I was running to keep myself warm. It was most awfully careless of me to go barging along like that."

"I'm not hurt. I was frightened—I thought you were a tramp."

She had a very pretty voice, rather high, very young, clear, and unmodulated like a child's voice. She went on:

"There was a tramp. I thought he had come back." The clear voice shook.

"Oh, I s-say—I must have frightened you dreadfully!"

Hugo's shyness and the little stammer which accompanied it were returning. They had been, as it were, knocked clean out of him when he bumped into the girl.

She came a step nearer.

"You didn't frighten me—it was the tramp. I wasn't frightened as soon as I heard your voice. The tramp had a horrid one—you know—*beery*." Her voice shook again on the unromantic word.

Hugo wanted to laugh, and felt like a tongue-tied fool. He began, "I'm s-so sorry," and was interrupted.

"You haven't seen him, have you? He went this way. I hid, and he went along here. That's why I thought you were him."

"I haven't s-seen anyone."

She came quite close.

"It's too dark to see anyone. He might be there." It was a very small whisper.

Hugo was not wanting in perception. He said, stammering very badly,

"Sh-shall I—w-would you—I m-mean—I—c-can't I do anything?"

A hand slipped into his arm. "Would you—walk a little way—with me? Would you really?"

"Of course."

"You were going the other way."

"I wasn't going anywhere really—I was just putting in t-time."

There was a little irrepressible laugh.

"So was I. How funny! Oh, do you know what the time is—because I'm most dreadfully afraid I shall miss my train."

Hugo turned up his wrist. The luminous dial showed like a faint moon.

"It's half-past ten."

"Then I shall catch it." She began to walk, keeping her hand on his arm. "I got so frightfully cold waiting. And I thought I should miss the train, and I thought about the tramp, and—don't you think when you're simply dreadfully frightened of doing something, it's better to do it?"

"S-sometimes," said Hugo.

"Not sometimes—*always*, or else you just get so frightened that you can't do anything—you can't even run away." The words came tumbling out. And then, with a sudden return of breathlessness, she demanded, "Do you live here?"

"No."

She pulled away her hand.

"Do you live near here?"

"No."

"Because I don't want you to tell anyone you've seen me."

Hugo gave his funny little laugh.

"But I haven't."

His arm was caught again.

"No, you haven't—you haven't seen anyone, because—you're sure you don't live here?"

"I s-swear it."

"Do you know people here?"

"No, I don't—really."

"Not anyone?"

"Not a soul."

"I'm running away. That's why I asked. You won't tell anyone—will you?"

Hugo stopped feeling shy. One might as well feel shy of a bird or a rabbit, or any other young, natural creature. He said quite seriously,

"I say, is that a good plan?"

"What?"

"Running away. Don't you think you'd better go home again?"

He stood still as he spoke. But she tugged at his arm.

"No—no. Oh, I'll miss my train! Do come on!"

Hugo began to feel rather middle-aged.

"Look here, what's the good of running away? Much better go home—they'll be in an awful state about you."

"Let them! I'm not going back." She laughed. "If I wouldn't go back for the beery tramp, d'you suppose I'll go back for you? Besides—Oh, anyhow, I'm not going back. You won't tell—will you?"

"I don't know," said Hugo.

"Oh! You *promised!*"

"Why are you running away?"

She laughed.

"I haven't murdered anyone or stolen anything, and nobody's going to break their hearts—they'll be all fussed up and shocked, but they won't worry, because I've got heaps of money and I know quite well how to look after myself, and I've told them I'm going to a job."

"L-look here," said Hugo.

"I won't go back."

"All right—don't. Only don't go telling strangers how much money you've got."

"I don't."

"You told me."

"Oh—*you!*"

Hugo burst out laughing.

"You needn't laugh! I can take care of myself. Why are you laughing? I *did* only tell you."

"And I—how many years have you known me?"

Something curious happened—silence; darkness; and a queer electric thrill. A whispering voice broke the silence. It spoke in the darkness quite close to him, and it said,

"I—don't—know."

Hugo went on trying to feel middle-aged, and become very much aware that he was only twenty-six and that for the first time in his life he was speaking to a girl without feeling shy. Susan, of course, didn't count.

They walked on.

She was quite right—you couldn't reckon by time.

She said, with a quick note of indignation, "Of *course* I told you."

"I see."

"You won't tell—will you?"

"Why did you run away?"

"Oh—because—"

She was walking about a yard away from him. Every now and then she turned in his direction—he could tell that by the sound of her voice. Her movements were all quick; her step was quick and springy; when she held his arm, her hand moved, quivered, and was alive. The yard of darkness between them was full of little live, warm, dancing things. Her voice was full of them too.

"I just *had* to run away. You know, she's only my cousin. She *says* it's second cousin three times removed, and you can't really count that sort of relation—can you?"

Hugo had not the faintest idea who *she* might be. He said so.

"Her name's Brown—Emily Brown. Isn't that frightful? And she's almost the only relation I've got. And her husband is a solicitor, and they're both most frightfully respectable and worthy, and managing and kind in a feather-bedy sort of way. If I'd stayed, they'd have smothered me into a sort of swoon, and I'd have waked up to find I'd married James."

"Who is James?"

"Another feather bed, just like them. They love him—he's Andrew's cousin. He used to come and play bridge every night and sing *Onaway, awake beloved!* and *Somewhere a voice is calling.* I suppose you think I ought to have married him?" The question came swiftly, lightly, eagerly.

There seemed to be nothing between marrying James and running away. All the cousins in the world cannot drag a girl to the altar.

"They couldn't have made you," said Hugo.

She laughed.

"They could have. But they can't now!" There was an excited triumph in the words. "What's the good of saying they couldn't make me? If you live on ditchwater and dullness, with feather beds all round you, and someone saying 'Oh!' in a shocked voice every time you want to do anything at all, and James asking you to marry him about seven times a week and twice on Sundays, and cold beef and pickles every day for lunch because Andrew likes them—and Emily would *murder* anyone if it would please Andrew—well, you wouldn't talk nonsense about their not being able to make you. I believe Emily said 'Oh!' at me a thousand times every day. And I used to wake up at night dreaming I was being married to James— you know, the perfectly awful sort of dream where everybody else talks and you can't say a word. And when the parson said, 'Speak now, or else forever hereafter hold your peace,' I couldn't. And the next thing I knew, he was saying, 'I pronounce you man and wife'— only just then I woke up. It was so frightful that I wrote straight off to Cissie and said I'd run away. Oh, look here, this is where I left my bag. I must just see if it's safe."

She made a dart into the hedge, then came running back.

"It's all right. The station's just round the corner. And I don't want to go there till the very last minute, till the train's in, because, you see, Emily will think I've gone to Ledlington—she'll never, never dream of me walking seven miles across the fields. You see, trains stop here because of Mr. Minstrel at Meade House. I don't want anyone to see me and tell Emily. We'll walk up and down till we see the train coming, and then just make a dash."

They had reached the corner; the lights of the tiny station showed below them at the foot of a sharp slope. The girl put a hand on his arm and pulled Hugo round.

He said, "Who is Cissie?" and did not stammer over the name.

"She was a girl I knew when I lived with old cousin Catherine— she went to London. And I wrote and told her about James, and she said, had I any money? And when I said I'd got lots, she said come along and she'd find me a job."

"How much money have you got?" said Hugh.

"Twenty pounds."

"Did you tell her how much you'd got?"

"No, I didn't."

"Who is she? What does she do?"

"I don't know. Cousin Catherine didn't like me to know her—but she was a very disapproving sort of person. I think Cissie was on the stage, or danced, or something like that. I should *love* to dance."

Hugo began to feel appalled. Twenty pounds—I told her I had lots of money—Cousin Catherine didn't like me to know her—

"I say, you know—"

"I can dance a little," the eager voice went on. "Of course I don't know if Cissie *is* dancing. I really knew her awfully little—only just for a fortnight last winter when Cousin Catherine and I were at Brighton. I got to know her because she dropped her bag and I picked it up, and she told me then she could get me a job if I ever wanted one. And she gave me an address to write to, so when I got desperate about being pronounced man and wife with James— *James*, I wrote."

"I say, you know, twenty pounds isn't such a lot of money."

"Oh it *is*—for me—it's a tremendous lot. Cousin Catherine gave it to me out of her silver teapot the night before she died. Emily got everything else because she was a niece and I was only an umpteenth cousin. Emily got the teapot. But I didn't mind about that, because it was a frightfully ugly one. I didn't tell her about the twenty pounds, and I didn't tell Cissie how much it was. So you see I don't tell everything, though you think I do."

"Why do you tell me?"

They turned and began to walk back towards the station.

"I don't know. It doesn't matter, does it? You don't mind?"

"No, I don't mind. But—"

"I don't even know your name, and you don't know mine. And if you met me to-morrow, you'd never, never know who I was. And perhaps some day you'll see me dance, and you'll never know that you nearly knocked me down in a dark lane and carried my bag and were very, very kind."

It was frightfully embarrassing; the whole situation was frightfully embarrassing.

"L-look here—"

"I've taken you frightfully out of your way. You needn't come any farther—there won't be any tramps now. I'll go close up to the station and wait. And you can go to wherever you're staying. They'll think you're lost."

"I'm not staying anywhere."

"You must be."

"I'm not. I've come down to look for a job. I came down to-night because I wanted to get in before anyone else to-morrow morning; but I had my pocket picked in the train, so I haven't any money till I get back to town."

He would not have any then, but this was a fact which he did not feel bound to explain. The lost pocket-book had contained his last fiver.

"They left my return ticket," he concluded cheerfully.

"Oh, I *hope* you'll get your job."

"So do I."

"What is it?"

"Secretary to an inventor."

He heard a little startled gasp:

"Not Ambrose Minstrel! Oh—you mustn't!"

"I say—"

"You mustn't! Oh, what shall I do? There's my train—I can't miss it! Quick—my bag!"

She was off. He heard the bag bump on the road; his hand, groping for it, met hers, bare like his own. He caught at the bag, and they began to run.

The train was coming into view along a raised embankment; the lighted windows seemed high up and very far away. A cloud of orange rosy smoke was blown backwards from the engine; it hung above the dead whiteness of the low fog.

"Run!" said the girl.

She took his left hand, and they raced down the hill. They reached the station whilst the train was still some hundreds of yards away.

"Get my ticket! Oh, I'm so glad I thought of that! Here's a pound—get it quickly!"

When he came back to her with the ticket, the train was in the station. Two men got out.

The girl took her ticket and the change, snatched up her bag, and ran across the platform. Hugo followed. The door slammed on her. The train began to move. She leaned out.

He felt an overwhelming desire to see her face. But she was only a slim black silhouette against the carriage lamp; it shone behind her head like a yellow aureole. She leaned out.

"Don't go there—you *mustn't* go there!"

"Why not?"

He walked beside the train, walked faster, began to run.

"I heard—there's no time—what's your name?"

He was being left behind. The engine snorted, and a great puff of steam came drifting back.

"Hugo Ross."

He seemed to be shouting it, but the wind took the words away. He heard her voice very faintly:

"You *mustn't*."

The steam hid her. The train went on.

Hugo turned and walked out of the station into the darkness. How astonishing! How extraordinary and astonishing! What on earth did she mean?

He walked to the corner from which they had seen the train. Its row of lighted windows had for a moment lighted up the sloping field from which the embankment rose. Six foot of fog and two black humps rising out of it—barns or haystacks. He thought he would go and prospect.

They were haystacks. Coldish comfort, but better than walking about all night. He sat down in the warmest spot he could find, leaned his back against the hay, and fumbled in an inside pocket.

There came out the two halves of a flute, his pride and his despair, practised by stealth, often abandoned, and as often resumed. The secret passion which drove him to make music was outraged by his lack of skill. Yesterday's exercise had been a teaser. He determined to get the better of it. For half an hour slow, melancholy notes followed one another into the fog.

At the end of half an hour he stopped playing the exercise and began to copy the high clear notes of a girl's laugh.

Chapter Two

AT HALF-PAST NINE next morning Hugo walked between the white gate-posts of Meade House and up the drive beneath the over-arching trees. The grounds were large and untidy. The house, when he came to it, was just such a house as he expected—square, flat, slate-roofed, and hung with leafless creepers. There were no curtains showing at the windows, and discoloured blinds hung unevenly, some up, some down, and one at least askew.

Oddly enough, Hugo's spirits rose. He was feeling quite horribly conscious of being unshaved, and it was a relief to find that the house did not set an exacting standard. As a matter of fact, no one would have suspected him of a night in a haystack. To their last thread Hugo's clothes would keep their shape and look neat, whilst his fair hair and fresh complexion gave him the air of having just emerged from a cold bath. His daily shave was a rite, not a necessity.

He rang the bell, and heard it clang far away in the recesses of the house. It had a hoarse, deep sound like a cracked gong.

Almost at once a middle-aged woman opened the door. She had a smudged face and a dirty apron. She carried a pail of water which slopped over on the step and wetted Hugo's shoe. He moved his foot and said politely,

"I've come to see Mr. Minstrel."

The woman set down the pail of water and left him standing at the open door. A minute passed—two minutes—quite a number of minutes. Hugo thought how cold the house must be getting. On any other morning his courage would have been cooling too. If he had been paying a call, now, and they had left him like this at an open door, he would probably have wanted to run away, and he would probably have stammered dreadfully when he began to speak. On this morning, unshaven and breakfastless, he had a feeling of assurance which was delightfully new and very supporting. He could have whistled; he could have played the flute openly and without a blush.

A door opened upstairs. Someone came running down into the hall—a man, large, young, with a blue chin, thick eyebrows, and a black moustache clipped short. He said, "Hullo!" in a tone of surprise; and Hugo said,

"I've come to see Mr. Minstrel."

The dark young man stared. He had eyes rather like bull's-eyes without the stripes; the comparison just passed through Hugo's mind.

"By appointment?"

"I'm applying for the post of secretary."

The dark young man laughed rather noisily.

"That's quick work! Did you come by wire? The advertisement's hardly out. All right, first come, first served. My name's Hacker. I'm Minstrel's assistant, and I shall be damn glad when he gets a secretary, because I've had all the correspondence on my hands since Mayhew left. Come along!"

He led the way to the back of the hall and threw open a door on the right.

Hugo came into a large, littered room with a faded carpet on the floor and ugly green curtains drawn rigidly back from a window which looked upon a straggle of leafless rose bushes. The walls were lined with bookshelves. There were two writing-tables and a cabinet gramophone.

"Sit down," said Mr. Hacker.

He went across to a door on the far side of the room, knocked on it, and waited. After a moment the door was opened and he went in, shutting it after him.

Hugo went and looked out of the window.

The room into which Mr. Hacker had disappeared was evidently a recent addition to the house; it could be seen from the window, a tall, long, featureless block set down on the remains of a rose garden. It was built of a hideous yellow brick and roofed with purplish slate—an offence to the eye. A skylight ran the whole length of it. Upon this side, at least, there were no windows.

Hugo turned at the sound of the opening door. Ambrose Minstrel was coming into the room—a tall, thin man with a stoop, and grey untidy hair and a grey untidy beard. He spoke over his shoulder to Hacker:

"Where is he? You shouldn't have left him."

"He's here." Mr. Hacker sounded quite meek.

Ambrose Minstrel turned, saw Hugo, swept him with a restless glance, and flung impatiently into an old leather-covered armchair. His eyes, under their bushy brows, came back to Hugo, and again shifted.

Mr. Hacker sat down at the nearest table.

Curiously enough, Hugo did not feel embarrassed. He was interested, stimulated, alert. He felt not the slightest inclination to stammer. It was immensely thrilling to meet Ambrose Minstrel—one didn't expect him to be like other people. He gazed with deep respect at the bulging brow, the hot restless eyes, the long nervous fingers, stained brown and yellow, scarred with the marks of epoch-making experiments. He felt very young and untried, and eager, and confident.

Ambrose Minstrel tugged at his ragged beard.

"You've come about the secretaryship?"

"Yes, sir."

He hadn't stammered at all; the 's,' his special enemy, had been surmounted without effort.

"Your name?"

The questions were being jerked at him in a dry, uneven voice. Hacker appeared to be taking down the answers.

"Hugo Ross."

"Age?"

"Twenty-six, sir."

Delightful—he hadn't stammered in the least. Why had he ever stammered? If one could say a thing like that, one could say anything; it was as easy as falling out of bed.

"Experience?"

That was rather a nasty snag, because of course he hadn't any experience to speak of. He flushed a little as he said,

"I used to do all my uncle's correspondence."

"Uncle? What uncle?"

Of course he oughtn't to have mentioned his uncle just like that. His cheeks had begun to burn.

"I lived with him, sir. He had a place in Devonshire."

"And you did the correspondence? And that's your experience?" The great man's tone was definitely sarcastic.

Hugo's ears burned as well as his cheeks; but he went on looking straight at Ambrose Minstrel. His eyes were a very bright blue.

Ambrose Minstrel laughed.

"Got that down, Hacker? Now where were you at school? And what have you been doing since you left school? Were you at the 'Varsity?"

Mr. Hacker wrote down the answers.

"You've been living with your uncle ever since you came down. What did you say his name was? Ross?"

"Trevelyan, sir. He was my mother's brother."

"*Was?*"

"He died three months ago."

"And left you the place?" Again the tone was sarcastic.

"No, sir."

"Cut you off with a shilling? Why?" The last word had a real stand-and-deliver sound.

Hugo did not look away.

"My uncle never made the will he meant to. I know he meant to do it, because when I went to live with him he told me so. I was meant for the Indian Civil, but he asked me to give it up and get into the ways of the place. I was practically agent the last three years. He meant to leave me everything. But the will couldn't be found— perhaps he never made it—and everything went, under an old will, to a distant cousin."

"Very interesting," said Minstrel.

There was a pause. Hugo felt himself cooling to the point of antagonism. If he had not had his pocket picked, he would have been tempted to say good-morning and walk out. He saw Hacker turn slightly. He could not see his face.

Minstrel looked round and said irritably,

"All right, all right! I wish to Heaven you'd attend to your job, Hacker! I tell you I won't be dictated to. I tell you I'll do things my own way or not at all. Am I engaging a secretary, or are you?"

Hacker turned back with a shrug of the shoulders. Hugo caught a glimpse of his side face—black eyebrow raised, exasperation plainly stamped.

Minstrel pulled his beard and went on interviewing Hugo after his own peculiar fashion.

"What relations have you?"

"Only a sister, sir. She's married to a man in India."

"Army?"

"Indian Army."

"Name?"

"Smith—John Warrington Smith."

"Rank?"

"Captain."

"No other relations?"

"Only distant cousins. I don't know any of them."

Minstrel nodded. The answer appeared to please him.

"You're not married?"

"No, sir."

"Engaged—entangled? You wouldn't tell me if you were, I suppose. I can't have my affairs talked about. D'you see? I don't want a secretary who's going to go home for week-ends and talk—or to go anywhere and talk. My affairs aren't to be talked about—my work isn't to be talked about. What d'you know about it already?" He shot this at Hugo with a sudden violence.

"Only what everyone knows."

"How discreet!" The violence slid into a sneer. "Well, what does everybody know?"

"It's in *Who's Who*, sir."

Minstrel laughed aloud.

"Where you've read it! A lot of tripe—half a column of it—from the Minstrel propeller to the Minstrel gyrostat! Half a column of cold-meat sentences! Bah! What do they know of the grind, the sweat, the brain I've put into my work? And for what? For what, I ask you? Letters after my name—paragraphs in the press—and the starvation wage which is all we've got to offer genius over here!"

Hacker turned again.

Minstrel pushed back his chair, got up, and went striding off to the end of the room. He took a book from a shelf, apparently at random, fluttered the pages, thrust it into its place again, and came striding back. He stopped by Hugo, looking down on him, and asked abruptly,

"What are your qualifications? Have you studied mechanics?"

"No, sir."

"Dynamics? Chemistry?"

"No, sir."

"Well, you've got a nerve—haven't you?"

Hugo began to think he had. Anyhow he had stopped blushing. Ambrose Minstrel reminded him of a weather report: "Squally. Some rain. Wind variable. Local thunderstorms. Very disturbed conditions. Further outlook highly uncertain." It was impossible to feel embarrassed by a weather report. He stood the scrutiny of those hot, restless eyes at very close quarters.

Then Minstrel turned away with a laugh.

"That's all right. I don't want an assistant—I want a secretary. I don't want brains—I want a writing-machine. I can do all the thinking that's needed in this house. I don't want anyone else butting in. D'you hear, Hacker? You can put that in your pipe and smoke it. Now look here, you—Ross, let's get down to business. What about your references? If you haven't got anything else, I suppose you've got a character. No—I apologize. You mayn't have brains or education, but you've got plenty of brass—I'll say that for you. Well—what about testimonials?"

He flung back into his chair with the envelope produced by Hugo in his hand, tore it roughly down one side, and proceeded most embarrassingly to read aloud the letters from Mr. Trevelyan's solicitor, the local parson, and a neighbouring J.P., in each one of which Hugo was praised as a young man of unblemished character, extreme trustworthiness, and unflagging industry. It sounded awful. In the midst of the last letter he stopped and flung the whole lot across the room.

"Lord! What stuff! Are you all that of a prig?"

"No, sir," said Hugo dryly.

Minstrel turned to his assistant.

"Hacker, get a move on, can't you? Pick up that tosh! See if any of 'em have got telephone numbers. Get on to 'em and ask 'em what about it. Meanwhile—here, you—Ross, have you got any objection to putting in a day's work without prejudice? You haven't? All right, go over there and begin. You'll find a pretty average silt, because Hacker's a lazy brute and hasn't done a hand's turn for days. I pay my secretary a hundred and fifty. If you don't suit, you can work out how much that comes to a day. I'll try you for a week if your references are all right. Now go over there and get down to it!"

Chapter Three

THAT NIGHT Hugo wrote to Susan in India:

"I am Ambrose Minstrel's secretary. Isn't it ripping? He's trying me for a week, but it's going to be all right. I came down over night and got in before anyone else. Manning gave me the tip. He knows Hacker who is Minstrel's assistant. It was awfully decent of him, because it really was a case of first come, first served. Hacker said that to me when I arrived, and I soon found out what he meant. Minstrel has taken me on for a week on the strength of my not having any relations to speak of. I had to take notes whilst he interviewed all the other fellows. Rather comic—wasn't it? As a matter of fact Minstrel only really interviewed two of them. In the middle of the second one he got fed up and dashed off into his laboratory and locked himself in, and left Hacker and me to carry on. It was awfully funny, because I'd only just come off the mat myself. As a matter of fact, Hacker and I did the job a lot better than old Minstrel. But when I handed in the beautiful notes I had taken, Minstrel just tore them across and flung them into the fire and said they could all go to blazes. Then he said, 'Hacker says your references are all right. If they are, you're probably too good to live; but if you survive, you can have the job—unless you get on my nerves. I'll soon tell you if you do.' He kept me busy all day. And then, just as I was wondering how I was to get my kit, he told me that there was a train at seven, and that I'd better clear out, get anything I wanted, and come down by the nine-thirty next day. So here I am, packing up."

He finished his letter and turned his mind to the problem of what to pawn. He was very glad he hadn't accepted Hacker's offer of a loan. Now why should Hacker have offered him a loan? It seemed odd. Why on earth should Hacker suppose that he needed a loan?

Hugo frowned, and, frowning, went and stared at himself in the glass. Did he look down and out? Did he look as if he needed a loan from a stranger? He did not. The grey suit was only a year old; a suit in the first flush of youth; a well cut suit; a reputable, decorous, secretarial suit; even a slightly priggish suit—not in the least the kind of suit to which the casual stranger offers loans. How could Hacker possibly have known that a return ticket to London was all that had saved him from having to confess to empty pockets? Hacker couldn't possibly have guessed. Hacker meant well.

Having thus damned Mr. Hacker, Hugo considered his pawnable possessions. Not his flute—certainly not his flute. He picked out Uncle Richard's field-glasses and wondered how much they would raise, and whether Minstrel paid by the week, the month, or the quarter? The field-glasses would certainly not last a quarter. He added a pocket aneroid in a worn leather case, a pair of skates, and a travelling clock. After which he packed everything else and went to bed, where he dreamt that he and Hacker were parachuting from the moon in the new Minstrel submarine. They were firing torpedoes out of catapults, and great flocks of birds with broad red wings went whirling down the sky in their track; they made a rushing sound like the rushing of the sea. And all at once the girl whispered in his ear, "You *mustn't* go there! Oh, you *mustn't* go there!" He woke up with the sound of the words in his ears.

The field-glasses, the barometer and the clock brought him three pound ten and the consciousness of having been done. If he had had more time, he would have walked out of the shop; but with the nine-thirty to catch, he pocketed the cash. It annoyed him to think that there had been a witness to his defeat. He thought the elderly man who had followed him into the shop regarded him with the sort of expression that says "had for a mug."

He was half-way to Meade Halt before he really recovered his spirits. He might not have recovered them then if he had known that at that very moment the elderly man was commenting on the incident over the telephone:

"Yes, I followed him. He pawned some old trash—field-glasses, an aneroid, and a clock. Got three ten for them. He went back to his room and paid the landlady. He only owed a week. Is that all? All right." The elderly man rang off.

Hugo left his luggage till the only porter at Meade Halt came off duty and could borrow a barrow. He walked up to Meade House. He had thirty-five shillings left. He had a job. He had a sense of adventure. Life was pretty good in spite of the pawnbroker.

The front door of the house stood open, and he walked in. The day was not cold for December, but the bare comfortless hall was as cold as draughts could make it. He went past the stairs to the study, and just short of the door he began to wonder whether he ought to have rung the bell.

There was a sound of voices in the room. The unlatched door moved in the draught, and he heard Minstrel's rasping voice raised angrily:

"I'll do things my own way or not at all. I tell you the young fool hasn't the brains. He's easy—easy—*easy*."

Hugo turned on his heel and walked back to the front door. Standing on the dirty doorstep, he rang the bell. It clanged; the sound echoed and died. No one came.

The violent disturbance in his mind settled. Minstrel's words might, or might not, refer to him. If they did, they meant no more than that Minstrel had a bee in his bonnet—probably thought everyone wanted to steal his ideas. It wasn't very flattering to get a job on the strength of being considered too great a fool to be dangerous; but there couldn't be any more to it than that.

He rang the bell again. Hacker looked round the study door and shouted, "All right—come in!"

Chapter Four

MINSTREL CERTAINLY HAD a bee in his bonnet. He set Hugo to work, disappeared into his laboratory, and then, ten minutes later, emerged abruptly.

Hugo heard the noise of the opening door, and Minstrel's voice from behind him:

"What am I working at in there—eh?"

"I don't know, sir."

"Get up! I like to look at a man when I talk to him. Get up and turn round! Let's see your face. You don't know what I'm working at?"

Hugo hesitated.

Minstrel dragged at his beard with a stained lean hand.

"Come! You could tell me what was in *Who's Who*. I'm a bit of print in a dictionary of biography? I'm a back number, am I? Is that what you think?"

"Of course not, sir."

"Then what do you think? What am I working at now? What's my brain thinking, and my will shaping, and my hand contriving—now—*now*?"

"That's not for me to say."

Minstrel broke into a laugh.

"What a discreet secretary I've got! You don't read the papers? They're not so discreet as you. Last week the *Daily Sensation* had a headline an inch high—'MINSTREL AGAIN—THE SUBMARINE OUTSUBMARINED.' You didn't see that?"

"Yes, I saw it."

"But you don't know what I'm working at?"

"Is it my business to know things you haven't told me, sir?"

Hacker had come into the room from the hall. Minstrel turned on him with a gust of laughter.

"D'you hear that? Who says I'm not a picker? Isn't it a treat to hear him? A paragon of secretaries! And I picked him—*I!* You can hold your tongue henceforward and forever, Hacker my friend." He came over to Hugo, put a hand on his arm, and spoke confidentially: "What's wrong with Hacker is that he fancies himself. You mayn't have noticed it; but he does. There—carry on. I'm busy."

He went back into his laboratory and banged the door.

Hugo wrote half a letter, and then found Hacker looking over his shoulder.

"What is it?"

"Nothing. Don't let him rattle you."

"He doesn't."

Hacker laughed.

"He's always jumpy when he's starting something new. The submarine's finished, you know—off the stocks. The Admiralty are taking it over. And if they don't give him a title this time, they ought to be ashamed of themselves."

"I shouldn't have thought he'd care for a title."

"He wouldn't. At the moment he only cares about the new idea, and he'll be like a cat on hot bricks till he's got it roughed out."

He strolled over to the other table and sat down.

Hugo went on with what he was writing; but before he reached the end of the letter the laboratory door was flung open with violence.

"Here you—Ross, d'you know a tune from a toasting fork? I want music—something loud—Wagner—yes, Wagner—he's full of ideas—he stimulates—better stick to Wagner. And mind you change the needle every time. Play 'em loud and keep 'em going. And you're not to leave the records about on the floor like Hacker does."

He swung round and disappeared, leaving the door ajar.

Hugo approached the gramophone and began to pick up the records which lay tumbled pell-mell on the floor beside it. The third one was *The Flying Dutchman Overture*, and he hastily put it on. Through the half-open door he caught a glimpse of Minstrel going to and fro with great plunging strides. He went on picking up the records, and chose *Siegfried's Funeral March* to follow *The Dutchman*.

Hacker came over and looked down at him with just the suspicion of a sneer on his heavy face.

"Tidy soul! He'll love you if you coddle his records. Oh, Lord! What a noise! It beats me how he can stick it. He always shouts for Wagner when he gets stuck. Loathsome stuff, I call it. If you want noise, why not a jazz band? But he can't bear jazz. Funny—isn't it?"

Hugo continued to feed the gramophone. In the middle of the *Fire Music* he was aware of Minstrel beside him; he had come in as soft-footed as a cat. He was smiling complacently and stroking his beard.

"Beautiful!" he said. "Beautiful! D'you like it?"

Hugo nodded. This was a new Minstrel. The restless eyes were restless no more; they dreamed.

"Beautiful!" he repeated: "Beautiful!" The words were just a whisper.

He stood there till the last note died away; then he said,

"That'll do. Finish your letters." He sighed and turned away. "Come on, Hacker! I want you."

They went away together.

Hugo went back to his letters. He thought he had come into an odd world. He thought it odder still as the days went on.

Minstrel and Hacker lived alone in the big neglected house. The woman who had slopped water on the doorstep came daily. She left pails on the stairs, brooms and mops all over the place, and called it "doing for the gentlemen." Another woman from the village came in to cook. She served up charred joints and smoked milk puddings, which Hacker supplemented with *pâté-de-foie-gras*, tinned asparagus, caviare, and salmon. Minstrel drank a particularly noxious brand of thick greasy cocoa with every meal, varied by an occasional outbreak of champagne. A third woman appeared at intervals, to perform a feat which she called "turning out." It seemed to Hugo to consist of taking all the furniture out of a room, stirring the dust into a thick cloud, and then bringing the furniture back again.

In the rather remote garage lived the chauffeur, Leonard. He took as much pains with the old Napier as if she had been a brand new car, and was, besides, kept busy on odd jobs for Minstrel. When the car went out, Hacker drove it. Mrs. Leonard was a dressy person who held herself very high and did no work outside her own two rooms.

Hugo had a large room looking to the front. It was next to Hacker's, and he had at once decided that it was Hacker's lighted window which he had seen from the lane. He slept in an old-fashioned four-post bed with a crooked tester and musty green hangings. The mattress and pillows smelt of mould, and the paper on the walls was peeling off with age and damp. There were no curtains at the two high windows, and the yellowed blinds were falling to bits.

Hugo dreamt strange dreams in the musty bed. He had never dreamed so much in his life before. The dreams were the most fantastic that could be imagined. He was in a sinking ship, and it blew up in a burst of scarlet flame. He was in a diving-bell, sinking down, down, down into blackening water that changed suddenly to boiling pitch. He was on an iceberg that broke into a million stars and whirled him into farthest space. The one thing common to these strange dreams was the element of danger; he was always on the brink of something terrible. Once he dreamt about the girl. She was walking just ahead of him in a black tunnel; he could not see her, but he knew very well that it was she. They walked on quite silently and as they walked, Hugo felt fear come close, and closer, until it touched him. He tried to cry out, and the girl turned and put her lips to his ear and whispered on a sobbing breath, "You *mustn't*! Oh, you *mustn't*!"

He woke. He knew that he was awake, because the girl was gone. The room was dark, but not as dark as it ought to have been; there was a little patch of light low down on the wall, a little shifting patch of light; it lit the stained edges of the paper, the rim of dust on the wainscot, and slipped lower to the floor. Hugo stared at it.

The light came from an electric torch. Someone was standing in the corner of the room, holding a torch so that the light shone downwards. It travelled to the lid of Hugo's trunk. He saw a hand come out of the darkness, and he saw the lid raised up. Then he called out.

The lid dropped, the light went out. There was no sound. He shouted, "Who's there?" sprang out of bed, and made for the corner where the box stood. He had the pleasure of barking his shins against it. There was no one there. He stood still and listened. No one moved or breathed.

By the time he got the candle lighted, he was beginning to wonder where his dream had left off. There was no one in the room.

Chapter Five

IT WAS NEXT DAY at lunch that Minstrel told Hugo curtly that he had no use for him till half-past four.

He took himself out of the house with a good deal of pleasure. The day was fine. The mist that would rise presently was only an inch deep in the low meadows; the pale arch of the sky was cloudless, and the sun, large and golden, had not yet touched the bank of purplish haze which would presently swallow it up.

Hugo left the lane cut across the fields, and climbed a little wooded hill. He did flute exercises for half an hour, and then ran to warm himself. There was going to be a frost, and the air had an edge already. The sun was gone; an orange glow suffused the haze; the mist was rising. He ran a mile along the road, timing himself, and then, turning, came back in a series of short sprints.

Just short of Meade House he fell into a walk, and almost as he did so, a man came round the corner, hesitated, half stopped, passed him, and then came quickly back.

"I beg your pardon, is that Meade House?"

"Yes, it is."

The man hesitated again.

"Excuse me—the light is bad—but are you Mr. Ross? Ah! I thought so."

Hugo was very much surprised. There was something just a little familiar about the man, but he didn't know him—a middle-aged person with clothes that looked odd in the country.

"Now, Mr. Ross, I would very much like to have a word with you if I may. I have a little matter of business which I would like to discuss—in fact, I may as well say that I came down here on purpose to see you. We have—well, not exactly met before, but—you don't recognize me?"

All of a sudden Hugo did recognize him. This was the middle-aged man who had witnessed his doing down at the hands of the pawnbroker. He went on feeling surprised, and the middle-aged man said,

"I'm here on a little matter of business. I believe you pawned a pair of field-glasses a week ago—no, please don't take offence—there's no need—I assure you there's no need. But the fact is, I have a client who collects such things. Curious hobby—isn't it? But there—we all have our hobbies, and this client of mine—well, he collects field-glasses."

"F-f-field-glasses?" said Hugo.

The man repeated the word with emphasis.

"Why does he c-collect them?"

"We all have our hobbies," said the middle-aged man in a deprecating voice.

"They are a p-p-perfectly ordinary p-p-p-pair of glasses."

"They belonged to your uncle, Mr. Trevelyan, I believe?" (What was the fellow driving at? What on earth was he driving at?) He went on speaking persuasively, "My client is very anxious to buy them. He would give a good price."

"What sort of p-p-price?"

"Well—what would you take for them?"

Hugo laughed.

"I d-d-don't want to sell them."

"Come, Mr. Ross! You wouldn't refuse a really good offer, I take it."

"Why does he want them?" said Hugo to himself. "What does it all mean? What's it all about?" Aloud he said, "Why does your man want them?"

"I'm not at liberty to say. Some association perhaps—a sentiment—I can't say more than that."

"Oh!" said Hugo with a sudden eagerness in his voice; he let his stammer go to a really reckless extent. "A s-s-s-sentiment! You d-don't mean—he's not—I s-say he's not one of the s-s-survivors of the *Trethewy*, is he?—not one of the people who s-s-subscribed for the glasses and presented them to m-m-m-y uncle for his s-services at the time of the wreck?"

The man hesitated.

"I'm really not at liberty—"

"A s-s-survivor might want to have the glasses of course," said Hugo. "I can't think why anyone else should. You m-might just tell me whether your man m-mentioned the *Trethewy*."

"Well, Mr. Ross, perhaps I might go so far as to say that he did."

"And my uncle's s-s-saving them? He r-risked his life a dozen times. He was a w-wonderful s-swimmer. Did he t-tell you how he s-swam—I mean my uncle swam—out to them with a r-rope after the b-b-boat foundered?"

"He mentioned it," said the middle-aged man guardedly.

Hugo subdued his stammer to a slight hesitation.

"Well—I didn't want to—sell them. But of course—"

"Under the circumstances, Mr. Ross—under the circumstances—"

"If he is one of the survivors—"

"Exactly—exactly. I may say, from what I know of him, that he will greatly appreciate the—er—feeling which you have—shall I say, evinced?"

Hugo had no objection to his saying evinced. He repressed the desire to take the middle-aged man's hand and wring it, whilst in a voice broken with emotion and stammering, he begged him to say evinced as often as he wanted to. Instead, he murmured something quite unintelligible and waited.

"As to terms now, Mr. Ross—"

Mr. Ross said nothing.

"Five pounds?" inquired the middle-aged man in a voice charged with feeling.

"Oh, n-no," said Hugo.

"Well, six."

"I'm afraid not—"

"Ten, then—and I don't mind telling you that ten's my limit."

"But I don't really want to s-sell."

"Would twelve be any good? Of course if you were to name your price, I could put the matter before my client."

Someone passed them, coming from the direction of Meade House—Leonard the chauffeur by his build; the light was too far gone to distinguish features.

"Look here," said Hugo, "I don't want to s-sell. It's g-getting late. I'm s-s-s-sorry you've had the trouble of coming down, and I'm s-s-sorry I can't ask you in."

"That's all right," said the man. "But see, Mr. Ross! You name a price, and I'll put it to my client."

Hugo had begun to walk away. He turned and looked over his shoulder.

"What about f-f-f-fifty pounds?" he said, and without waiting for an answer broke into a run.

In another moment laughter would have overcome him. He ran, and laughed as he ran. Of all the absurd affairs! How much more would the fellow have swallowed? And then, all of a sudden, halfway up the drive, the laughter went clean out of him and left him cold and empty, with a prickle of fear somewhere in the dark corners of his mind. What did it mean? There had never been any *Trethewy*; there had never been any wreck that he knew of. The field-glasses had been bought by Richard Trevelyan in a shop in Exeter not ten years ago; there was no story attached to them, and three or four pounds was the outside price that anyone would pay for them. What on earth did it mean?

Hugo went soberly back to the house.

Chapter Six

AN HOUR LATER there was a knock on the study door. Minstrel and Hacker were in the laboratory. Hugo said, "Come in!" and looking over his shoulder, saw the door open a scant six inches; the woman who left brushes and pails about peered through the crack with an aggravated air of embarrassment. When it became obvious that she would not come in, Hugo got up. She backed away from him into the hall, and at a safe distance from the door said in a piercing whisper,

"There's a young person as wants to see you."

"Wants to see *me*?"

The woman sniffed.

"She says as she wants to see Mr. Hugo, and seeing as the name was on the letter I give you this morning—"

Hugo looked past her. Everyone in the house invariably left the front door open; it was open now. The young person was standing on the doorstep. The hall lamp flaring in the draught disclosed a plump rustic girl who shifted from one foot to another. He came forward. She had unbelievably round red cheeks and incredibly round blue eyes. She wore a brick-red coat, a felt hat of the brightest shade of periwinkle mauve, and her hands were encased in sky-blue knitted gloves.

Hugo was quite sure that he had never set eyes on her before. He said "Good-evening," and waited, conscious that Mrs. Parford was dusting the banisters with unaccustomed zeal.

"Please," said the girl with a gasp. "Please, sir, are you Mr. Hugo?"

"My name's Hugo Ross."

The girl also was aware of Mrs. Parford. She dropped her voice to a mumble:

"Because she said, sir, as I was to be sure and not give it to no one but Mr. Hugo hisself."

"Give what?"

"Not on no account," said the girl.

Hugo took out of his pocket the letter which he had received that morning from his uncle's solicitor. It was addressed very clearly to Hugo Ross, Esq. He held it out for the girl to see. The blue eyes stared at it. After a moment she stared at Hugo.

"She says if it was Mr. Hugo, he'd say what her cousin's name was. And she said not on no account I wasn't to give it to no one else"—she paused, and added with a gasp—"*nohow.*"

Hugo's thoughts jumped to the girl in the lane. She had asked his name; he had shouted it after her as the train moved off in its cloud of steam, and the wind had carried his voice away. She must have heard just "Hugo," and no more. And she had written or sent a message.

He said eagerly, "You've got a letter for me."

"Not if you don't know her cousin's name, I haven't."

Brown was the name—yes, Brown—Emily Brown; and her husband was a solicitor; his name was Andrew. He said,

"Mrs. Andrew Brown—Christian name Emily. Is that right?"

The girl relaxed into a giggle.

"That's her! And it's all right about your being Mr. Hugo, I suppose?"

"Yes, it's all right."

She dived into the pocket of the brick-red coat and produced a letter.

"She said to find out for sure and certain whether you was living here, and not to give it to no one else."

"Who's *she?*" said Hugo quickly.

He had forgotten Mrs. Parford, but the girl's round stare dwelt on her.

"That woman's a-listening," she said.

Hugo looked round impatiently.

"That's all right, Mrs. Parford—you needn't wait."

Mrs. Parford sniffed, and faded resentfully. Later on she took away Hugo's character in the village with a good deal of the "Who'd ha' thought it?" and "I'm sure I don't know what the world's coming to" type of innuendo.

"She was a-listening," said the girl. "I know her sort. And I don't want no one listening to Miss Loveday's business."

Hugo's heart gave a funny little jump at the name. He had not the slightest idea why this should happen. It had the effect of making him stammer.

"I s-s-say, d-do give me the letter."

The girl went on clutching it.

"Miss Loveday she wrote to me Tuesday; but I couldn't come afore, because I don't get no more than the one afternoon and evenin' off."

"Do you live with Mrs. Brown?"

"I don't live in—I obloiges her. And Miss Loveday wrote me to come along to Meade House and find out whether there was a gentleman living here by the name of Mr. Hugo. And Miss Loveday she said very partickler not to give her letter to no one else."

"All right, I'm Mr. Hugo. Give it to me."

The girl still clutched it.

"They were in an awful way about Miss Loveday going off," she said. "And she said not to tell no one as I'd heard from her—and I haven't neither." Then, without the slightest pause, "Please, sir, I must be getting along, or my friend that's waiting for me will be in a reg'lar taking—he gets that jealous. So I'll be going."

She pushed the letter at him and ran away into the dark. Hugo heard a man's voice on a deep growl, and heard her giggling answer. Then he shut the door and ran upstairs to his own room.

It was pitch dark, the uncurtained windows as black as the walls. He lit his candle and sat down on the edge of the four-post bed. His heart gave another of those odd jumps as he turned the envelope to the light. There was just his Christian name written on it in a round childish hand—"Hugo." He tore it open and took out the letter with a most vivid sense of expectation.

The letter was written in pencil. There was no heading to it; it just began,

"I've told Gertie to find out if you're at Meade House, and to give you this if you are. If you are, please leave it and come away at once. I can't tell you why in a letter. I want to see you, but you can't come here. Cissie says"—this was scratched out but quite legible—"you can't come here. And you mustn't, mustn't, *mustn't* stay at Meade House. Do come away quickly. If I can think of somewhere to see you, I'll write again. I can't tell you in a letter, but you mustn't stay. Please burn this."

A long sentence followed, which had been so successfully scratched out that he could only distinguish the name Cissie at the beginning and guess at something which looked like "promised" at the end. She had signed her name after that:

"Loveday Leigh."

Hugo sat and looked at the letter until he heard Minstrel roaring for him below. Even then he took time to hold the letter to the candle and to watch the flame catch the edge of the paper. The sheet curled up and blazed. Loveday's name went out in a blue flame. The black ash fell into the trough of the candlestick and fluttered there.

He pushed the envelope into his pocket and went down.

Chapter Seven

IT WAS ALL very odd. The more Hugo thought about it, the odder it seemed. He thought a good deal. And he wished that Miss Loveday Leigh had been less discreet and had told him why she thought that he mustn't stay at Meade House. As a matter of fact, he was more or less bound to stay there, since he possessed no more than thirty shillings in hard cash. You cannot go very far or live for very long on thirty shillings.

All next day Minstrel's temper raged. Hugo marvelled at Hacker's patience. One would not, somehow, have supposed that Hacker would be patient. The weather was cold and dreary. Everything that Hugo did was wrong; the evening found him wondering whether he would not be told to pack up and be off. Instead, Hacker seized a moment when they were alone to say some really very decent things:

"You're sticking it very well. He gets like this every now and again, but it doesn't last. He likes you, you know, or he wouldn't let himself go like this. You're treated as one of the family. I get my share. I don't say he's easy; but he's a big man, and I'd rather be cursed by him than soft-sawdered by one of your mediocrities."

It was next day that the letter came. Hugo found Mrs. Parford studying the envelope in the hall. He took it from her and went on into the study, wondering who his correspondent might be.

The letter was signed "Brice," or "Rice," or some such name, and it appeared to be from the middle-aged man who wanted to buy Uncle Richard's field-glasses. Hugo looked at a page covered with characterless copper-plate and read:

"DEAR SIR,

"I am instructed to say that my client does not consider the sum you mentioned too large in view of the nature, and the value to him, of the article in question. I am therefore empowered to make you an offer of £50.

"Yours faithfully,"

There followed the scrawl that might have been "Brice" or "Rice."

How astonishing! Fifty pounds for a pair of old field-glasses. If it had been five, Hugo would have been tempted. But fifty gave him the sensation of being out of his depth in dangerous waters; there were currents running of which he knew nothing. He put the letter away and thought that he would take a day or two before he answered it.

It happened that he was alone when the telephone bell rang. He took up the receiver and, to his surprise, heard his own name:

"Is that Mr. Ross?"

"Speaking."

"Oh, Mr. Ross"—it was a man's voice—"I rang up to ask if you had received my letter—the one in which my client made you an offer."

"Yes, I've got the letter."

"And you accept my client's offer?"

Hugo was silent.

"Come, Mr. Ross, you fixed the price yourself."

Hugo laughed.

"If you call that fixing it! I wasn't serious."

"Are you not satisfied with the amount?"

"It seems to me to be a perfectly ridiculous amount," said Hugo.

"Well, well, I won't say that my client would not raise it. He attaches great importance—Come, Mr. Ross, name your own terms—in writing. I can't say fairer than that." There was a click and the line went dead.

Hugo put back the receiver. He was to name his own terms. If fifty pounds was not enough, he could have more. What sort of fool did they take him for? And who were they? For the hundredth time, what did it all mean?

Hacker came in presently.

"He's going to town to-morrow for a couple of days. I'm going with him, worse luck! And he says you can stay here, or go away, or do any blessed thing you please. I should clear out if I were you, or you'll be dead of boredom by the time we get back. It's only his temper that keeps us going. Whatever else he is, he's not dull— is he?"

Hugo took a look at Mr. Rice's letter—he had decided that the name was Rice. It gave an address in north-east London. It occurred to him that he might do worse than run up to town and make some discreet inquiries about Mr. Rice. He could get a bed at his old lodgings if he wanted one. He could—yes, he thought he would go to town. But he didn't say so to Hacker.

About one o'clock the telephone went again. This time it was a woman speaking.

"Can I speak to Mr. Hugo?"

Hugo jumped. Who was it? It didn't sound—and yet—

He said, "Speaking," and had trouble with the "p."

"It's me," said the voice. "Oh—is it you? Oh, *do* say quickly if it is, because I can't stop a moment—I can't really."

"I'm Hugo Ross. Who are you?" But by now he knew that it was the girl in the lane.

"I'm Loveday. You know—you carried my bag. Is your name Ross? I didn't get that part of it—only the Hugo. It *is* Hugo, isn't it? Did you get my letter—the one I sent by Gertie?"

"Yes, I g-got it. Look here, what does it mean?"

"I can't tell you on the telephone. I want to see you—I *must* see you. Can you come up to town and meet me at Waterloo, by the end platform where you go down to the Tube? It's nineteen, or twenty or something like that. Can you meet me there?"

"I c-could—to-morrow."

"At one o'clock? Could you meet me at one o'clock? Cissie's going out to lunch. I think I could manage to get away—I *must*. Can you manage one o'clock?"

"Yes."

"You'll wait if I'm late—won't you? Because I must see you. Are you alone, or is there anyone in the room?" Her voice dropped to a whisper. "Mr. Hacker isn't in the room, is he?"

Hugo was startled.

"Why do you ask that? Do you know him?"

"Cissie knows him. Is he there?"

"No—I'm quite alone. Look here, how shall I know you? I mean I've heard your voice, but—"

He heard a little breathless laugh.

"I'll wear a chrysanthemum—a yellow one. Oh—" It was just the sharp beginning of a sound, cut off almost as it reached him. He waited; but there was no more life in the line.

As he hung up the receiver, Hacker came into the room.

Chapter Eight

HUGO SLEPT that night heavily and dreamlessly. He woke late, and came down to find that Minstrel and Hacker were already away.

"Gone this half-hour," said Mrs. Parford with a morose sniff. She was slopping water on the hall floor and messing it about with a mop. She regarded Hugo with an air of virtuous distrust, sniffed again, and inquired, "Might you be wanting anything?"

"B-b-breakfast," said Hugo meekly.

Mrs. Parford tipped the pail in his direction.

"*On* the table—*in* the dining-room. And I'd be glad if you'd make the tea do, seeing I'm in the middle of me floor and it isn't but half an hour made—and what's half an hour when all's said and done?"

Hugo caught the next train. He had the luck to get a carriage to himself, and presently it occurred to him to take out his pocket-book and have another look at Mr. Rice's extraordinary letter. He had pushed it down behind the last letter he had had from his uncle's solicitor.

The solicitor's letter was there, a thick, stiff wad—but Mr. Rice's thin blue sheet was not where he had put it. It was neither behind Mr. Gray's letter, nor in front of it, nor anywhere else in the pocket-book. It was gone. Something else had gone too—those pawn-tickets. Never mind about them.

Hugo sat looking down at the pocket-book on his knee. The telephone bell had rung. He had talked to Rice, and after Rice had rung off, he had taken a look at the letter; and then he had put it back. He was quite sure that he had put it back. He remembered pulling Gray's letter forward so as to make room for it. He had certainly put the letter back, and, as certainly, the letter was gone. The address—yes, fortunately he remembered the address—107 Finch Street, N.E. He thought he would go and have a look at 107 Finch Street after he had talked to Miss Loveday Leigh.

At ten minutes to one he took up his stand between platform 21 and the Tube entrance. An intense shyness had fallen upon him like a fog. He knew quite well that he ought to be feeling adventurous, excited, romantic. Instead, he was merely in a blue funk. Suppose he spoke to the wrong girl. Suppose she never came. Suppose there were half a dozen girls all wearing yellow chrysanthemums. Suppose there wasn't anyone wearing a yellow chrysanthemum at all. In any case, he was quite sure that he was going to have one of his worst stammering fits. A horrified glance at his watch showed him that it was a minute passed one. He would have given anything in the world to be somewhere else, and for four minutes he hoped earnestly that she would not come; after which he became desperately afraid that she had changed her mind, that she had been kept, that she was not coming after all.

He began to walk up and down, twenty yards in the direction of the flower-stall, and twenty yards back again. Perhaps she meant to buy her chrysanthemum at the stall. He walked nearer to it, and when a girl stopped and bought flowers he broke into a cold perspiration. She was a pretty girl with red hair. She bought a sheaf of bronze chrysanthemums and ran past him as if she were afraid of losing her train.

He heaved a sigh of relief. Quite definitely he did not want Loveday to have red hair. And then, right in front of him, coming towards him with a look of inquiry on her face, he saw a girl with a yellow chrysanthemum pinned conspicuously on the left of her coat. She was thinner than he had thought she would be, and older. But perhaps this was because she was made up so pale. He hadn't, somehow, expected her to be made up at all. Why couldn't girls leave their faces alone?

The girl with the yellow chrysanthemum had rather bright blue eyes and very long black lashes. Her face was white with powder, and her mouth was painted a very brilliant shade of cerise. She wore a black coat with some grey fur on it, and a bright scarlet hat. The yellow chrysanthemum struck a vivid, jarring note.

She came up to Hugo with the beginning of a smile. And then, just as she was about to speak, she began to cough; her hand went to her sleeve and out came a bright green handkerchief and a waft of scent. She pressed the handkerchief to her lips and went on coughing, but with less violence. After a moment she made an effort to speak.

"Mr. Hugo?"

Then she began coughing again.

"Yes, I'm Hugo Ross. Are you—?"

"Loveday Leigh." The bright blue eyes looked up at him, and then were veiled in an affectation of embarrassment. "I've got such a shocking cold. You must excuse me." Her voice was hoarse and weak. She coughed again.

Something odd had happened to Hugo. His shyness was gone; he no longer felt the slightest inclination to stammer; he was coldly alert. He said,

"I'm so sorry. Perhaps you'll feel better when you've had some lunch. Where would you like to go?"

Lunch for two would make rather a hole in his very small balance. He wondered what she would say.

She looked over her shoulder and back again. Then she said, "I can't stay."

"But you must have lunch somewhere."

Another glance, slightly more coquettish.

"Oh, I've got an engagement."

"With someone more fortunate?"

She giggled, and then coughed again.

"Well, if you won't have lunch, what about a cup of coffee?"

"I can't—really." She came dangerously near to saying "Reelly."
Hugo gazed at the yellow chrysanthemum.

"Well, where shall we talk? You said you wanted to talk to me,
didn't you?"

"Oh, Mr. Hugo! How that sounds!"

"Yes, doesn't it? But then I want to talk to you."

She slid a hand into his arm.

"Do you really?"

"Of course I do."

"Well, there's a seat over there."

They went over to it and sat down. Station seats are not made
for comfort; they are works more of necessity than of mercy. There
was a dampness on the pavement and on the seat itself. There was a
cold rushing draught. He continued to look at the chrysanthemum.
He was conscious of some curiously mixed feelings. Anger was one
of them.

The girl fidgeted with the corner of her green handkerchief,
looked sideways at him, and said, still in that weak, hoarse voice,

"You were sweet to me the other night."

"Was I? Was that why you wanted to see me?"

"Of *course*. Didn't you want to see me?"

"Very much. But you had something to tell me, hadn't you?"

She laughed rather consciously and looked down. Her features
were pretty in spite of their pallor; the down-dropped lashes were
dark and silky.

"Hadn't you something to tell me?" said Hugo.

"Oh—well—"

"You said you had."

She looked up at him again archly.

"Oh well, a girl says—I mean—well, perhaps I wanted to *see* you."

"That was very nice of you. But I think there was something
more than that."

"More?"

"You said I mustn't go to Meade House. Aren't you going to tell
me what you meant when you said that?"

She gave a little conscious laugh, and then broke off to cough. "Oh dear—this cold! What did you say?"

"I asked what you meant when you said I mustn't go to Meade House?"

The blue eyes looked at him meltingly.

"It's such a long way off," she whispered.

"Was that the reason?"

"I oughtn't to have said so."

"Why not?"

"You'll think—" She coughed. "Oh, you'll think—I must go—really I must."

She jumped up as she spoke and began to walk away.

Hugo followed.

"Then there isn't really a reason why I oughtn't to stay at Meade House?"

"Not if you don't think so."

"You were just pulling my leg in fact." There was a little offence in his tone.

The girl burst out laughing.

"Perhaps I was. You swallowed it all beautifully—didn't you?"

"Oh—well—"

Her eyes teased him.

"Come! You believed it all. You thought there was some deadly secret. You never thought you were just being had."

"It wasn't very k-kind of you—w-was it?"

She laughed again.

"Poor Mr. Hugo! Never mind—perhaps it wasn't all teasing—perhaps I did really want to see you again. Will you come up and meet me another day if I ask you? Will you?"

Hugo met the challenge of her eyes, and began to stammer very much. It was quite easy tó stammer if you wanted to.

"I'd l-l-love to."

The girl pressed his arm.

"We'll fix it up. I must go. Don't come any farther. No, you mustn't—*reelly*." It *was* "reelly" this time.

She pressed his arm again and ran off down the incline that led to the Tube.

Hugo watched her out of sight. He did not follow her, because there was no need to follow her. He knew very well that he had not met Loveday Leigh at all. He walked out of the station and over the bridge in a mood of bleak, cold anger. What a fool they must think him! What an utter prize fool and mug! The girl was undoubtedly Cissie—Cissie, who knew Hacker.

He remembered Loveday's little interrupted cry at the telephone. Someone had come in—probably Cissie. How much had Cissie heard? Enough to make her turn up at the meeting place which Loveday had suggested, with a yellow chrysanthemum pinned on her coat. They *must* think him a mug!

It consoled him slightly to remember that the first glance had roused an inward protest, and that the scented green handkerchief had finished him. Miss Cissie probably thought she had been frightfully clever. He could imagine her being terribly pleased with the idea of getting over the difference in voices by pretending to have a very bad cold—she did it quite well too. But from the very first moment he had been furiously certain that she wasn't Loveday.

Concern for Loveday sprang up suddenly and stopped his thinking of himself. Where was Loveday, and why hadn't she come? And what sort of friend was Cissie for the child who had run hand in hand with him down the dark lane to Meade Halt?

He hadn't any answer to these questions.

Chapter Nine

HUGO LUNCHED economically at an A.B.C. on the other side of the bridge. As he sat at the small marble-topped table, he was wondering what he was going to do next. He went over all the things that had happened in the last fortnight. Any one of them, taken by itself, could be explained away with the greatest ease; but, taken together, they simply could not be explained at all. Some of them were trivial, some annoying; others bizarre and apparently purposeless. Taken in a lump, you couldn't explain them—you simply couldn't. And behind the feeling of being up against something inexplicable there was the constantly recurring prick that says. "Look out!"

He drank his coffee slowly and took time over the tongue, roll, and butter. What was he going to do about it? The name of Mr. Benbow Collingwood Horatio Smith presented itself, and not for the first time. It went on presenting itself, supported by reason and common sense.

Hugo frowned at reason and common sense. The idea of obtruding himself upon the notice of one of Susan's in-laws, and a bit of a bigwig at that, made him feel hot all over. Benbow Collingwood Horatio probably didn't even know of his existence. That is to say, he probably knew that Susan had a brother, and might be vaguely aware of having shaken hands with him at Susan's wedding. Perfectly horrible to trade on being Susan's brother and to thrust one's jumbled affairs upon an unwilling bigwig. The question was, were these jumbled affairs his, Hugo's, private affairs, or was he by some odd chance caught up into a tangle which might concern even bigger people than Benbow Collingwood Horatio Smith.

Hugo could make nothing of this line of thought. He began to think he was a fool not to have followed Cissie. He ought to have followed her. He ought to have found out where she was living; because then he might have met Loveday after all; and if he had met Loveday, she would have told him why he mustn't stay at Meade House.

He paid his bill and set out to look for 107 Finch Street and the elusive Mr. Rice. It was one of those grey days when the air is so wet that it is a constant surprise to discover that rain is not actually falling. It does not fall, because it remains in the air, on your face, your hands, your clothes. This wet air was as warm as if it had been July instead of January.

As Hugo approached Finch Street, his way lay amongst streets that grew steadily greyer, poorer, and, as it seemed, damper. The houses, the pavements, and the people were all damp and dirty. When he had asked his way for about the tenth time, the dampness seemed to be getting into his mind. Why was he looking for Mr. Rice? What did he want with him? What would he say if he found him? What, in fact, was the good of anything?

He came into Finch Street, and found it a place of dismal little shops. It smelt of fish and old clothes. About every tenth shop appeared to sell fish and chips. 105 was a slop shop; 106 a pawnbroker; 107 a tobacconist.

Hugo went in and asked for Mr. Rice. The answer did not surprise him—there was no Mr. Rice there. He tried Price, and Brice, and was looked at coldly by the handsome hook-nosed damsel behind the counter.

"Don't know him."

"He gave this address."

She shrugged her shoulders.

"Do you take letters for people?"

"And what if we do? We don't have to ask your leave, I suppose?"

"To be c-called for?"

Hugo could have killed himself for stammering. The girl mimicked him.

"Yes, Mr. C-c-clever. Too c-c-clever to live—aren't you?"

Hugo walked back through the dreary streets. What was he going to do next? He had not answered the question, when the lights of a Tube station caught his eye. He stood and frowned at the lights for a minute. Then he crossed over, entered a telephone booth, and rang up Mr. Benbow Collingwood Horatio Smith.

Chapter Ten

WHEN THE telephone bell rang, Mr. Smith was looking out of the window. He stood with his hands behind him and his head a little on one side. A very tall, thin man, with the forward stoop and slightly peering gaze of a scholar. He wore large horn-rimmed glasses pushed up on to his forehead. He appeared to be looking at the rain. On a perch, about a yard away, sat a grey and rose-coloured parrot very busy with its toilet. It stretched a wing, said "Awk!" in a loud peremptory manner, and then, with the wing still spread to its utmost reach, observed conversationally, "I parted from her on the pier the first day of July."

Mr. Smith said "Ssh!" and the parrot looked at him reproachfully. After a moment it slowly folded its wing, said "Awk!" again rather angrily, and began to recite at the top of its voice:

"Three jolly admirals all of a row;

Collingwood, Nelson, and bold Benbow—"

It stopped abruptly, flapped both wings, and said "Yah!"

The telephone bell rang. Mr. Smith went slowly to the table and took up the receiver.

"Who's that?...Who did you say?...Susan's brother? Yes, of course I knew Susan had a brother. I suppose I met you, didn't I?...What do you want?...Yes, I'm in...Yes, you can come along... All right."

He listened for the click at the other end and put the instrument back. Then he walked to the window and went on watching the rain.

A less nautical figure could hardly have been imagined. It was as if his whole appearance protested against the names thrust upon him in unconscious infancy. Even the enthusiastic parents responsible for them had not seriously considered the sea as a profession after he was five years old. He had distinguished himself greatly both at school and college, and then, like so many brilliant boys, had passed into obscurity. Ample means allowed him to indulge a taste for desultory rambling through the old cities of Europe. He became known as a collector of prints, and published a small monograph on Russian icons, followed a year or two later by another upon early German woodcuts. Then, quite suddenly, he emerged from this cultured obscurity as the author of a book with a commonplace title and a daring content. *The European Problem* set more than its author in the lime-light. It was at once an analysis and a forecast. In every country it was read, talked of, criticized, and attacked. Written fifteen years before the war, it forecast not only the war itself, but its social and economic consequences. And if he chose, Mr. Smith might at the present moment have indulged himself by observing, "I told you so." As a matter of fact, he never referred to the subject.

During the war his intimate knowledge of almost every European country brought him very closely into touch with more than one government department. As to his present position and activities, most people were as much in the dark as Hugo Ross, who had merely a vague impression that John Smith's uncle was no end of a distinguished old fellow with some sort of mysterious—or shall we say undefined—connection with the Foreign Office. For the rest, he was a bachelor and an eccentric; and he had given Susan, as a wedding present, a string of pearls worth five thousand pounds. Susan was therefore a prejudiced witness when she declared fervently that he was a dinky old duck.

Hugo came into the study to find the curtains still undrawn and Mr. Smith still contemplating the falling rain. He turned round when the parrot flapped, and said,

"Ssh, Ananias!" and then, "That you, Ross?"

Hugo came forward and lent a hand with the curtains, which his host now proceeded to draw. Ananias watched them with a sarcastic eye.

"It's very good of you to s-see me," said Hugo when the subsequent silence had gone on for some time.

"Well," said Mr. Smith, "I'm not doing anything for you—am I?" He began to walk away from the window, talking as he went. "Of course the question is, do you want me to do anything for you?— and if you do, what is it?—and if you don't, why have you come to see me at all? Because of course—" He reached the mantelpiece and, turning, stood with his back against it. "Let me see—I suppose I met you at Susan's wedding, didn't I?"

"Yes, sir."

It was pretty awful. How on earth was he to begin? How on earth did one begin confiding in a sister's uncle-in-law who just wandered round the room talking vaguely, not to you, but to the carpet at his feet?

He gazed at Mr. Smith's long drooping form and Mr. Smith's rather classic and quite expressionless features surmounted by the horn-rimmed spectacles and a mass of very thick iron-grey hair, and wondered why he had come.

Mr. Smith continued to look at the carpet; but for the moment he had ceased to wander.

"The further question arises as to whether one is justified in recommending anyone for a job when you don't know anything about them except a sister—a very charming sister. Susan is undoubtedly a very charming girl. And though I disapprove of marriage in the abstract, I find that, in the concrete, I do approve of Susan. I suppose you want a job."

"N-no, sir."

Mr. Smith pushed the glasses up farther. He had a long, thin, carefully tended hand, and the gesture had a certain weary grace. He said,

"How remarkable! Young men are always coming to me and asking me to recommend them because I knew their grandfathers—or their grandmothers. A grandmother is, of course, the stronger recommendation of the two; and if I ever danced with her, the young man is, naturally, perfectly competent to go anywhere or do anything."

"I've got a job," said Hugo.

"Do you want a better one?"

"Not exactly."

Mr. Smith began to drift off towards the window again.

"It wasn't exactly raining this afternoon, but it's raining now," he observed. "And it isn't exactly Christmas yet, but it will be in about eleven months—eh, Ananias?"

The parrot rose on his toes and said "Awk!" Then in a rapid monotone it began:

"'Three jolly admirals all a row;
Collingwood, Nelson, and old Benbow—'

Hard a-port! Hard a-port, I say! Give us a kiss, ducky! Give us a kiss, ducky—do!"

The sound of a resounding smack followed. Mr. Smith said, "Ssh, Ananias!" and drifted back again to the fire.

Hugo was ready for him.

"It m-must seem awful cheek to you, sir, my c-coming to see you like this. I've come because I want advice. I w-wouldn't bother you with my affairs, b-but—"

"There always is a but," said Mr. Smith.

"I'm not sure where my affairs stop and s-something that I ought to have advice about begins."

"I am not a solicitor," said Mr. Smith.

His tone was dreamy, not sarcastic; but Hugo stiffened; the flush which rose so easily to the roots of his fair hair subsided.

"May I tell you what my job is, sir?"

"By all means."

"I'm Minstrel's secretary."

Mr. Smith gazed in the direction of Ananias.

"Minstrel?" he said. "Ambrose Minstrel?"

"Yes, sir."

"And you want advice. What sort of advice?"

"I've been there a fortnight—and odd things keep happening."

"Ah—odd things. What sort of odd things?"

His tone was abstracted, and he continued to look at Ananias; yet somehow Hugo felt that he was being attended to.

"I was very glad to get the job, because I wanted a job pretty badly, and I was most awfully pleased at being taken on by a big man like Minstrel."

"Yes—how did you get the job?"

"A friend told me that Minstrel was going to advertise, so I got down to his place before anyone else. I didn't think I had an earthly chance, because I thought he'd want someone with shorthand and a lot of other qualifications that I haven't got. But he t-took me."

"Straight away—without seeing anyone else?"

Hugo laughed.

"He k-kept me to interview the others."

Mr. Smith took up the tongs, selected a large lump of coal, and put it on the fire. With his back to Hugo, he said,

"Was that one of the odd things?"

"N-not exactly, sir."

"He took you without references? Did he know anything about you?"

"I believe Hacker telephoned about my references. Hacker's his assistant."

Mr. Smith turned round again. He still held the tongs, and kept opening and shutting them in an absent sort of way. He seemed to be looking at Hugo's boot-laces.

"Well, well," he said. "Are you so inherently modest as to consider that there must be something odd about a person who engages you as a secretary?"

"No, sir. I haven't really got to the odd things yet. It—it's difficult to begin. They don't s-seem so odd when you take them one by one."

"I see. Well—begin. Let us have these oddments. Produce them."

Hugo began to produce them. It was frightful to feel that his cheeks were burning. The things that he had to produce shrivelled into absurdity under Mr. Smith's attention.

"Someone came into my room in the night and opened my box."

"Dear me!"

Hugo described the incident in detail. It was a ridiculous incident. He described the half-caught words which he had heard when he first arrived at Meade House: "He's easy—easy;—*easy*." Minstrel's rasping voice came back to him: "The young fool hasn't got the brains." The words might have referred to anyone.

He went on to Mr. Rice, and felt on firmer ground. It was impossible to deny the oddness of Mr. Rice and of the client who offered fifty pounds, and was prepared to raise it, for a pair of field-glasses that were not worth five. Mr. Rice's visit, Mr. Rice's letter, and Mr. Rice's telephone call were most undeniably odd.

"You've got this letter?"

"No, sir—that's another thing—it's gone. I p-put it in my pocket-book, and it isn't there."

"Awk!" said Ananias very loudly.

Mr. Smith laid down the tongs and put his hands behind him. "Sure?"

"Quite sure, sir." A pause, and then, "I really am quite sure."

Ananias began to dance up and down and flap his wings.

"If he hollers, let him go.

Eena, meena, meena, *meena*, MEENA!"

Mr. Smith went over and cuffed him. When he came back again, he asked,

"That all?"

"N-no, sir."

"Go on."

"There was a girl, sir."

"There always is. What about her?"

"I m-met her in the lane when I went down about the job—I ran into her in the dark—she was running away—" Hugo stuck there because Mr. Smith was looking at him for the first time.

"Oh, she was running away?"

"Y-yes, sir. And I c-c-carried her b-bag." He was stammering badly.

"Interesting—but hardly odd," said Mr. Smith.

"That wasn't the odd p-part. We had to run for the train—her train—and she said I m-mustn't go to M-meade House. I'm t-telling it awfully badly. We were talking and I s-said I hoped I was going to get a job at Meade House. And we saw the train and had to run—and just as the train was g-going out, she s-said, 'You m-mustn't go there—you *m-mustn't* go to M-meade House!'"

Mr. Smith's eyebrows rose until they touched the horn-rimmed glasses.

"How romantic! Continue."

"She wrote to me."

"How did she know you'd got the job?"

"She wrote to a girl who worked for her cousin, and the girl came to the house to find out if I was there. She g-gave me the letter."

"Got it?"

"No, sir—I burned it. She s-said I m-mustn't s-stay at Meade House—" He hesitated and then repeated Loveday's letter verbatim; after which he found himself explaining about Cissie, who had been encountered on the pier at Brighton; and so on, through the interrupted telephone call to the meeting that afternoon with the girl who wasn't Loveday.

When he had finished, there was a pause. With his back to them, Ananias was swearing softly in Spanish; his back was humped, his feathers ruffled.

Mr. Smith strolled across and scratched the back of his head. Ananias sidled away and swore a little louder. Mr. Smith came back.

"You're sure about the girl? Why?"

"I'm quite sure, sir. That is, I'm quite sure it wasn't the girl I talked to in the lane."

"How can you be sure? You didn't see her face."

"I'm quite sure, sir."

"Tell me why you're sure?"

"I d-don't think I can. They were d-different. Loveday was l-like a n-nice sort of child—the other one—w-wasn't."

Mr. Smith walked over to his writing-table and sat down.

"Are you staying in town?"

"Yes, sir."

"Where?"

Hugo gave him the address.

"I expect they'll be able to take me in—I was there for some weeks while I was looking for a job."

"Well, you might give me the references you gave Minstrel."

Hugo gave them. Mr. Smith took up a pencil and wrote.

"How long are you staying up?"

"Only till to-morrow afternoon."

"It's a short time. But I suppose—let me see, you were at school with John—his fag, weren't you?"

"Yes, sir."

"Have you told me everything?"

"I went to the address that man Rice gave, and it was only a place where you call for letters—a dirty little tobacconist's in Finch Street."

"Number, please?"

"A hundred and seven."

Mr. Smith wrote it down with an absent air.

"Come and see me at twelve to-morrow," he said, and getting up, went over and began to make his peace with Ananias.

Chapter Eleven

HUGO'S OLD LANDLADY seemed very pleased to see him.

"I'm sure, sir, we've quite missed you. Ella was only sayin' to me last night, 'I'm sure, Aunt, I wish to gracious we'd got Mr. Ross back, instead of that there fidgeting, ferreting, philandering foreigner—*that* I do.'"

"Have you got a foreigner, Mrs. Miles? I say, *not* in my old room! Because I want it to-night."

"You shall have it, Mr. Ross, if I'd fifty foreigners—which thank goodness I haven't, seeing one's enough and to spare. 'Ella,' I says, 'if it's my last dying word I won't say different—foreigners is foreign, and what I say is, let 'em stay foreign where everyone's used to it, pore things, and can't help 'emselves.'"

"What sort of foreigner is he?"

It was pleasant to be looked at comfortably by Mrs. Miles after being sniffed at for a fortnight by Mrs. Parford. Mrs. Miles didn't sniff. She was a hearty, buxom creature who had come up from the country in her youth and never quite lost the look of it.

"What sort, did you say? The sort that's best somewhere else, with his fidgety ways and his ferrety eyes, and never done asking questions. And, as I said to Ella, red hair is what I've no stomach for, neither in man nor woman. And 'Thank goodness,' I says, 'yours is a decent brown, for I couldn't never have took to a child with red hair.' And Miles had an aunt as was carrots through and through, and you couldn't get from it." She sunk her voice to a penetrating whisper, "Would you say there'd be many of those Bolshevist Russians with red hair?"

"I don't know."

Mrs. Miles looked disappointed.

"I says to Ella, 'Miller he may call himself, but it's my belief he's one of those there Russian Bolshevists.' Mr. Bolshy Miller is what I'd like to call him to his face—only with red hair you got to be careful—especially when they're foreign and used to knives and all manner of nasty horrors. Why, only last week Ella and me went to the pictures, and there was a pore girl that was carried off by a Bolshevist and served something crool. And I says to Ella then, 'Money or no money, and rent or no rent, I don't keep that there Miller a day longer than what I can help.'"

Hugo found it quite pleasant to be in his old room again. He wondered if he had done any good by going to Mr. Smith. There was a certain relief in having spoken of the things which had been troubling him—a certain sense of having shifted some part of a growing burden of responsibility. He slept without dreams and woke refreshed.

In the morning Mrs. Miles knocked at the door.

He said, "Come in," and she brought hot water into the room and then shut the door. Her round face was red with anger.

"That there Miller!" she began.

"I say, what's the matter?"

"I've always been one to mind my own business, and as I says to Ella, 'A busybody nor a interferer is what I never was and never will be.' But when I sees my duty, I sees it—and a duty I feel it to be."

Hugo's head went round a little. That the duty was in some way connected with himself was to be discerned from the manner in which Mrs. Miles was looking at him.

"And my advice is—not as you're asking it; and p'r'aps I'd do better not to give none, but seeing as I feels it a duty, I will. For, as I says to Ella, 'Who's a-going to warn him if I don't? Tell me that, Ella,' I says. And she hadn't a word to say."

Hugo did not think that Ella very often got a chance of saying a word. He laughed, and said,

"What do you want to warn me about, Mrs. Miles?"

"It's not a case of wanting to," said Mrs. Miles darkly; "it's a case of feeling it a duty—and what I feels to be a duty I'll do, if it costs me a neffort, or if it don't cost me a neffort." She was still very red in the face.

Hugo put on an ingratiating smile.

"I s-say, Mrs. Miles, w-would you mind warning me before my sh-sh-shaving water gets cold?"

"And what you wants to shave for, the Lord knows!" said Mrs. Miles.

Hugo blushed.

"I s-say, d-do warn me, and let me get up. I w-w-want to get up—I really do."

"You may take it light, Mr. Ross, but it's my bounden belief that that there Miller isn't up to no good."

"Why?"

Mrs. Miles snorted.

"What's the good of asking me why? Because he's a creeping, crawling ferret, and a foreign Bolshevist Russian, if he do call himself Miller—that's why."

She leaned forward and went on in scornful tones, "And if he isn't, what's he want asking questions like he does—'Where's Mr. Ross gone?' and, 'What kind of a job has Mr. Ross got?' and, 'When's he going out?' and, 'When's he coming home?' and, 'Did he pay his rent?' and, 'How much money did he have?' and, 'Wasn't he very hard up?' There! I don't rightly know how I kep' myself. I says to Ella, 'Ella,' I says, 'I thought I should ha' burst!' And Ella says, 'Oh, lor, Aunt! Don't say such horful things!' And I says, 'I do say it, and I won't go from it. And what's more, I shall tell Mr. Ross.'"

"Well," said Hugo, "you've told me."

Mrs. Miles looked at him with a pitying eye and shook her head.

"Ah! There's more to come," she said. "What's he want to see you for? Tell me that!"

"He can't see me," said Hugo—"I'm g-going out—that is if you'll l-let me get up."

Mrs. Miles retired.

On his way downstairs Hugo passed a pale, red-haired man whom he supposed to be Mr. Miller. He didn't like the look of him, and he felt distinctly annoyed when, instead of making way, the man addressed him.

"Mr. Ross, is it not?"

"Yes."

"I have a wish to speak to you." The fellow had a very decided accent; but whether it was Russian or not, Hugo did not know.

"What do you want?"

Ella was coming upstairs. Mr. Miller spoke quite loud enough for her to hear.

"It is that little matter of business—the offer we make you. If it is not high enough—"

"I don't know what you mean."

Hugo pushed past him furiously and went on down the stairs. Miller's voice followed him:

"Oh come, Mr. Ross! You know very well what I mean."

Hugo went out into the street and banged the door.

Chapter Twelve

HUGO FOUND Mr. Benbow Smith very busy teaching Ananias what, he explained, was a very ancient Slav greeting. From the gusto with which Ananias delivered it, it was quite obvious that he considered himself to have acquired a new and impressive malediction. He continued to recite it softly but fervently as Mr. Smith drifted down the room and took up a position on the hearth-rug.

Hugo waited to be addressed. He noticed that Mr. Smith's horn-rimmed glasses were now in his coat pocket.

"Of course," said Mr. Smith, as if continuing a conversation which had already lasted some time, "the question is, who am I going to advise? Because there are, naturally, two of you. You see that, I suppose?"

Hugo didn't see it in the least. He said,

"N-no, sir."

Mr. Smith looked over the top of his head and went on speaking in a dreamy voice:

"Or perhaps I should say three—yes, I think three—yes, decidedly."

Ananias repeated the greeting after the manner of one who says, "Cursed be he in his rising up and in his lying down."

"Ssh, Ananias!" said Mr. Smith.

Ananias said it all over again in a whisper, with one red eye fixed indignantly on Hugo.

"He's really only saying how pleased he is to see you. Yes—I think three. You see, there's Susan's brother—and a young fellow whom I don't know personally—and—there's Minstrel's secretary. And the question is, which of them do you want me to advise?"

"N-not Susan's brother," said Hugo quickly.

Mr. Smith nodded.

"You see what I mean—you come to—well, you come to me as Susan's brother, and you tell me you're Minstrel's secretary, and you hand me over a parcel of odd happenings to sort out, and you ask for my advice. Well, if I'm advising Susan's brother, it's quite simple—I do it in two words—'Clear out!' There—you've got it. And the quicker the better."

"I don't want you to advise Susan's brother, sir."

I should give the same advice to Minstrel's secretary. Without going into particulars, I should advise Minstrel's secretary that the job is not likely to be a particularly healthy one."

Hugo looked at Mr. Smith.

"I want to know just what you think I ought to do, sir."

"I shouldn't use the word ought. And I don't think I'm going to give any advice to the third person I spoke of. It might—no, I don't think I'll give him any advice. But perhaps I'll just put a hypothetical case—quite without prejudice, you know, and without reference to anyone in this room or outside it. You understand—don't you?"

Hugo went on looking at him.

"Yes."

"Very well, we take a young fellow who comes of a decent family and has been decently brought up. He finds himself in a position which he doesn't quite like—a position in which a number of odd things keep happening one after another. He doesn't know what to make of them, and he doesn't understand their trend. But he doesn't like them; he feels a vague sense of being threatened—of something ominous. But he is not sure that it is only he himself who is threatened. If he were sure, he could just clear out. But he's not sure. I don't like using high-falutin words; but he has some sort of an idea that something vastly more important than himself is being threatened, and that he has got a duty in the matter. I suppose one might put a case like that without getting out of touch with the facts?"

"Yes, sir," said Hugo.

Mr. Smith went over to the book-case, took from the lowest shelf a large volume marked "Maps," and came back with it under his arm. He laid the book on the writing-table and stood looking down at it. Then quite suddenly the drawl went out of his voice. He asked,

"What do you know of Minstrel's work?"

Hugo had turned to face him. He coloured a little in surprise.

"I don't know anything at all. There was a paragraph—'The Submarine Outsubmarined.'"

Mr. Smith nodded. "It went the round of the papers. Is that all you know?"

"He's working at something now, but I don't know what it is."

"He's always working at something. It's the 'submarine' that's in question; only—I'm trusting you, Hugo Ross—it's not a submarine at all. It's convenient sometimes, you know, to call a thing by another name—take 'Tanks.' That's why that paragraph went round the papers."

He opened the atlas, turned a leaf or two, and pointed.

"They're pretty far away—aren't they?" With Minstrel's 'submarine,' there won't be any distance in that old, comfortable sense of the word. If they had Minstrel's 'submarine,' we could never say again, 'They're mad, and they're bad, and their idea of world politics is a nightmare; but after all, they're so far away that it doesn't really concern us.' If they have Minstrel's 'submarine,' sooner or later it's going to concern us."

He closed the atlas gently and walked back to the hearth. There was a long pause. Ananias filled it with Slavonic syllables.

"Ssh, Ananias!"

Hugo spoke quickly and eagerly.

"How could they have it, sir?"

"Well," said Mr. Smith in non-committal tones, "they might steal it or they might buy it. You see, there really isn't anything to prevent any inventor from selling any invention to the highest bidder except—it is, of course, quite a big exception—patriotism and, alternatively, fear of public opinion. One or other of these considerations usually operates to prevent the sale of naval and military inventions to a foreign power. Of course, if a man's own government turns his invention down, the case is a little different."

A vivid colour rose to Hugo's cheeks. He dropped his voice.

"Has the Government turned the 'submarine' down?"

"No," said Mr. Smith. "No—not at all—in fact, quite the contrary. I believe they are negotiating."

"Then—"

Mr. Smith took out his horn-rimmed glasses and began to polish them with a silk handkerchief.

"Perhaps one might put another hypothetical case." He breathed on the right-hand lens and held it up to the light. "Let me see—yes, a hypothetical case. Let us suppose that a man is known to have something very valuable to sell. Whilst he is negotiating for its disposal it—disappears. We will say that it has been stolen— the owner will certainly say that it has been stolen. The man in the street says, 'All right—but if it has been stolen, where's your thief?'"

He breathed on the other lens, polished it, and looked through it at Ananias, who was scratching the back of his head. "I seem to remember a story about a ram in a thicket—Abraham and Isaac. Isaac wasn't sacrificed; but I believe the ram was." He slipped the glasses back into his pocket. "That, at least, is my recollection of the story; and I am inclined to ask myself whether Meade House is, or is not, a thicket within the meaning of the tale."

There was a moment's pause. Then Hugo asked, with a flash of humour,

"Am I the r-ram, sir?"

Mr. Smith nodded.

"I think you might be. That is, of course, if you were a character in this purely hypothetical tale."

Hugo felt a curious excitement. His mind was very busy piecing things together.

"May I ask you something, sir?"

"Oh yes."

"Who's got the plans of the 'submarine'?"

"Yes—that's quite an intelligent question. Well, so far as I know the—er—inventor has them. That, you see, is the point. The negotiations between such high contracting parties as a government department and an eminent inventor who does not—er—underestimate the value of his work, are inclined to be of a somewhat protracted nature. That is the point. If the plans were—stolen, and it was necessary to put the blame on somebody, the position of the unfortunate ram would be very unenviable."

There was a pause, broken by Ananias, who had tired of his Slavonic sentence. He burst into a loud screech and produced a round, full-flavoured oath of unimpeachably British origin.

"Ssh, Ananias!" said Mr. Smith. Then he asked in quiet conversational tones:

"What's your impression of Hacker?"

Hugo hesitated.

"He's been quite d-decent to me."

"If Hacker meant to sell the plans, it would certainly suit him to have someone handy to put the blame on." Mr. Smith seemed to have abandoned his hypothetical case. He stood half turned from Hugo, looking down into the fire, and spoke in a slightly dreamy voice: "Say he sells them, and there's a row—there'd be bound to be a row, you know, and somebody's got to be suspected, and it's not going to be Hacker, who's been Minstrel's assistant for five years. No, I don't think it would be Hacker—I feel sure that Hacker would see to it that it wasn't Hacker. I feel sure that it would be the new boy—the secretary who had been taken on in a hurry. And then a number of interestingly damaging facts would come out. One; the new secretary might reasonably be supposed to have a grievance—it would come out, you see, that he had been disappointed of his succession to a property. I seem to have got a little mixed. Let me begin again. One; the new secretary is a disappointed man. Two; he is so hard up that he has been obliged to pawn some of his possessions—pawn-tickets are always very damaging. Three; a letter will be produced—I think Hacker has it—yes, I feel sure Hacker has it—in which somebody offered the secretary a sum of fifty pounds for an article not specified. A nought or two is easily added to fifty."

Hugo gave a sharp exclamation.

"The letter about the field-glasses?"

"It didn't mention field-glasses, did it? I think you said it didn't. I think you said it offered to pay the price you had asked for something you had named. You remember I asked you whether the field-glasses were mentioned in the letter?"

"No, they weren't."

Mr. Smith poked the fire with his foot.

"I expect Hacker has the pawn-tickets, too," he said quietly.

Just for a moment Hugo had the sense which had been with him in his dreams at Meade House—that bewildering sense of danger, formless and unescapable. He said "Hacker!" under his breath, and saw how all the odd happenings fitted into place as threads in the meshes of a horrible net.

"*Probably* Hacker," said Mr. Smith. Then suddenly he straightened up and changed his voice. "Well, there you are. What about it?"

"I—don't—know."

"I told you what my advice would be—to two of you. To the third"—he began to speak very slowly—"to the third, if he were prepared to take the sort of risk which one man isn't justified in asking another to take—well, I'd give different advice."

Hugo coloured.

"The *risk*, sir?"

"One is justified in asking a man to risk a good deal for his country—his interest—his prospects—in time of war, his life—yes. And in time of peace, how much? How much am I justified in asking you to risk? And how much are you prepared to risk? That's the question. And if you'd like time to think it over, well, take what time you want."

"I don't want time—I want to know what the risk is."

Mr. Smith looked straight at him for the first time. His eyes were different; they were not dreamy now, but vividly intent.

"The biggest risk in the world, Hugo," he said.

"Yes, sir."

"I haven't asked you to do anything yet. But if I asked you to stay where you are, I should be asking you to risk being branded as a thief who stole a military secret of the first importance to his country and sold it to an enemy country. I don't know if I'm justified in asking anyone to take that risk. But it's this way—We know nothing; we suspect a good deal. We have no evidence. If you remain where you are, the evidence might come your way—you might do a great service, an almost incalculable service, or—you might fail, and take the consequences of failure. We couldn't do anything to help you— we couldn't appear in the matter at all—and you'd never be able to show your face again. I said it was a big risk for a big stake in a big game. But it won't look like that; it'll look like the dirtiest trick in the world, in the dirtiest game in the world."

He stopped, his eyes on Hugo's eyes. There was a silence. Then he said,

"Well, Hugo Ross?"

Chapter Thirteen

HUGO EXPERIENCED some rather strange feelings. To begin with, he felt as if he were standing up to his knees in ice-cold water. And then he was at the same time horribly afraid and curiously uplifted; he felt as if he were going to do something that he didn't want to do, but to which he was impelled by some quite irresistible force, and he was tingling with excitement. Yet when he spoke, his voice was sober and steady.

"What do you want me to do?"

"What are you willing to do?"

"I'd like to know a little more about it, sir."

Mr. Smith put a long, thin hand on Hugo's shoulder.

"I can't tell you any more unless you mean to go through with it."

Hugo heard himself laugh, and heard himself say.

"I'll go through with it, sir."

He had no idea why he had laughed. But he felt a certain relief; he had said he would do it, and it was easier to do a thing than to make up your mind whether you would do it or not. Now that he had made up his mind, there was that sense of relief. He said,

I'd like to know as much as you can tell me, sir."

"Why—yes," said Mr. Smith. He turned back to the fire and began to put some coal upon it. "Why—yes." He stood up, dusting his fingers, and looked distastefully at a smear of coal-dust on the left forefinger. "The question is," he said, "how much is there to tell? Not very much, you know—not very much, really. Perhaps I might begin with Mayhew—yes, I think I could tell you about Mayhew. You know the name, I see."

"Hacker—he was the last secretary—Hacker mentioned him. I don't know anything about him."

"He was a secret service agent," said Mr. Smith calmly. "He found Hacker rummaging in his box one day—there wasn't anything there of course—and next day Minstrel sacked him—him, not Hacker. I think that's all I can tell you about Mayhew. He had been with Minstrel for about a year—it was thought advisable. And now I'm afraid I shall have to fall back on another hypothetical case in order to illustrate the present situation. We will postulate an important invention and someone we will call A who is interested in selling the invention to a foreign government. The invention is already the subject of negotiations with a government department in this country. Now the question is, what moment would A choose for his coup? He has to let the foreign agent have the plans, and he has to do it in such a way as to secure the highest price and incur the least amount of suspicion. I think he would wait till the last moment, because this would enable him to raise the price, and it would also give him time to get his plans cut and dried for diverting suspicion. He has to find someone on whom suspicion can reasonably fall, and to arrange matters so that this someone shall have had the opportunity of stealing the plans. I think it would be a necessary part of the scheme that the substitute should actually have the plans in his possession. Yes, I think they would try to arrange that—I think so."

Mr. Smith rubbed his forefinger with a fine white silk handkerchief, but the smudge remained. He frowned at it and went on speaking in low, introspective tones:

"We are in a very weak position—no legal status. If anyone asks why we don't go to Minstrel direct, what's the answer? Well?"

"Hacker has a lot of influence with him."

Mr. Smith nodded.

"And Ambrose Minstrel has one of the most irritable tempers in Europe. We have no legal status. He could put his plans in his pocket and cross the Channel and sell them to anyone he chose, and we couldn't stop him. And then"—Mr. Smith's voice faded to a dreamy whisper—"there'd be questions in the House, and leaders in the Press and, generally speaking, the devil to pay. And after that—I don't know how long after—perhaps two years, or three, or five, or even ten—a very great judgment, a very great and ruinous judgment."

There was a long pause. Then Hugo said hopefully,

"They think I'm an absolute m-m-mug, sir."

Mr. Smith put his hands behind him. He conveyed the suggestion that he couldn't bear to look at them any longer.

"That, of course, is an asset. Now let me see—yes, this is the position. The negotiations were practically concluded just before Mayhew got the sack. There was at once a hitch. A fortnight ago—I think you've been in your present job for a fortnight—the negotiations were resumed. To-day they are practically concluded. Minstrel was at the Air Ministry yesterday. They had expected that he would bring the complete specifications with him, but he did not do so. He is seeing them again to-day." Mr. Smith hesitated. "It's not a matter of ordinary plans, you must understand. There's a new—I don't know what to call it—process—that's the blessed word that covers a lot. It's the formula for this which is in question. Until it has been handed over, the whole thing is in the air. Well, I can't tell you any more. Let's come down to brass tacks. Where do you come in? Well, there'll be that moment when the actual transfer to a foreign power takes place. That's a scene in which you are bound to be on, because if you're not there, you can't be compromised—and they want to compromise you, and they think you're a mug. That's the position as I see it. No one can help you, and you may not be able to help yourself. There it is."

Hugo did not say anything. He was looking at the position as defined by Mr. Smith. It seemed to consist entirely of pitfalls and wire entanglements.

"There it is," said Mr. Smith. "You mustn't come and see me, and you certainly mustn't write to me. Steps were taken to ascertain that you were not followed here to-day. But you must understand that you might be followed at any time. You had better understand that. Don't use the telephone for anything confidential. If you have anything urgent to report, write for information as to motor-cycles to this address. If it is very urgent, telephone, giving your name and address, and three hours later be at the crossroads on the Ledlington-London road two miles from Ledlington. And make sure—*sure*, mind—that you're not followed. By the way, have you come across Mme. de Lara?"

"No," said Hugo.

"No—she's been away. But she's going back—you wouldn't have met her yet, but I expect you will. She—er—specializes in young men." Hugo was enraged to feel that he had coloured. "She lives at Torring House—she is, in fact, Minstrel's next door neighbour. I believe they were once great friends. I am told they are not on speaking terms now. I do not always believe everything that I am told."

"Who is she?" said Hugo, frowning. He hoped that the frown would convey a complete lack of any except a business interest in Mme. de Lara.

"Oh, a very charming lady. The sort of lady who has had a foreign husband—no one has ever met the husband, but he always has a pleasantly romantic name, and the lady is usually attractive. Mme. de Lara is very attractive. Have you memorized that address and the telephone number? Because if so, we'll put it in the fire. The place really *is* a cycle shop, you know. Now one thing more—if I want to see you, you will receive a gushing little note from a young lady called Daisy, with whom you are on very intimate terms. You needn't take any notice of what's in the note—it will be all—er—eyewash. But a number will be mentioned in some way. Let me illustrate. If Daisy says, 'I saw three cows to-day,' you will go to those cross-roads outside Ledlington at three o'clock on the day you get the letter. If the three is spelt out, it means P.M.—if it's a numeral it means A.M. If she says 'I hope to see two friends of yours to-morrow,' then you go to the cross-roads at two p.m. on the day after you get the letter. Now repeat all that, and let's see if you've got it right."

Hugo repeated it very accurately.

"In an extreme case Daisy might telephone, using the same formula. Nothing else she said would be of any importance. I think that's all. I can't give you any advice, you know. It would probably be very dangerous for you to go to Mme. de Lara's house; but on the other hand it might be very advantageous. The only bit of advice I can give is, 'Don't fall in love with her.' It would be agreeable, but I'm afraid it would be a handicap."

Hugo could not think of anything to say. He blushed and said, "Thank you, sir."

Ananias rose upon his toes, flapped his wings, and said "Awk!"

"That's all," said Mr. Smith thoughtfully—"except as regards funds. The question is, how hard up are you?"

"Not very."

"What does that mean? You pawned some things for five pounds a fortnight ago. How much have you got left?"

"About a pound, sir."

"That's not enough. On the other hand, any considerable sum might be an embarrassment to you. I think"—he paused to consider—"I think you may reasonably be supposed to have a friend whom you can touch for a fiver." He took five extremely crumpled notes out of a very battered pocket-book. "You needn't say thank you—it's not a personal matter."

To Hugo's surprise he found himself shaking hands.

"Good luck, Hugo," said Mr. Smith. Then he looked over his shoulder. "Wish him good luck, Ananias."

Ananias lifted his wings and displayed their rose-coloured lining.

"*Vaya con Dios*," he observed a trifle morosely.

Chapter Fourteen

HUGO RETURNED to his lodgings, and was met by Mrs. Miles in a state of agitated dignity.

"If you'd come this way, Mr. Ross. If it's not troubling you too much, there's a matter I'd like for to speak about."

She led the way into her sitting-room and shut the door. It was a dingy room with a large round mahogany table in the middle of it, and a suite covered in green plush ranged round the walls. One of the green chairs was drawn up to the table. Ella Miles sat on the edge of it looking the picture of misery. Her eyes were red, and so was the tip of her little sharp nose; she held a sodden green handkerchief in one hand and sniffed into it.

"*Well* you may!" said Mrs. Miles addressing her in awful tones. "*Well* you may, Ella my girl! And you that wrote 'Least said, soonest mended' in your copy-book times and times under my very own blessed eyes!"

Ella sniffed and gazed tearfully at Hugo. She was a little slip of a thing, small-featured and pale. She looked younger than her seventeen years.

"Look at her!" said Mrs. Miles. "Look at her, Mr. Ross—a setting there and sniffing instead of holding her tongue when she hadn't no call to talk!"

"What's the m-m-matter?"

"That's what I asked you in here to tell. You hadn't been gone more than half an hour, when a gentleman comes to the door and asks for you." She turned on Ella. "He asked for Mr. Ross, didn't he?"

"Yes, h'Aunt."

"And what call had you to say anything more than what Mr. Ross was out? I ask you *that*, Ella Miles!"

Ella sniffed.

"A bad end is what you'll come to—same as any girl'll come to as stands gossiping on doorsteps."

"'Twasn't the doorstep," said Ella with a gasp.

"Passages is *worse*," said Mrs. Miles. "And gossip is what's brought many a girl to her ruin—as I hope and trust you won't find out." She turned to Hugo. "Hacker was the name."

"Hacker!"

"Said he'd took a chance of finding you, seeing as how you'd mentioned where you'd been living afore. And then he asks if he can write a note, and he writes it. And Ella she stands there a-gossiping while he done it."

"Oh, *h'Aunt*!"

"Don't you go answering me, Ella Miles! Well, Mr. Ross, I come down the stairs, and I heard him say as bold as brass, 'And is the foreign gentleman a friend of yours?' And Ella she giggles and says, 'I don't know, I'm sure.' And what I don't know is how I kep' myself from going in and giving her what for—only I thought I'd get to the bottom of her goings-on, so I waited. And that there Hacker asks her if she ever heard you a-talking to the foreigner, and she ups and says she heard him offering to buy something off of you this morning, and she ups and says she wondered you didn't say 'Yes' straight away, because you was pore enough and that there Miller seemed to want whatever it was pretty bad. And with that I opens the door, and I comes in, and I gives her a *look*."

"Oh, *h'Aunt*!"

"And I says to that there Hacker, '*Good*-morning, sir,' and he up and went. And I told Ella what I thought about her—and here's your note, Mr. Ross."

Hugo tore it open. It was quite short.

"DEAR ROSS,

"We are staying another day, so don't hurry back if it doesn't suit you. I was passing, and took a chance of finding you.

"Yours,

"J. HACKER."

He turned back to Ella.

"I s-say, Ella, d'you mind telling me how you and Hacker came to be talking about Miller?"

"And mind you answer truthful, Ella my girl," said Mrs. Miles.

"Mr. Miller come down the stairs," she said in an injured voice. "It wasn't my fault he come down the stairs, and it wasn't my fault if Mr. Hacker asked me who he was, and I didn't see no harm in saying he was a foreign gentleman. And then Mr. Hacker asked me was you and him friends, and I didn't see no harm in what I said. I only wish somebody would say they didn't mind what they paid for something as belonged to *me*."

"Listen to her!" said Mrs. Miles.

Hugo went upstairs and considered. Hacker wanted him to stay in town—he wouldn't have taken the trouble to come round if he hadn't wanted him to stay. At the first glance then, it would be better not to stay. Hacker probably wanted to compromise him with Miller. Already Ella would be able to say that she had heard Miller offer him money.

Hugo considered.

The mischief was already done. As he read the situation, it was no good running away; he had to run into danger as the only possible road to safety, and the one thing that he must not do was to show that he suspected anything. The slightest sign of awareness, and his one asset went by the board. They thought him a mug, and they must without fail go on thinking him a mug; it was his one chance of bringing anything off.

He began to think about Loveday. He really had been a mug not to follow Cissie. He wanted to see Loveday very badly; he wanted to hear what she had to tell him; and he wanted to tell her that she mustn't stay with Cissie, and—well, he just wanted to see her.

Chapter Fifteen

HUGO HAD A stroke of luck that evening, unlooked for and quite undeserved. He was walking along a little street in Soho, when he saw Cissie. She was in a taxi, leaning forward and calling out of the window to the driver. He recognized her at once.

The taxi went on and turned the corner; and Hugo ran after it. He turned the corner too, and there was the taxi drawn up at the kerb in front of a small restaurant. Miss Cissie was halfway across the pavement. She was bare-headed and wore a thick dark coat with a fur collar. She disappeared into the restaurant, and Hugo followed her. He found her sitting at a little table in an alcove.

The room was very hot and full of the ghosts of dead meals. Cissie had slipped off her coat, and sat there in a very short, thin dress of a bright shade of petunia. A spotted mirror in a gilt frame behind her showed the set of her head with its carefully waved hair. She was made up to a startling pallor, and the lashes that surrounded her bright blue eyes had been heavily darkened. She gave a jump when she saw Hugo, and said "Oh!" with a sort of gasp.

Hugo had wondered what he was going to say, but, to his surprise, he found it quite easy.

"I s-say, this is ripping! I saw you get out of your taxi, Miss Leigh."

"You didn't!" She had hold of the table edge, and her breath came quickly.

"I d-did—really. I s-say, this is ripping—isn't it?"

Cissie was recovering her self-possession.

"You quite frightened me."

"D-did I?"

"Yes, you *did*."

"I s-say, won't you dine with me?"

Cissie looked at him sideways.

"Did you think I'd come here by myself? *Reelly*, Mr. Hugo, I'm sure I don't know what you must think of me! No *indeed*—I'm meeting a friend, and I shall have to be dreadfully angry with him for being so late—and you mustn't stay talking to me, because he's ever so jealous, and if there is an awkward thing, it's a man being jealous of you in a restaurant." She pronounced the "t" at the end of this word.

Hugo wondered if the friend was Hacker.

"You must go—*reelly*, Mr. Hugo."

"But when am I going to s-see you again?"

"Oh, I don't know. Do you *reelly* want to see me?" Hugo got a very arch glance indeed.

"Of course I do."

It was at this point that Cissie remembered that she ought to have a bad cold. She had been speaking in her natural voice, rather high-pitched, rather bright; and then suddenly she remembered about the cold and began to cough.

Hugo wanted to laugh so badly that, like Mrs. Miles, he didn't know how he "kep'" himself.

"This horrible cold!" said Cissie. "Oh, Mr. Hugo, you *reelly* mustn't stay. You don't know what my friend's like—you wouldn't believe anyone could be so jealous."

Hugo had not the slightest desire to meet Hacker. He wondered whether Cissie would tell Hacker that she had met him. He only wanted one thing, and he wanted it very badly—he wanted Cissie's address. He looked eagerly at her.

"When can I see you? Give me your address, and I can write to you."

"Oh, I don't know."

"*Please*," said Hugo.

He was not playing a part; he had really forgotten everything except how much he wanted that address.

"If I give it you, you mustn't come and see me. It wouldn't do. You must promise you won't come and see me."

"I promise I won't come and see you."

"All right then."

She scribbled on the menu-card and tore off the written slip.

"Don't tell Jim Hacker, will you, Mr. Hugo."

"Of course not."

He thought she meant that; he thought she was playing her own game, not Hacker's for the moment. He thought, with an odd little thrill, that she liked him—"*reelly.*" He felt a momentary softness towards Cissie.

She gave him a little push.

"Oh, *do* go! I don't want him to see you," she whispered.

That sounded genuine enough. Hugo went away wondering what he should say if he were to meet Hacker on the doorstep. He certainly didn't want to meet Hacker.

He walked briskly along for a hundred yards or so, and then looked at the address which Cissie had given him. It conveyed nothing to him. He walked on until he came to a tobacconist's, where he bought a box of matches and asked for information.

The girl behind the counter was very affable.

"Morrington Road? Why, that's up off the Bayswater Road. I've got an aunt lives up that way, and this Lexley Grove must be one of the small turnings out of it. Oh, not at all—only too pleased to be any help." This in response to Hugo's stammered thanks.

As he left the shop, he heard her remarking that she wouldn't half mind taking up with a nice young fellow like that.

He took a bus to the Bayswater Road, and then walked. He had a bit of thinking to do, because at every turn it seemed as if he had to find the one right thing amidst a hundred chances of doing the wrong one. He must see Loveday. But Hacker mustn't know that he had seen her. He must be warned; but if it were known that he had been warned, the value of the warning would be gone. He must know, and not appear to know. If he went to the door and asked for Loveday, he ran the risk of Cissie finding out that he had called; and if Cissie knew that, she would also know that her pretence of being Loveday hadn't deceived him. He couldn't afford to take that risk; there was too much at stake. But he had to see Loveday.

He decided to find the house and reconnoitre.

Morrington Road was one of those streets which have gone down in the world. Its tall houses had once been inhabited by well-to-do people. They were now let out as tenements, and the pavement in front of them was crowded with children at play—very dirty and uncared for, some of them.

Hugo found Lexley Grove at the less populated end of Morrington Road. It was a dark street with a row of tall houses on both sides, the even numbers on the right. The number Cissie had given him was fifty. He started to count the houses, for it was much too dark to read any number, and many of the houses showed no light.

Hugo did not like the street; he did not like to think of Loveday living there. He had counted sixteen houses, when he saw that the row on the other side had been interrupted; some dozen or more houses were gone, and in their place a dim street lamp showed a hoarding and dark, gaunt scaffolding poles.

He counted on. At twenty a policeman passed him—at least he guessed it to be a policeman from the measured tread. He had reached the twenty-fourth house, when he heard steps coming from the opposite direction. Someone ran up the steps of number fifty and put a key in the latch. Hugo heard it grate, heard the door swing in and the man enter. He heard these things, but he didn't see anything; it was too dark to see; the opening door showed no light within.

All the way along the street Hugo had been wondering what he was going to do—thinking. Now he didn't think at all. He ran up the steps, pushed the door, and found it, as he knew he would find it, ajar. He came into a dark hall, and heard hurrying footsteps on the stair above him. The man who had entered must be very familiar with the house, for he was running up the stairs without a light.

Hugo felt his way forward. It was black dark, and it was a darkness that could be felt. The house gave out darkness. He groped, and his hands touched the balustrade, his foot struck the bottom stair. He went up, moving quickly, quietly, listening for the steps that climbed above him. The man had left the door ajar—he had not waited to strike a light—he ran. These things meant great haste and the probability of as hasty a return.

Hugo turned a bend in the stair and, looking up, saw a narrow yellow beam of light high above him. Somewhere at the top of the house a door had opened. The hurrying steps had ceased. He heard voices.

He kept his hand on the banister and went on up the stair. It was uncarpeted, and he had to take the greatest care to move quietly. He came on to the landing immediately under the half-open door from which the light still streamed; and as he stood there, the door was drawn to. But the murmur of voices still went on; he heard a woman say, "How long?" and he heard a man answer her, "Ten minutes will be safe. You're sure she's off? We don't want a row."

Hugo stood in the dark, and was afraid for Loveday.

The man spoke again; he had a foreign accent.

"Answer me—is she asleep?"

The woman cringed and answered him, "I don't know—I gave it to her."

"Then she's off—and so am I."

He came running down the stairs. Hugo slipped across the landing out of his way, and the man passed, hurrying down, down into the darkness. The front door banged, and overhead the woman gave a sort of gasp and began to sob. Hugo heard her whisper, "I can't—I *can't!*" and then he heard her fumble at the handle. The light streamed out again.

He ran up a dozen steps and came on to a narrow landing. A door on the left was open about a foot. The light was within, and he saw the woman's shoulder and arm against it. She turned with another gasp.

"Why have you come back? They haven't come—*already?* Oh, don't—*don't!*"

Hugo had his hand over her arm. It was very thin. She clutched at him with a hot, dry hand.

"Don't let them come! Don't—who—who are you? I thought—" The terrified whisper died in her throat.

"Where's Loveday? Is she here?"

"Who are you?" She was trembling violently.

"I'm Loveday's friend. What's happening?"

Her hand tightened on his.

"They're going to take her away."

"Who?"—he felt her tremble—"Where?"

She spoke in a dry whisper.

"They're going to take her away. If you're her friend, why didn't you come before? They'll take her away and get her on board the ship, and no one will ever see her again. And she looks like Min!"

Hugo shook the arm he held.

"Where is she? I've come to take her away."

"You can't—they're watching the house. They'll wait till the policeman's out of the street, and then they'll come. She knows too much."

"Where is she? Quick!"

He was remembering that the policeman had passed him just as he reached the house.

"In there." She pointed across the landing.

"Is she drugged? What have you given her? I heard—"

She wrenched her arm away sobbing.

"I couldn't do it. She looked like Min. He said, 'Put it in her coffee.' And Cissie went out, and I gave her the coffee—but I threw the stuff away—I thought I'd give her a chance—Min didn't have any chance."

Afterwards he wondered who Min might have been. He had no time to wonder now; whilst she was gasping out her broken sentences he was across the landing trying the other door. It was locked.

"Who's got the key?"

"I've got it—but—"

"Give it to me!" He ran back and took her by the arm again. "Quick! Give it to me! Is there a back way out?"

"Yes—but they'll kill me."

"Come too!"

He had the key and was half across the landing, when they both heard the front door open; there was a sound of feet, a sound of voices.

"It's too late." It was the most agonized thread of a whisper.

Hugo turned the key in the door, and as it turned, he felt the woman snatch at it.

"He'll kill me!"

The steps and the voices were coming up. There was a flashing light below. Hugo wrenched open the door and stumbled into utter darkness; for a moment he lost his balance. And in that moment the door was shut and locked behind him.

Chapter Sixteen

THE JERK with which he recovered his balance and the click of the turning key came together. As he stared into the blackness, he heard a sobbing breath from the other side of the locked door and the soft patter of the woman's hurrying feet; he heard her door shut, away across the landing.

He called into the darkness.

"Loveday! Loveday! Loveday!" And then, on the same low urgent note, "Loveday, it's Hugo Ross. Are you there?"

Ahead of him a door was pulled open.

"Loveday, are you there? It's Hugo Ross."

The door opened wide. The room was dark, but the windows showed the sky—a black sky, but not so black as the blackness of the house—and through the open window half a gale blew in, not cold, but wet with the breath of rain.

With the opening of the door and the blowing of the wind there came Loveday's voice—the voice that he remembered in the lane:

"I'm frightened. Where are you? I'm frightened."

He said, "Loveday!" and she ran to him with a quick, light rush as if the wind was blowing her. He felt her touch him, and it was like being caught in a soft flurry of snow; her touch was so light and so cold. He put his arm about her, ran to the inner room, and shut the door upon them both.

"They're coming. Is there anything we can jam up against the door?"

"The chest of drawers."

"Where?"

"Here."

He barked his shins against it. They pushed and pulled. It was heavy. They got it to the door.

"I'm frightened!" said Loveday panting. "What is it? Who's coming? Cissie—"

He cut her short.

"The window! What's outside?"

"A bit of roof. We can't—"

"We *must*." There was an urgency beyond his safety or hers—
the bigger game—the game he had set himself to play—the game
that would be lost if he were found here.

Hugo was at the window, leaning out, staring, straining to see.
After the darkness of the house the night outside seemed clear; it
was a black night, but the air was clear instead of dense; things
could be seen, if only as strange, formless shadows.

The window was in the side of the house. Hugo looked down on
the roofs of other houses a story lower. If one hung by one's hands,
there would be a six-foot drop. Too much for Loveday. But he could
let her down. He called her.

"Quick! I must let you down." And then as he still stared over
the drop, he discovered that it was not sheer. The wall went down
four feet or so, and then a piece of roof slanted to meet the roof of
the lower house.

Loveday was climbing out on to the sill, and as she turned to face
him and he caught her wrists, they both heard a woman's scream.
It came through the two closed doors, and terror came with it. She
gasped and swung down from the sill. Hugo leaned over, taking
her weight until her feet were on the slanting roof and he caught a
whispered "All right." He let go with a horrible feeling at his heart.

Loveday slid into the gutter between the houses, and as he
climbed through the window he heard the outer door open. He
let himself down and dropped slithering on wet slate that slipped
away from his clutching fingers. He went down four or five feet and
fetched up sprawling in the gutter. His hands were out in front of
him. He lay all along and looked down—a most horrible, long way
down. His hands were over the edge, his head was over the edge. He
looked down, and saw the street below him. He could see two faint
lamps a long way apart, and, immediately beneath him, the lights
of a taxi. He could hear the ticking of the engine. He must have
been dizzy, because a shadow seemed to pass when he heard the
ticking and saw the lights. And immediately Loveday touched him
and he drew back his hands and scrambled up. She pressed against

him and said "Hugo!" and laughed, the least little ghost of a laugh. And then, through the open window, there came a banging sound and the grate of the heavy chest of drawers which they had rammed against the door. He felt her shiver. And then they were climbing a low parapet on to the roof of the next house.

There were four of these lower houses, each divided from the next by a parapet. Looking back over his shoulder, Hugo could see the house they had left rising in a black mass. Voices came from it, and a light flashed at the window. In front of them there was a narrow gangway from which the roof rose slanting on either side. These four houses had been built with lofts to front and rear. The gangway ran between the lofts. Faint oblongs of windows showed here and there against the slate, and the chimneys stuck up like masts.

He held Loveday, and they ran. The loft windows were all empty, all dark. They climbed three more parapets, and then the low roofs ended. The next house was tall; it rose in their path and blocked the way. They stopped running, holding one another and listening. How far would they be followed? Would they be followed at all? Would the men who were following them risk showing a light? And without a light how far would they come?

Someone slipped on the next roof—slipped and swore. Loveday pressed close to Hugo in the dark. The side of the house rose up before them with its slant of slated roof, slippery and unclimbable; behind them, footsteps and gruff murmuring voices, but, thank Heaven, no light. And then all of a sudden there was a light; not where the voices and the footsteps were, but overhead in a window like the window out of which they had climbed. Someone had lighted the gas in the room just above them, and through the open window came the sound of a man singing in a lusty bass:

"The animals went in two by two.

Hurrah! Hurrah!"

He paused, struck a match and sucked at a pipe, puffed, and went on:

"The animals went in two by two,
The elephant and the kangaroo.
They *all—went—into* the ark
For to get out of the *rain*."

Hugo felt Loveday tremble. She stood close to him, very close, and they heard the silence. Everything seemed to be holding its breath out here. Their roof was still, and the next roof was still, and all the roofs beyond were still, with the stillness of suspense; but overhead in the lighted room there were all manner of cheerful sounds—pleasant everyday sounds of a man pushing the fire with his foot, moving a chair, whistling, and presently breaking again into song:

"The animals went in three by three,
Hurrah! Hurrah!
The animals went in three by three,
Hurrah! Hurrah!
The animals went in three by three,
The hippopotamus and the flea.
They *all—went—into* the ark
For to get out of the *rain*."

Loveday put her lips so close to Hugo's ear that the soft breath tickled him. The soft breath said, "I don't sing it to that tune—I sing 'One more river to cross' for the chorus."

Hugo slipped his hand up and covered the whispering lips. He was afraid to say "Hush" because of the silence. They stood very close together. He felt her lips move against the palm of his hand. And then the silence broke. From the next roof came the sound of feet moving, slipping, going away.

Hugo watched the other window, the window of No. 50. It was dark. He watched it until a light sprang up in the room behind it. Figures moved to and fro against the light; one of them was a woman. He wondered if Cissie had come back—he thought it was Cissie. Then someone came to the window and shut it, and a hand pulled down the blind. All this time they had stood there motionless and tense; now all of a sudden Hugo became aware of how strange it was to be standing there in the dark, so close to Loveday, with her lips against his hand. His palm burned.

He stepped back, and he heard the little tiny ghost of a laugh and felt Loveday's hand on his arm.

"Where are you? Don't go away."

"Ssh!"

"I am—Hugo, I am. Don't go away and I'll whisper." Her lips were at his ear again. "No one can possibly hear me, and I'm bursting to know what it's all about. I don't know anything. I've been frightfully good. Why are we running away?"

"Ssh!" said Hugo again.

"They've gone away."

"I'm not sure. They'd want us to think so."

"D'you mean that someone's *lurking*? How *horrid!*"

"Yes."

"Who are they?"

"I don't know. They meant to carry you off—they had a taxi."

She pressed up against him.

"Why?"

"I don't know. Look here, Loveday, we've got to try and get out of this."

The little laugh tickled his ear.

"How?"

"I don't know."

"We really want a parachute, or an aeroplane, or—Hugo"—she pinched him—"we might get through one of those little windows, the funny little slopy ones in the roof—we might do that."

"They'll be shut."

"One of them is nearly always open—I see it from my window. It's open first thing in the morning, and it's open at sunset, and I believe it stays open all night except when there's a frost. They keep plaints there, and they put them out on the roof when it rains—I've often watched them."

"Which roof is it?"

"The next, I think." She tugged at his arm. "Do come and see."

It would not be very dangerous to venture on to the next roof. They climbed over the parapet, and then stood waiting, listening in a breathless hush for a sound that did not come. There was no sound.

They crept between the sloping roofs to where one of the oblongs of window showed against the slate. It caught a faint reflection and looked pale. It looked different from the other windows; it looked pale and it looked different because it was propped open a couple of inches, catching some faint diffusion of light.

Hugo knelt, slipped his hand through the gap, found and loosened the metal stay, and lifted the window. There was a space big enough to climb through; but so dark—if you stepped on pots, they would make all the noise in the world and bring an enraged gardener-householder on the scene with the police to his aid. Beastly things pots!

He let himself down very gingerly indeed. Down was only about three feet, and there were no pots where his feet landed He felt with his hands, found the space beneath the window clear, and whispered to Loveday. She slid down, gave a little gasp of surprise when she found the floor so near. And then on the top of that sound there was another. Someone moved on the roof over there by the parapet. Someone—

Hugo pulled the window down noiselessly, using his own hand as a pad. He slipped his fingers out, found the bolt, and slid it home. They crouched below the window and heard a slow, slow foot go by. Loveday pinched him so hard that he very nearly cried out.

The step went by, and suddenly from beneath them there arose a sound of splashing. They crouched motionless. The splashing went on. Hugo strained to listen for the step, and after a long, slow time it came again and passed them by and was gone. From the bathroom below came the sound of the bath running out; someone moved to and fro; the water gurgled noisily. Presently it stopped gurgling. The door shut with a bang.

Chapter Seventeen

LOVEDAY DREW a long breath. Then she shook the arm that she had pinched.

"*Now* we can talk! I'm bursting—simply *bursting*."

Hugo was feeling his way. Twice his hand touched pots—finally a packing-case. He wanted to get away from the sky-light, and he too wanted to talk. He felt as if he had come a long way and through strange places to talk to Loveday.

He said, "Here"; and she fetched up beside him with a whispered "Now—Hugo, tell me—quick—why are we running away?"

"I don't quite know. I had to get you away. Who's the woman in the room opposite yours?"

"She's a friend of Cissie's. I don't like her husband very much."

"She had been told to drug you."

"Oh!" Loveday gave a gasp and came closer. "How horrid! She brought me some coffee—I thought she was *kind*—I *drank* it."

He felt her shiver, and put his arm round her as they sat there leaning against the packing-case. It seemed quite natural to put his arm round Loveday.

"It's all right. I say, don't be frightened—she didn't do it—she said she couldn't—she said she wanted to give you a chance. And she opened the door and let me in."

He felt her tremble and relax.

"How did you get there? Tell me—tell me from the beginning. I don't know anything at all, and it makes me feel like when you wake up in the dark and don't know which side of the room the window is or—anything. It's *horrid*."

"But I want *you* to tell me things. You said you had things to tell me."

"Oh yes, I have. But you must begin. We can't escape out of here until everyone is asleep in the house—can we? So begin right at the very beginning and tell me."

It came over Hugo how crass it was of Cissie to think that anyone who had ever heard Loveday speak could forget the quick, tripping way that the words came tumbling out, like a lot of breathless children at play; she had a soft, eager way with her even when she whispered. He wrote Cissie down as a fool, and he wondered what he should tell Loveday and where he should begin.

"Oh, you're wasting time!" said the soft whispering voice. "Do begin!"

Hugo went back to Meade House.

"There's such a lot of it. But—you remember you telephoned to me."

"Yes, I did, and—"

"Something happened—someone interrupted you, didn't they? Was it Cissie?"

"Yes, it *was*. But I don't see how you knew. It was in a shop. It was the only chance I ever got. She was trying things on. And then she came in and pulled the receiver out of my hand and she was frightfully angry. And afterwards she cried and said I'd get her into dreadful trouble if I met you. And she said you were just leaving Meade House anyhow—she knew all about it because of Mr. Hacker being a friend of hers—so I promised I wouldn't."

"She was telling you lies. I'm not leaving. I'm up in town because Minstrel's away and doesn't want me. And—I kept that appointment, Loveday."

"Oh—did you wait long?"

"No," said Hugo dryly, "I didn't wait long. Miss Cissie met me and pretended to be you."

"Oh, she *didn't!*"

"Oh, she *did*. She's got a nerve. She pretended she'd got a bad cold, and she actually thought I was mug enough to believe she was you." He laughed a little. "I suppose I must look like a mug, because they all seem to think I'm one."

"Go on," said Loveday. She pressed up against him like an eager child. "Go on. Tell me how you got here—tell me everything."

He did not tell her everything; but he told her how he had met Cissie that evening, and how he had come to the house and found it dark, and how he had followed a man he did not know up the unlighted stair.

"Now it's your turn," he said. "Tell me why I wasn't to go to Meade House. You said it three times, and I want to know why you said it."

She said, "Three times, did I?"

"Yes, you did—in the lane, and in your letter, and when you telephoned. *Now* I want to know why."

She drew away a little.

"I'll tell you. I've wanted to tell you frightfully badly. It was just before I met you in the lane—I told you about running away so as not to wake up and find I was married to James or anything like that. I did tell you that."

"Yes."

"Well, I ran away. And I just missed the train I wanted to catch, and there I was with hours to wait. So I just put my bag in the hedge, and I began to walk up and down. And then there was a horrible beery tramp. And he was between me and the station, so I had to run the other way. And when I got to Meade House I ran inside the gate because it felt safer. And then I heard people coming, and I crouched right down behind a hedge. And there were two men, and they were talking."

"Yes—go on."

"They came from the direction of the house, and they were talking about a secretary who had gone, and they said he was a good riddance—they said he knew too much. And I thought that was funny, because I should think you'd want your secretary to know things. They stood there just inside the gate, and they talked. And this is the bit about you. One of them said, 'Manning's boy sounds just what we want—no relations, no connections.' And the other one laughed, and *he* said, 'He sounds almost too good to be true—the disinherited nephew touch is a real stroke of genius.' And then they walked a little way and came back. And when they came back, the one who laughed was saying, 'He'll be as easy as mud. Everyone'll believe he took them. There'll be no one to kick up a fuss.' Then they walked a little way again, and when they came back one of them said, 'Well, he'll be for it'; and the other said, 'Poor devil!' And then they went right away. That's what I heard."

"I see," said Hugo. He spoke slowly. "They knew I was coming—it was all a plant. Manning—no, I swear Manning's straight—he didn't know—I swear he didn't know—he thought he was doing me a good turn—but it was all a plant from the beginning. I say, what swabs! And, I say—I haven't thanked you—but I do thank you most awfully. I knew some of it, but you've cleared up a bit I didn't know."

"You knew some of it? Oh!"

"Yes—some—" He gave a low, sudden laugh. "I say, they do think me a mug—a prize, first-class mug! It's not flattering, because I suppose I *must* look like one."

Loveday laughed too, just in a whisper; but even in a whisper her laugh was pretty, like a trickle of water.

"I don't know what you look like. Isn't that *funny?* I haven't seen you, and you haven't seen me, and—why, didn't you think Cissie was me?"

"I'm not such a mug as I look," said Hugo.

Loveday laughed again.

"I want to see you. It's so silly not to know what you look like."

"G-guess!" said Hugo. His stammer had returned suddenly, but he did not feel embarrassed by it. He felt an eager excitement.

"Guessing's silly. I want to see you. Haven't you got a match? Do you think that horrid lurking man would find us if you struck a match?"

"He m-might."

"I don't believe he would—I believe he's gone away. Besides, if he tried to get in here, I could scream, and the people in the house would come and help us."

"No, you mustn't. Nobody's got to see me—nobody's got to know that I've been here, or that I know anything."

"Why?"

"Because they've got to go on thinking I'm a mug. I can't tell you any more than that. I've got to go on at Meade House; and they've got to go on thinking I don't know anything. It's most awfully important."

She came quite close.

"Well, *I* may see you. Do strike a match—I do want to see you so badly."

"I want to s-see you, Loveday."

Hugo liked saying her name. It was a very easy name to say; it said itself when he thought about her.

Loveday drew back.

"I'm all on end like a hedgehog, and I expect my face is all slatey—my hands are, and I'm sure it's got on to my nose—things do."

Hugo took out of his pocket the matches which he had bought from the friendly damsel in the tobacconist's. It seemed a long time ago. He struck a match and saw it flare up, a little yellow tongue of flame on a tiny stick. He held it up, and by its light he and Loveday saw each other for the first time.

They both saw the match, with its yellow light rising up into a pointed tongue of flame, and they both saw Hugo's hand holding it. Loveday saw Hugo's face, very eager and earnest, his fair hair all ruffled, his eyes very blue and intent. Hugo saw brown short hair, pushed back, wide-set eyes which he thought were grey, a soft little nose, and a wide mouth that trembled and laughed. There was a smudge on her chin and another high up on her left cheek. Under the smudges the chin was very white and the cheek was rather pale. Each saw the other, and then both of them saw the same thing happen, because at one and the same moment the colour ran up to the roots of the fair hair and the brown. Loveday blushed, and Hugo blushed; each saw the scarlet colour rise and felt it burn.

The match dropped because Hugo's finger burned too. The flame touched it. The match dropped.

Loveday gave a little gasp. They drew away, and were glad of the darkness.

Chapter Eighteen

LOVEDAY WAS the first to recover. She drew a long unsteady breath and said,

"Have I got a smut on my nose?"

"N-not on your nose," said Hugo.

"Where? Oh! How horrid of you!"

"There's one on your chin, and one up near your eyelashes."

He could hear her rubbing vigorously.

"You'll only m-make it w-worse," he said.

"I always get smudges," said Loveday. "Some people never do; but if there's one single smut in a whole town, it gets on to my nose."

"It wasn't on your nose."

"Why don't you get smuts? You were simply *horribly* clean."

"I know." He spoke despondently. "It's one of the things that make people think I'm a m-mug."

Loveday nodded in the dark.

"And you blushed," she added most unfairly.

Hugo blushed again.

"S-so did you."

"Lots of people can't blush," said Loveday—"*lots* of them. I think it's rather dull to be the same colour always. James was always exactly the same colour—rather like soap, you know—and I got awfully bored with it."

Hugo felt a certain impatience of James. He looked at the dial of his watch and saw that it was nearly eleven. He wondered how soon it would be safe to try and get away, and he wondered, quite suddenly he wondered, what on earth he was to do with Loveday. The thought rushed into words:

"Loveday—do stop talking about James."

"Why?"

"Why do you w-want to talk about him? I w-want to talk about you. I w-want to talk about what we're going to do with you."

"With me?"

"Yes. It's eleven o'clock. By the time we get anywhere it'll be about midnight. What are we going to do with you?"

"I don't know." She did not sound seriously concerned.

"Have you got any f-friends in London?"

"Only Cissie."

"Cissie's not a f-friend. Look here, Loveday, I don't want to f-frighten you—but you mustn't make f-friends with girls like Cissie."

"She wasn't as nice as I thought she was," said Loveday mournfully.

"I c-can't think how you ever thought she was nice."

"It was James."

"J-James?"

"Yes—because he was so dull. That's the awful part of James. It's like being driven to drink—he's so deadly that anyone who isn't deadly seems to be most frightfully nice. That's why I thought Cissie was nice."

"What am I going to do with you?" said Hugo.

He felt her come a little nearer.

"You won't let them!" Her hand touched his and clung to it.

"Of c-course not."

She came closer still, her shoulder touched his shoulder.

"It sounds silly, but I got frightened of Cissie. She said such odd things, and she wouldn't let me go out alone, and she gave me such a horrid feeling sometimes"—he felt her hand tremble—"the sort of feeling you get when horrid things are going to happen. I've really only had it in dreams before—the horrid sort where quite nice things suddenly turn into something frightening. I used to get that sort of feeling with Cissie, and it was *horrid*."

Hugo put his arm round her.

"I shouldn't think about it. I'll find somewhere safe for you," he said.

They stayed like that quite silently for a time. Loveday felt very safe, and Hugo very sure that he could keep her safe. The silence and the peace of the sleeping house seemed to rise up around them. The attic was a friendly place. They sat quite still.

At last Hugo said, "Loveday—" and then, "Are you awake?"

"Is it time to go?"

"I think so." He lit a match. The light showed a sloping roof, a packing-case or two, the corner of a cistern, and rows of pots, some just bare earth, and others pierced with the green shoots of growing bulbs. A second match discovered a trap-door a yard or two from where they sat.

"What shall we do if it's bolted?" said Loveday in a whisper.

Hugo had no idea. He could only hope that it would not be bolted, and found his hope rewarded; the trap came up and showed a ladder running down to a bathroom below.

They crawled down the ladder and opened the bathroom door. It was like opening the door into a new adventure. Here was a strange house full of strange people—people who were not really there at all, because their thoughts were wandering in some far-off dream.

Hugo struck one match, and made out the staircase; after which they went down in the dark, step by step, waiting with held breath to hear if any of those dreaming people had been called back through the ivory gate.

No one moved but themselves; no one waked or stirred. The house had a sleepy, peaceful, friendly feeling. They went down, and down, and down to the foot of the stairs and along a yard or two of passage to the bolted and locked front-door. The bolt creaked once, and they stood there with a most dreadful sense of guilt until the silence had settled again.

The key turned easily in the lock, and the door swung open and let in the warm wet air.

Chapter Nineteen

HUGO SHUT the door behind them. It made a little sound like a farewell. The house that it guarded slept on.

They came into a dark street where nothing moved. Everything was still and dim. They crossed the road. There was no light in any window of No. 50, and the taxi that had ticked before the door was gone. The way was clear.

Morrington Road was not quite so deserted. When they came to it, there were still people abroad and a taxi or two plying. Here each lamp as they passed it showed them to each other. Hugo saw that Loveday wore a grey jumper and skirt. She was coatless and hatless. Two of the people they met turned and stared as the light fell on the brown tumbled hair. She caught his arm.

"Have I still got a smut on my face?"

"No—it's gone. I mean *they're* gone—there were two."

"Then why did they stare?"

"Well, you know you haven't got a hat or a coat, and you're not in evening clothes—the hat wouldn't matter if you were."

The lamplight shone on them. He saw her wide, delightful smile and the dimple in her chin.

"Give me yours. Will you?"

Hugo blushed, because he hadn't thought of this for himself, and it was so simple.

She crammed the old felt well down on her head and laughed.

"Is it becoming?"

"Not v-very. You've got it on crooked."

He put it straight for her quite seriously, and was disconcerted because she laughed again. It was very important that she should not be noticed. A man without a hat is nothing; but a girl in a grey jumper suit, hatless at midnight in the Bays-water Road, with wildly tumbled hair, would go on being stared at until he could get her into shelter. His hat made all the difference; in the Bayswater Road the few people whom they met did not stare at all.

They stopped at Notting Hill Gate Tube station.

"Where are we going? What *are* you going to do with me, Hugo?"

Hugo had made up his mind. He would have to try and get Mr. Smith on the telephone. Something had to be done with Loveday, and Mr. Smith would have to take a hand. Besides, there were things he ought to know.

Having picked out Mr. Smith's remarkable name from amongst several closely printed pages of other Smiths, Hugo asked for the number and put his pennies in the slot. He rather blessed the godfathers and godmothers who had so conveniently afflicted Benbow Collingwood Horatio. He hoped and trusted with all his heart that Mr. Smith sat late amongst his books.

The telephone rattled and a voice said, "Who is there?"

"I want to speak to Mr. Smith." This was to make assurance doubly sure, for he recognized the calm, dreamy tones.

"I am Mr. Smith."

"Hugo speaking."

"Where from?" The question came with astonishing sharpness.

"Notting Hill Gate Tube station. I thought that wouldn't m-matter. It's v-very important."

"Very well—go on. What has happened?"

Hugo felt a sudden conviction that Mr. Smith would disapprove very much of his interview with Cissie and the whole of this Lexley Grove adventure. He began to stammer a good deal.

Mr. Smith did not help him at all. He let Hugo get his story out in embarrassed jerks, and maintained a most complete and unhelpful silence until the end.

The ensuing pause was broken by the voice of the operator, who demanded two more pennies.

"Are you there, s-sir?"

"Yes," said Mr. Smith dryly. "Is that, may I ask, the full tale of your indiscretions?"

"Yes, s-sir."

"You shouldn't have gone—I suppose you know that. The question is, did anyone recognize you?"

"No one s-saw me."

"The woman who gave you the key?"

Hugo was beginning to feel better.

"She didn't see me—it was dark."

"That makes no difference. You had just got the address from Miss Cissie. If the woman tells tales, I think we may suppose that Miss Cissie will put two and two together; and then, as far as you are concerned, the game is up—you are of no further use."

"I don't think she'd tell—she was scared stiff."

"Well, that remains to be seen. I'll find out and let you know. Now what about this young woman you've run off with? Where is she?"

"She's here, sir."

"And what do you propose to do with her?"

"I don't know, sir."

Mr. Smith appeared to be considering. There was quite a long pause. Then he said,

"She must go back to the cousin she was living with."

"Will that be safe, sir?"

"Perfectly—if she does what she's told. I'll arrange for her to have police protection. Let me see—the cousin lives at Ledlington, I think you said. Well, the young woman is to stay in Ledlington. No traipsing about—no gadding. She's to keep to frequented places and not go out alone at night or talk to strangers."

Hugo felt a most unjustifiable annoyance. Loveday was not a young woman. She was Loveday. It was revolting to think of her being forced back into the society of James. The conviction that Mr. Smith's advice was good merely heightened the annoyance.

Mr. Smith went on speaking.

"For to-night take her to 105 Meeson Street. It's about five minutes' walk from where you are. Ask for Miss Agnes and say Ananias sent you. She'll take the girl in for the night and pack her off to her relations to-morrow."

"S-supposing she won't go, sir?"

Mr. Smith made no reply to this.

"That's all. And please remember that you are on no account to use the telephone again."

Hugo came out of the telephone box.

"What ages you were—what simply *ages!* What are we going to do?"

"I'm going to take you to a house near here."

"Whose house?"

"A Miss Agnes. And—and he s-says you m-must go back to Ledlington to-morrow."

Loveday turned on him with her chin in the air and her eyes very bright under the brim of his old hat—it really was quite becoming enough.

"Who says?"

"Well, I can't tell you. But we've b-both got to do what we're told."

"I haven't!" said Loveday.

"Yes, you have. It's f-frightfully important. I can't explain."

The eyes became tragic.

"Do you want me to go back to Ledlington and marry James?"

Hugo didn't want anything of the kind, but he clutched at common sense.

"Why should you m-marry James?"

"I've never been able to think of any reason why I shouldn't— that's just it."

"Then nobody can m-make you."

Loveday broke into an unexpected gurgle of laughter.

"You don't know much about girls—do you?"

"Why should I?"

"Some people do. *James* does—at least he thinks he does. James thinks that any girl can be made to do anything if you're only persevering enough. And he just goes on being persevering, and singing awful sentimental slosh at me, and taking about ten minutes to shake hands every time I see him, and calling me 'Loveday' in the sort of voice that treacle would have if it could talk. And perhaps—perhaps he'll end by converting me, and then I shall marry him in a sort of treacly trance. Do you *want* me to marry James in a treacly trance?"

They had been walking along the street. When Loveday asked this ridiculous question, she stood still and took hold of Hugo's arm with both hands. She shook the arm and said,

"Do you *want* me to marry James?"

They were out of the thoroughfare. The street was dark and empty. Loveday's face was turned up to him. Hugo did the sort of bold thing that only very shy people do. He said, "I'd hate you to m-marry James," and he kissed her. The kiss landed near her eyelashes where the smudge had been.

Loveday said "Oh!" pinched him very hard, and then let go and began to run away. Her heart was beating so fast that she didn't really know what she was doing. She did not run very fast, and Hugo caught her quite easily. His heart was beating too. He did not know what he was going to say, but he heard himself saying, "I'm *f-frightfully* sorry." And then Loveday said, "*Are* you?" and his heart beat harder still, and he said, "*No.*"

Loveday stopped and stamped her foot.

"You're *not!*"

"N-no."

Quite suddenly Hugo stopped being shy. He took Loveday's hands and said,

"Oh, Loveday, do you w-want me to be sorry?"

Loveday said, "I don't know," and then she began to cry.

Hugo had always thought of her laughing. Now she was crying, and it was he who had made her cry. He ought to have been struck to the heart. Actually, he felt very large and strong and uplifted by the fact that he had made Loveday cry; it made him feel about six foot high and as strong as Samson.

When Loveday snatched away her hands and covered her face, he put his arms round her and kissed the little bare, cold fingers and the point of her chin.

"Oh!" said Loveday with a heartrending little sob. And then all at once she put her head on his shoulder and clung to him.

Hugo said all the words he had never said to anyone before; words like darling and sweetheart just crowded into his mind and said themselves into Loveday's ear. It was the most astonishing thing that had ever happened.

"Darling love! Darling love!"

Loveday pinched him with all her might.

"I'm so frightened!" she sobbed.

"Don't be frightened. Darling, don't be frightened."

"I *am* frightened—I'm dreadfully frightened. Oh, please hold me."

"I am holding you. You needn't be frightened any more."

"Why did they want to carry me off? I'm frightened about it."

"You're quite safe. I think they wanted to get you out of the way. Did Cissie know what you overheard about me?"

"Yes—I told her. Wasn't I an *idiot?*"

"Yes," said Hugo. He kissed her again.

"I told Cissie, and it was after that she wouldn't let me go out alone, and she used to lock the door when she went out. She *said* it was because the other people in the house weren't very nice; and that gave me a horrid sort of frightened feeling. She said Maggie's husband wasn't very nice—and I don't think he was."

"Maggie?"

"She let you in. She has the room across the landing. I liked her—I thought she was kind."

Hugo frowned in the dark.

"It was a beastly house for you to be in. I s-say, darling, I wouldn't t-tell anyone about it if I were you."

"Of *course* not. You're different—aren't you?"

"Of course I am. You can tell me anything."

Loveday gave a little whispering laugh.

"I shan't. I shall tell you just what I want to."

"You've got to be good—you've got to be frightfully good and go back to your cousin Emily. She was Emily, wasn't she?"

"Emily Brown—Emily—featherbed—Brown. If I go back, she'll simply smother me with things like 'I told you so,' and 'Look before you leap,' and masses and masses of good advice and more things like 'It isn't done,' and 'Just see what comes of it, my dear,' till I'm choked. And when I'm choked perfectly dumb and helpless, James will come along and propose to me in about five volumes, and I shan't be able to say 'No.'"

Hugo actually laughed.

"I'm not really afraid of James," he said.

"Suppose I marry him?"

"You won't."

"How d'you know?"

"Because some day you're going to marry me."

The street was dark and empty; the wind came down it in gusts. Hugo had the thought that it was like someone laughing—shouting and laughing and rushing by; he felt as if it were a natural thing for the wind to laugh and shout for him and for Loveday, because they were young, and strong, and poor, and immensely happy. He kissed Loveday, and he laughed as he kissed her. And she pinched him and laughed too, and said in a whisper—

"Hugo, why do you laugh? Why?"

"Because I've got everything in the world to laugh at."

Loveday did not laugh again. She put her lips close to Hugo's ear and said,

"You're not going back?"

"Back where?"

"To that horrible house."

He had both arms round her. He shook her a little, gently.

"Of course I'm going back."

"You're not! You *mustn't!*"

"Silly little thing! I must."

"I'm not silly. I'm sensible. It's silly to go back to a horrible house where you know people have got some horrid plan to get you into trouble."

"Loveday—listen. I m-must go back. I can't tell you why, and you m-mustn't ask. I've got a job of work to do, and I've simply got to go back. I c-can't tell you any more than that."

Loveday went on pinching.

"You said that just like James. James is frightfully earnest. If you're going to be earnest and secretive, and like James, I won't ever marry you. Why must you go back? They'll get you into some horrible, horrible trouble if you do. They felt all horrible and wicked when they were talking. It made me feel cold all down the back of my neck and horribly frightened inside. If you go back, they'll do something horrid to you—I know they will."

"No, they won't. Look here, Loveday—don't you see it makes all the difference my knowing that they're going to try it on? I know what they're up to; and they don't know that I know. And as long as they think I don't know, I'm safe. Do you see?"

"I don't see anything."

Footsteps sounded, so close to them that they started apart; a man went by with a shuffling tread. Hugo realized with a start how late it was.

The house they were looking for was no more than two minutes' walk. On the doorstep he asked,

"Have you any money?"

"Cissie's got it," said Loveday. "I had twenty pounds, and she said it wasn't safe to leave it about. And yesterday, when I asked for some, she said it had gone to pay my board and lodging till the end of the month and that I was very lucky to be taken in for so little in London. But I don't think it was a little—I think it was a frightful lot—don't you?"

Hugo didn't say what he thought about Cissie; he rang the bell instead. There was a tinkle of sound.

Loveday came close.

"Someone will come, and you'll go *away*."

"I must."

"Oh, Hugo!"

"Darling, I must."

"Will you come and see me?"

"I can't."

"Or write to me?"

"No—I can't."

"And mustn't I write to you?"

"N-no, darling."

He kissed her, and she kissed him back. The door began to open. It opened about six inches and then stopped.

"Who's there?" said a voice.

What was one to answer? It was no good saying "Miss Leigh"; but what was one to say? Hugo began to stammer:

"W-we were s-sent—I mean t-told—I mean he s-said to ask f-for M-miss Agnes."

"I am Miss Agnes. Who sent you?"

"Ananias," said Hugo, and thought how mad it sounded.

The door opened wider. A woman in a black dress stood there holding a candle.

"Better come in," she said.

Chapter Twenty

Hugo went back to Meade House in the morning. A curious incident happened when he was saying good-bye to Mrs. Miles. He had shaken hands with her and was picking up his suitcase, when the red-haired Mr. Miller came running down the stairs. Mrs. Miles opened the door, and when Hugo said, "Good-bye, Mrs. Miles," she said she was sure it was a pleasure and she hoped it wouldn't be no time before they were seeing him again. It was just at this moment that Mr. Miller reached the third step from the bottom. He leant on the banister and called out in a familiar tone,

"Hullo! Are you off? Well, so long—and I expect you'll get your price all right, though I must say you pitched it pretty high. Still there's nothing like asking—is there?"

"I don't know what you're talking about," said Hugo; and as he shut the door, he thought to himself that he knew very well. Mr. Miller could now bring Mrs. Miles as well as Ella to testify that he had had conversations with Hugo as to the price of some unnamed article. It was a crude device, and its crudity showed plainly how low they rated him. He hoped that they would continue to rate him insultingly low. He went back to Meade House in extraordinarily high spirits. The whole thing had become a great adventure.

He found a letter from Mr. Rice waiting for him. He read it up in his own room. Mr. Rice wrote:

"DEAR SIR,

"I see no reason whatever why we should not be at an agreement. As I have said to you before, if the price that you ask is a high one, still those for whom I am acting are quite willing to pay a high price, because, as I have said, they put a very high value on what you have to sell. The matter must be concluded within a short time. I should be glad to hear from you whether you are satisfied with what we have offered."

That was all the letter.

Hugo read it three times. It contained just one piece of useful information—something was due to happen quite soon, or as Mr. Rice put it, "within a short time." He hoped that Mr. Rice was right, for he wanted the adventure to go ahead.

Minstrel and Hacker returned at dusk; Hacker very much pleased with himself, Minstrel morose and acid. He vanished into his laboratory, emerged to bolt a horrible meal consisting of tinned mackerel and greasy cocoa, and then disappeared for good. Hacker, in a genial mood, regaled Hugo with scandalous stories about prominent personages, becoming steadily more patronizing and well informed as the evening wore on. Hugo allowed himself to stammer a good deal.

Next day was dry and windy. Minstrel remained locked in his laboratory until noon, when he burst out and demanded music; after which he walked to and fro between the two rooms scowling and pulling at his beard. As he walked, he muttered to himself. Once he stopped by the gramophone and spoke through the tumult of *The Flying Dutchman Overture:*

"Does he speak to you? Or are you deaf and idiotic like Hacker? Hacker likes noise—jazz—a storm in a teacup. No, not a teacup—he hasn't any use for tea—a storm in a champagne glass and plenty of silly tinkling laughter—that's Hacker's taste! Is it yours?"

"N-no, sir."

Minstrel's lip lifted.

"The virtuous apprentice!" he sneered. "Do you think that commends itself to me? I hate a prig!" He stopped suddenly and held up his hand. The tumult and the storm had melted into an enchanted calm. He seemed to listen with caught breath till the record ended with the grating of the needle in an empty groove. Then he fetched a deep sigh, looked past Hugo for a moment, and with an abrupt turn stalked back into the laboratory and banged the door.

In the afternoon Hugo went down to the post with some letters. After some consideration he had decided to leave Mr. Rice's communication unanswered. He burnt it to a fine ash, and wondered what they would make of his silence.

The letters he took to the post were Minstrel's. One of them was addressed to the Air Ministry. If it was not a holograph letter, it must have been taken down by Hacker; certainly it had not been dictated to Hugo.

He posted the letters and began to walk back. The distance was about three-quarters of a mile. He had gone about half the way and had reached a long straight stretch of lonely road, when a girl on a bicycle passed him slowly and then, with an exclamation, jumped off her machine and began to feel the back tyre. It was certainly very flat. She poked it, made a vexed little sound, and then in a very fumbling manner she began to do something incompetent with her pump. The tyre remained flat. Hugo received a glance of appeal, and before he quite knew how it happened, he was pumping the tyre.

The girl had a London look; her shoes were thin, and so were her stockings; she had pretty fluffy fair hair and pretty blue eyes, which she used with some effect. She thanked Hugo profusely:

"I'm so stupid with a cycle. I can ride it, you know, but if anything goes wrong—well, I'm in the soup as sure as my name's Daisy."

Hugo gave ever so slight a start. It was a coincidence of course; if he were not all strung up and on the lookout for things to happen, he would never have noticed it. If Mr. Smith wanted to send him a message, it would be signed Daisy. But then Daisy was a very common name. It was just a coincidence.

"I'm sure it's ever so stupid of me. You *are* clever at it—aren't you? And I'm keeping you, and perhaps you're in a hurry. Do you live near here?"

"N-not very far. I'll pump the other one whilst I'm at it."

"Oh, *thank* you! You *are* clever at it, Mr. Ross."

This time Hugo's start was a very definite one.

"Why do you think m-my name is Ross?" he said, and stopped pumping to stare at her.

The blue eyes opened very wide.

"*Isn't* it? I thought it was. Mine's Daisy."

They looked at each other.

"*Daisy?*" said Hugo.

"Isn't it a pretty name?" said the damsel.

"*Daisy?*" said Hugo again.

She nodded.

"You're Hugo Ross, aren't you?"

He saw no harm in admitting it, so he said "Yes."

"Good gracious! What a fuss about saying so! You've got a sister, haven't you? What's *her* name?"

"S-Susan," said Hugo.

"And what's the parrot's name?"

It wasn't a coincidence; it was a message from Mr. Smith.

Hugo said, "Ananias," and the girl nodded.

"Just as well to be on the safe side, though I recognized you from your photograph."

"My photograph?"

"The one in your sister's wedding group—only you don't look so cross in real life. Well, I've got a message for you. He thought you'd better know that Maggie Plane didn't give you away."

"I didn't know her name," he began, and then he remembered that Loveday had called the woman across the landing at No. 50 Maggie. It was a great relief to be sure she had held her tongue.

"He thought you'd better know," said Daisy. "Oh—and Ananias thought you'd better have this—he thought it might be useful." She put a long envelope into his hand. "Don't open it now—there's no particular point in anyone coming along and seeing us. Well, I must be getting along. And thank you ever so for pumping my tyre. The front one isn't really flat, you know."

Hugo watched her ride away. He pushed the envelope down inside his pocket and walked back through the dusk. When he reached the house he went up to his own room. After the first glance at the contents of the envelope he went and stood with his back against the door. They were not at all what he wished Hacker or anyone else in the house to see. He looked at them for a minute or two, turned them over, and finally put them back into the envelope and put the envelope back into his pocket. Then he slipped down the stairs and went out again. It was dark enough on the drive, but it was darker still in the shrubbery. It took him five minutes or so to find what he was looking for.

He returned to the house, to find Minstrel angrily demanding of heaven, earth, and Mr. Hacker why he paid a secretary if that secretary was not to be there when he was wanted. He began to dictate letters with great volubility; one to a Swedish professor concerning several extremely abstruse and technical matters, another to a publisher, and a third to an American agent refusing a lecture tour.

This last was so exceedingly vituperative that Hugo wondered whether Minstrel really meant to send it. He walked about all the time that he was dictating and appeared to be in a state of extreme nervous tension. When the letters were written, he made Hugo read them over. In the end he tore up two out of the three and began all over again. Then, suddenly breaking off, he said.

"They can wait! Why should I answer letters? Fools with all the time in the world on their hands write to me and expect me to answer them. They expect me to waste time which is worth, not just money, but ideas—unminted, unrealized, and unassayed ideas worth more than any wretched sordid gold that was ever mined. They expect me to take these ideas and pay them out—sweat for them, work for them, and then pay them out to any fool who writes to me and begs. Pah! They make me sick!"

He walked down the room and back again.

"What's the good of you if you can't answer this sort of pettifogging stuff without bothering me?"

He picked up the American's letter and thrust it into Hugo's face.

"Like to like! Tell him I'll see him dead before I'll cheapen my wits to put money in his pocket!"

He flung over to the bookshelf, plucked forth a book, and opening it, stood there reading, his back to the room.

Hugo wrote briefly that Mr. Ambrose Minstrel could not at present contemplate a lecture tour in the United States. It was nine o'clock before he was free.

He went up to his room and looked out at the night. There was a strong, warm wind blowing; clouds that had hung low all day were piled high in the east. The south and west were clear, and there was moonlight, though he could not see the moon. The house oppressed him. He put his flute into his pocket and went out. The front-door shut behind him with a bang.

He was perhaps halfway down the drive, when the door opened and shut again noiselessly. Mr. James Hacker took the same way. He wore tennis shoes and moved with caution.

Hugo went on, and presently climbed to the top of the wooded hill which had become his place of refuge. He liked being high up, and he liked the trees. The wind blew through them to-night, and their many moving shadows made patterns in the moonlight. He settled himself in the crook of a branch and began to play.

Mr. Hacker turned and went over the hill towards Torring House.

Chapter Fourteen

THE WOOD was a very nice place. The notes of the flute dropped into the wind like water, and the wind went on, now loud, now soft, with great rushes and sudden lulls. From where Hugo sat he could see a little glade opening before him. The trees stood all round it in a ring. It was carpeted with dry leaves that rustled in the wind. Overhead there were branches, and then a space of clear moonlit sky.

Hugo began to feel very happy. He had opened a door and walked right out of his adventure into a place which was full of wind and music and the rustle of leaves. Presently he would go back through the door and go on with the adventure again. He did not know that the door had opened of itself, and that the adventure was following him.

He began to think about Loveday. He felt immensely happy when he thought about her. He did not mind not being able to go and see her—she was here. His thought was so full of her, and he was so uplifted by it, that he wanted to shout with the wind and make better music than he had ever been able to make before. It was a most exhilarating feeling.

He began to play a tune that he had picked out for himself. He and Susan had an Irish nurse who had crooned them to sleep with it, and if he had ever known the words, he had lost them again. It was just a tune that reminded him of Loveday, and he played it and played with it, and put little turns and twirls to it, and quite forgot to play in a whisper for fear of being overheard. Then all at once, just as he was beginning the tune again, he had the most curious sensation; the flute seemed to be playing by itself. He stopped in the middle of a bar, and the air went on, very sweet and clear but rather far away. The hand that held the flute dropped down upon his knee; the other hand gripped the branch on which he sat. The clear fluting sound came from the other side of the glade. He heard a twig snap. The wind blew and the leaves rustled. The tune took words to itself:

"New hope may bloom, and days may come,
Of milder, calmer beam;
But there's nothing half so sweet in life as
Love's young dream.
Oh, there's nothing half so sweet in life as
Love's young dream."

Hugo leaned forward on his branch. The far side of the glade was in black shadow. On the edge of the shadow something moved and came out into the misty moonlight. There it stood still, a small dark shadow. A high, clear voice called,

"Where are you?"

It wasn't Loveday. Hugo had known all along that it wasn't Loveday; and yet he felt the queerest sense of disappointment. What was anyone else doing to come into this enchantment of wind and shadow and moonlight and call to him? It should have been Loveday; and it wasn't Loveday.

He stayed still, leaning forward, holding on to the branch on which he sat.

"Where are you?" asked the clear, high voice.

Hugo remembered his manners. He dropped to the ground and said,

"I'm here;" and then as he walked towards her, "D-d-did you w-want anything?"

He could hear her humming the air he had played. As he came nearer, he saw that she was wrapped in a long velvet cloak. He thought it was velvet because it looked so black and soft, blacker and softer even than the shadow out of which she had come. The wind blew the cloak and showed a gleam of silver, the turn of a bare arm, the flash of a ring where she held the folds together.

"C-can I do anything for you?"

He stopped a couple of yards away, and got a queer half glance.

"You can tell me who you are."

No one could have said that she had a brogue, but there was just the least soft Irish touch on the words; it was rather like the something that isn't quite rain in the West of Ireland breeze. The voice was not without its charm.

"My n-name is Ross."

The little cloaked lady sketched a curtsey.

"Mine is Hélène de Lara. And now we're introduced, and you're wondering what in the world I'm doing interrupting you like this."

She pushed back the hood as she spoke. The moonlight showed him a curious little face which reminded him of a monkey, and the palest hair he had ever seen. The monkey was rather a pretty monkey, and it had a pair of eyes like black pools; altogether an elfin apparition and quite at home in a forest glade.

"I heard you playing," she said.

Hugo said nothing. One bit of him was feeling shy and tongue-tied, and another bit suspicious and alert. He wondered what Mme. de Lara wanted, and he thought he would wait and see. She went on speaking, and all the time that she was speaking, the big dark eyes looked him over mournfully.

"I heard you playing, and I came because I've done mad things all my life when I've wanted to—and sometimes when I haven't." She paused and laughed a little laugh as mournful as her eyes. "Ah well, if you've never done a mad thing just to please yourself, you won't know what I'm talking about, and I'll just say goodnight and go home." All at once her voice changed; she went on without any pause, "Who taught you to play Irish melodies? For you're not Irish—are you?"

"N-no. I didn't know it was an Irish tune—at least—"

"Didn't you know that you were playing *Love's Young Dream?*" She laughed again. "Perhaps we none of us know till it's over and the dream is gone."

"My nurse used to s-sing it—n-not the words—just the tune. She called it *The Old Woman.*"

Hélène de Lara nodded. Her cloak slipped and showed a silver dress.

"That's the name of the tune. Tommy Moore wrote sentimental words to it and called it *Love's Young Dream.* He was an arch sentimentalist, you know, and everyone laughs at him now. I laugh at him by daylight or lamplight; but he goes very well with the moon, and I've a soft spot somewhere for him and his sentimentalities. Won't you go on playing?"

The idea filled Hugo with horror; it also touched his sense of humour.

"I'm af-f-fraid—" He did not try to stammer, but he did not try not to stammer.

"Poor romance!" said Hélène de Lara. "It has been killed, like all beautiful things, by fear. Everyone to-day is afraid of romance and poetry and beauty and youth and love—I'm afraid of them myself. Just for this moment, of course, I am mad, so I am not afraid—mad people are never afraid of being ridiculous—but when I am not mad I am just as much afraid as anybody else—I ask just as carefully, 'Is it done?' And if it is not done—*Fi donc!* I do not do it. And if it is done, it does not matter in the least how ugly and stupid and dull it is—I do, it, and everybody else does it too, and we are bored. Only every now and then I have a mad moment, and I please myself and say what I think, or run out into the moonlight to listen to an old Irish song." She spoke at first in a light, soft tone that gradually fell away into sadness. Her voice had an extraordinary charm, the charm of laughter and tears.

Hugo did not know what to say. For the matter of that, it was best to say nothing—to be stupid and shy was the safest rôle in the world.

"Ah well," she said, and pulled her cloak about her—"we mustn't be mad for more than just a moment—must we?" Just above her breath she sang:

"Oh, the days are past when beauty bright
Our hearts' chain wove,
When our dream of life from morn to night
Was love—still love."

She put out her hand—a little hand with a great diamond that caught the light.

"Good-bye, Mr. Ross."

He saw her turn to go with the swirl of the wind in the full black cloak; and then she looked round at him over her shoulder.

"You're at Meade House, aren't you? How is Ambrose?"

The question was, as it were, tossed at him, lightly and as if the answer mattered less than nothing; yet she turned back for the answer, and he saw that the hand with the diamond on it was pressed against her throat. He spoke as if he noticed nothing, but he thought perhaps he need not stammer any more; he was feeling too much interested to be shy. He said,

"Oh, he's just as usual."

Mme. de Lara caught him up.

"As usual? What do you mean by that now?"

Hugo said, "Oh—I don't know," and she took her hand from her throat to make a little gesture with it.

"What is usual with him—now? Is he ill? Is he well? Is he sad—or cross—or mad? Or is he only trying to drive everyone round him into Bedlam?" She laughed, a hard little laugh with an edge to it. "Any of these things might be usual with Ambrose."

Hugo was very decidedly interested. Mr. Smith had hinted at something more than a friendship between these two odd people. He wondered why the lady should be at so much pains to give the fact away. And then it seemed to him that it was clever of her, because Hugo might have heard rumours, and she was conveying the impression of a complete breach. He did not think it necessary to say anything.

Mme. de Lara came a step nearer.

"How discreet you are! You won't talk about Ambrose. *I see.* Am I allowed to inquire for Mr. Hacker? Or is that also *pays défendu*?"

Hugo looked puzzled. He still held his flute, but he began now to take it apart and slip it into his pocket. He said doubtfully,

"Are they friends of yours?—Mr. Minstrel. I mean, and Hacker?"

He saw her lift her chin. She had the monkey is trick of sudden grimace. The odd, pretty face became vividly ugly for an instant.

"Perhaps we were friends—once. Ah now, there's a bad word!" Her face wrinkled again. She said, "*Once*" on what sounded like an angry sob; and then, very quickly and passionately, "I was young—once. And I was gay—once. And once—once—*once*—oh, once I was loved!"

Hugo felt like an actor who is suddenly carried away by his part—and he had forgotten that it was his part to be stupid and tongue-tied. He said, speaking quickly and low,

"Why not 'I was *sad* once'?"

She brushed her hand across her mournful eyes and laughed.

"Only *once?* Fortunate Mr. Ross! But you are young. What a lot of time there is for you to be sad in!" She laughed again. "Ah now, that's unkind of me—I'll take it back. And I'll go before we quarrel. It's so stupid to quarrel—but one doesn't think of that until it's too late. We'll be wiser. Good-bye." The last word had a sort of sober sadness.

Hugo said good-bye, and watched her walk away. The acting had moved him. He had never watched acting that had moved him more. If the world was Hélène de Lara's stage, she brought to it a surprising gift.

She went slowly away down the glade, moving with a grace that touched the imagination. Hugo watched her, and wondered if the curtain were really going to fall. He thought not.

It seemed that he was right, for just short of the deep shadow at the edge of the glade the lady tripped, cried out, and fell. When Hugo reached her, she was trying to rise, but not making much of a success of it. She laughed up at him.

"This is what comes of being mad! I've twisted my foot. That is to teach me not to run out in the moonlight, I expect. Ouf! How stupid of me! Will you give me your arm?"

He had to do more than that; he had to put his arm round her waist. She was incredibly small and light and soft to hold. He could have carried her, and said so; but she laughed again and protested that she could walk.

"Just your arm—yes. How clever you are! Like that—so that I need not put my weight on the foot."

Her weight! He could have laughed. She didn't seem to have any; she was as soft and light as thistledown. This part of the play was decidedly pleasant. He wondered what came next. He would see her home, she would ask him in, and—Mr. Smith's words came back warningly: "It might be very dangerous for you to go to Mme. de Lara's house; but on the other hand it might be very advantageous."

"Am I very heavy?" said Hélène de Lara. "We're just on the path. I think I can manage once I get to the path—unless you are going to be so kind as to see me home."

Hugo made the answer that was expected of him. He was thanked very prettily and allowed to afford just as much support as was graceful and agreeable. The feeling of being in a play became stronger and stronger.

The path wound gently down between the trees. The moon looked through upon it, and the woods were full of the sighing noises of the night. He lifted her down half a dozen steps, unlatched a rustic gate, and came out upon the drive of Torring House.

"We will go round to the side," said Mme. de Lara. She laughed, and caught her breath in the middle of the laugh. "I do not always tell my butler when I do mad things—he is as proper as Mrs. Grundy. Come round to the side of the house."

Chapter Twenty-Two

"I CAN'T SEE a thing," said Hugo.

They had turned into very deep shadow, the shadow of the house and the shadow of overhanging trees. He felt Hélène de Lara lean towards him, and he felt the pressure of her hand high up on his arm, where it clung for support.

"I can see," she said. "But no one can see us. There is something about being quite, quite in the dark that makes me feel very safe. Do you know what I mean? We are here; but we are not here, because no one can see us—we are like invisible ghosts. It makes me feel safe." Her voice had a whispering sweetness.

"I like to s-see where I'm going," said Hugo.

"How dull!" said Mme. de Lara.

They had some steps to mount, and came out upon a terrace. His feet felt gravel, and all at once he felt, rather than saw, the black mass of the house.

"Two more steps," said Mme. de Lara. "The glass door is not latched. Push it!"

They came into a dark room with a glow of firelight in it. It was warm, and it smelt of violets. Hélène de Lara steadied herself against his shoulder and touched the wall. The light came on and showed a little room full of flowers and soft chairs with bright coloured cushions. The light itself came from three lamps with shades of blue and primrose and violet. A very large orange cat rose from before the fire, stretched himself, and fixed a cold regardful eye upon Hugo.

Mme. de Lara sank into a chair and let her head fall back against an emerald cushion.

"O-o-oh!" she said. It was a sigh of pain.

With a groping movement she undid her cloak and pushed it back. The black folds covered the chair; her head with its silver flaxen hair lay back on the emerald brocade; her eyes were closed. The light above her, filtered through a pale blue shade, made her look ghastly; only her lips were brightly, unnaturally red.

Hugo thought the play was very well staged—the silver hair and the silver dress, and the little silver slippers stained with woodland damp; the pale blue light, and the soft sigh of pain. He thought it very well done and he hoped that he carried his own part as well. It was quite an easy part really—up to a point. He had to be shy, to stammer a little, to seem stupid, to notice everything—and to keep his head.

Hélène de Lara opened her eyes.

"Shall I c-call someone?" said Hugo.

"Oh no." She sat up. "I'm all right. I only want to sit still and not meet anyone for just a minute or two." A smile touched her eyes. "I want a minute or two to come back—out of the woods. Sit down and we'll come back together."

Hugo remained standing.

"I m-must be g-going."

"Ah, you don't want to come back! And you're lucky, because you needn't. I—must! You don't know how I envy you."

She looked up at him and down again—the old trick that shows how long and dark the lashes are and gives just a hint of dark depths in the eyes.

Hugo began, "I m-must—" and she laughed a little sadly.

"I wanted you to stay—just for a little—just while I came back. It's so lonely coming back alone." Then she said quickly, "Will you get into trouble if you stay? Will Ambrose scold you for being late? Does he scold you much? He's got a frightful temper—hasn't he?"

"Oh, I don't know."

She lifted her eyebrows.

"Don't you? *I* do. He nearly strangled me once"—Hugo thought she turned a little paler—"he did really. You'd better not offend him—he's a dangerous man to offend." She was sitting up now and looking at him anxiously. "You'd better go. But will you come again in quite a respectable, ordinary way? I've got some people coming to dinner to-morrow. Will you come? And will you bring your flute?"

Hugo was furious because he felt himself blushing scarlet. The idea of being asked to play the flute at a dinner-party was inconceivably horrible. That the blush was most excellently in keeping with his part did not console him in the least. He said, "I c-couldn't!" in such panic-stricken tones that she laughed.

"Then you shan't—you shall only play to the moon and to me." She put up her left hand with a graceful gesture. "You'll come to-morrow? Ah, *do* now! I think we might be friends. You'll come?"

As he took the hand, he wondered what he was to say. It might be dangerous to come; but it might be more dangerous to stay away and be suspected of being on his guard. He looked at the great diamond that almost hid a fragile wedding ring. It was curiously set in a circle of tiny emerald points. He thought it would be safer to seem the fool they thought he was and to come.

He said, "Th-thank you," and felt the little hand press his before it slipped away.

He went out through the glass door and, looking back, saw Hélène de Lara standing there with her hand on the emerald curtain that hung before it. The light shone on her hair and on her silver dress. The curtains framed her for a moment before they fell. He was in the dark, and had to grope his way down the steps.

At the bottom of the steps he stood still and looked back at the house. The moon was behind it, not high enough to clear the roof. He was marking the position of the door through which he had come, when a window sprang into view, above it and a little to the right. Someone had opened the window and was pulling back the curtains; light streamed from it. A girl leaned out; and Hugo's heart gave a sudden thump because the girl looked like Loveday. It was not Hélène de Lara. But how frightfully stupid of him to think of Loveday at Torring House! Loveday was at Ledlington with her cousin Emily Brown—Emily—featherbed—Brown. Loveday could not conceivably be here. He frowned because it would not do at all for him to start imagining things.

And then his heart gave another thump, because the girl turned back from the window. She had been leaning out of the corner of it, and as she turned back, the light inside the room fell on her slantwise and Hugo saw her face. And it was Loveday—beyond all mistake or cavil it was Loveday.

A bewildered moment passed. His mind would not work. Loveday was at Ledlington—Loveday was here—Loveday couldn't possibly be here—Loveday *was* here. His mind simply would not work at all. His eyes stared at the window and saw Loveday pass slowly across it. She was there—and then she wasn't there any longer. He felt the need to get away and think. He simply had to think.

He plunged into the deep shadow of the over-arching trees, walked a few paces, and then stood still. What did it mean?

What *could* it possibly mean? The suddenness of the thing was like the suddenness of a blow that knocks all the sense out of you. He had to steady himself and recover; he had to think. And quite suddenly he was able to think again.

Mme. de Lara had asked him to her house. Why? He didn't think it was for his *beaux yeux*. He didn't think that she had come on him by accident. She had asked him to her house because Loveday was there—she had asked him to her house because she, or someone else, wanted to see him meet Loveday. That meant that someone wasn't sure—He broke off and began again.

Daisy had come to him with a message from Mr. Smith. Mr. Smith had sent him a message to say that Maggie had held her tongue. If Maggie had held her tongue, no one knew that he had come to No. 50 in the dark and taken Loveday away. No one knew that he and Loveday had met since their first meeting in the lane. Cissie didn't know, and Hacker didn't know; so Mme. de Lara couldn't know. They didn't know that Loveday had warned him, or that she had had any opportunity of warning him. Why did they want him to meet Loveday? He went back farther for the answer.

If Hacker was planning to sell Minstrel's invention, and planning to make a scapegoat of a convenient Hugo Ross, he would need to be absolutely sure that Hugo had no suspicions, because— the more Hugo thought of it the more certain he became on this point—if Hacker meant to make a scapegoat of him, Hacker would have to take a certain amount of risk. If Hacker meant to sell the plans of Minstrel's invention and make it appear that it was Hugo who had sold them, then he would have to risk allowing the plans to pass through Hugo's hands; there would have to be a moment when they were actually in Hugo's possession, because unless there was some proof of this, it would be difficult to make a really satisfactory scapegoat of him. Every time he thought it over, he felt more certain that the moment would come when the plans would actually be in his hands. And it was obvious that Mr. Smith thought so too. Hacker would just have to take the risk; but before he took it, he would want to make sure that Hugo had not been warned. Maggie hadn't spoken. But had Cissie spoken? Had Cissie told Hacker that she had seen Hugo—and had given him her address on the night of Loveday's escape? If Cissie had told Hacker that, he might very well have suspicions, and take steps to confirm or remove those suspicions. It might be Hacker's idea to bring Hugo and Loveday together and see what happened. It might be Hacker's idea, or it might be just coincidence that made Mme. de Lara invite Hugo to dinner when Loveday Leigh was in her house.

Hugo didn't think it was coincidence. He thought it was no more of a coincidence than the overtures of Mr. Rice, the odd behaviour of Mr. Miller, and the disappearance of Mr. Rice's letter. He thought they were all exactly the same sort of coincidence. And he suspected Mr. Hacker of producing them, after the manner of a conjuror, out of his hat.

Well—what about Loveday? It was no use wondering how she had got to Torring House. At Torring House she was; and he felt quite sure that when he walked into the drawing-room tomorrow evening, he would find Loveday there, and that their meeting would be a matter of considerable interest to someone else who would be present.

He had got as far as this, when he heard a sound. It came from the direction of the house. He couldn't put a name to it—it was just a sound, and he stopped his thoughts to listen. It came again, and it was nearer—a whisper of voices, a footfall on the path, the sound of the wind blowing the dry leaves, and then voices again; a man's voice and a woman's, coming nearer.

Hugo was in black shadow. He had stepped off the narrow winding path and stood in a deep recess between dark holly and darker yew. The wind blew among the leaves, and he heard Mme. de Lara say, "I must go back."

It was Hacker's voice that answered—Hacker's voice, but a different voice to the voice of the everyday Hacker; its tones were deep and angry, and charged with some violence of feeling which Hugo did not understand at all.

"Go back then!"

"How angry you are," said Hélène de Lara. The words came mournfully from her unseen lips.

She stood a bare yard from Hugo Hacker, beyond her, answered roughly:

"Some day you'll push a man too far and he'll swing for you."

She gave a little cry of protest that was half a laugh:

"Come, come, my friend—"

He broke in, "Are you going back to him?"

She laughed again.

"You know very well that he went ten minutes ago. Alas! I shall not see him till to-morrow. I've lost my heart to him, you know. He has such innocent eyes, and he blushes so divinely."

For once Hugo found himself in one mind with Mr. Hacker; he felt that Mme. de Lara was the sort of person who might very easily get herself murdered. He heard Hacker take a stride forward, and he heard Hélène say quickly,

"Don't eat me, James! Oh! How rough you are! No, I will not kiss you if you are rough. Put me down!"

Hugo had not bargained for this. It was frightfully embarrassing. To his relief the interlude was of the briefest. There was a kiss or two, and then the lady said,

"Come, James—enough! Let me go, and attend! To-morrow I will send you a formal invitation—one to you and one to him. You will open yours when he is there. And you will say what a pleasant neighbour I am, and any other *politesse* that may occur to you— not too *empressé*, you understand. And you will say what a bear Ambrose is, and what a pity there has been a quarrel, but that, for your part, you mean to accept the olive branch and dine with me. Then you can watch with your own jealous eyes to see how Master Hugo meets my cousin Loveday. For my part, I believe you have found a mare's nest."

"I don't know." The violence had gone from Hacker's voice; it was merely puzzled. He went on quickly, "You haven't said anything to her?"

"Not a word. I have not said his name. She does not even know that I have ever heard of him. It will be a complete surprise."

"It must be, or it's no good. We come in together, and she must be there. I want to see—I must see—if there's the least recognition. If they only met the once in that dark lane, there won't be any recognition. But if, somehow, they've contrived to meet since, one of them's bound to show some sign."

"Well—they meet. And then? What next?"

"You introduce him. If he's really innocent, he'll be just mildly struck with the name, and no more. But she'll be taken aback and excited. She'll want a chance of speaking to him, and it's up to you to see that she doesn't get it. If he's really innocent, then he believes that the girl he met in London was Miss Leigh. You see?"

Hélène de Lara laughed her mournful laugh.

"Ah, James," she said, "I think I'd give the world and all to be as innocent. Wouldn't you?"

Mr. Hacker grew impatient.

"Don't talk such nonsense! Who wants to be innocent? The point is—is he a fool, or isn't he? And is it safe to bank on his being just the fool he seems?"

"He's not a fool—he's a boy."

"The same thing."

"You mean it will serve you as well." Her voice was a little scornful.

"Come, Hélène, be rational for once! You always say you can read men—you've certainly had plenty of practice. I want to know, seriously, whether you think it's safe to bank on his being a fool."

Her answer came a thought indignantly:

"Yes—I've had practice. And I tell you, just as seriously as you want, that your Hugo Ross isn't a fool at all. He's a boy. He doesn't suspect people, because he's friendly like a boy, and shy like a boy. And I think you are safe—oh yes, quite safe—to bank on being able to ruin this friendly boy." Her voice lost its rather tragic note and became light with laughter. "I will tell you something else—something that you haven't asked me. I will tell you that Hugo Ross will make a most adorable lover, and that I think that's a better use for him than to be mixed up in your dirty affairs."

She blew him a kiss and began to run away.

"Good-night, James!" she said and was gone.

Chapter Twenty-Three

WITH A VIOLENT WORD Mr. Hacker flung away in the opposite direction.

Hugo stood where he was and considered the situation. How on earth was he to warn Loveday? And if she wasn't warned, what would happen? The odds were that she would show that she recognized him when he came into the room. For his own part, he was warned. But if he hadn't been warned—if he had come into Mme. de Lara's drawing-room and found Loveday there—he couldn't be sure that he would have escaped the trap that had been laid for him. A single look, a stammer, a change of colour—no, he couldn't be sure. And if he couldn't be sure of himself, he couldn't be sure of Loveday. They must both pass Hacker's test, or it was all up with his job.

There was a sound of flying footsteps, and Mme. de Lara passed him, running. Her cloak blew against him, and she ran on. He heard her call, "James! James! *James!*" in a panting whisper, and he heard Hacker come striding back. They met, and Hélène said, still panting,

"Why did you go away like that? See how nice and forgiving I am. I'll go up through the wood with you if you ask me nicely."

"I won't ask you at all." Hacker's voice was rough.

"Then I'll come to see you don't get into mischief, and we'll talk about Hugo, for indeed, and really, I've lost a little bit of my heart to him."

Hugo didn't wait to hear any more. He stepped out upon the path and moved silently in the direction of the house. He had no plan, but the feeling that Loveday was there and that she must be warned drove him. If he were to slip in through the unlatched sitting-room door...No—far too dangerous. It would be ruin, sheer blank ruin, if he were seen.

He stopped by the steps and looked up to where he had seen the lighted square of her window. The curtains had been drawn across it, but they did not meet; a vertical shaft of light divided them. She was still awake. He thought of throwing up a pebble; and then he thought of Hélène de Lara coming up soft-footed out of the shadows and finding him under Loveday's window.

It was not as dark as it had been; the moon was near to topping the house. To do nothing might be dangerous; but anything that he could do might be more dangerous still. He could see the sitting-room door. Here too a line of light showed like a thin bright wire. He was looking at it, when in a moment it widened, showed the bright room within, and against the bright room—someone who stood there whilst he breathed twice. They were quick breaths, because the someone was Loveday.

She dropped the curtains behind her and came running forward for a dozen steps, then stopped, came on slowly, groped with her foot for the topmost step, and called,

"Hélène!"

The sound died away as if it were afraid of the dark.

Hugo said, "Loveday! Loveday!" and she said, "Oh!" in a soft, glad, laughing, surprised way and ran right down the steps into his arms. There was just a rapturous moment of being together again, and then they both said, "Ssh!" and Loveday laughed her little whispering laugh and put her face against his shoulder so that no one else should hear.

At the foot of the steps on either side there was a tall yew pyramid. Hugo pulled Loveday behind the farther one and said "Ssh!" again.

"We haven't a minute. I've got something frightfully important to tell you."

Loveday was still quivering with laughter.

"We always seem to be running into each other in the dark! It's so *funny*."

Hugo shook her.

"Don't laugh! You must listen. I'm coming to dinner to-morrow night. It's a put-up job to see whether we recognize each other. I was just wondering how I could warn you."

"Oh! How *exciting!*"

He had his arm round her shoulders. He shook her again.

"Listen! It's frightfully important. It's a put-up job. They want to see how we meet each other."

Loveday rubbed her head against his cheek.

"Well—how *do* we meet each other?"

"Not like this. Loveday—listen! It really is frightfully important. You see, as far as they know, we've only met once—in the lane, when it was dark and we couldn't see each other. That's what you told Cissie—isn't it?"

"Yes, I did."

"Well, what Cissie knows Hacker knows, and what Hacker knows Mme. de Lara knows. They know we met in the lane, and they know you wanted to see me again because you wanted to warn me about something. Did you tell Cissie just why you wanted to warn me?"

"No, I didn't. I told her I'd heard things about Meade House, and that I didn't think you ought to go there. And when I saw she really wanted to find out, I wouldn't tell her. I said you might be blown up in an explosion—but of course she knew it wasn't that. But I wouldn't tell her what it was."

"That's all right. Now, so far as they know, you never did see me or warn me. But they want to be quite, quite sure about it, because it's tremendously important for them to be sure that I haven't been warned; so they've put up this dinner-party business, and they're going to spring us on each other and watch to see whether we give ourselves away."

Loveday wasn't laughing now. She gave a little shiver and said, "Tell me what to do."

"You mustn't recognize me, of course—we mustn't recognize each other—but when I'm introduced to you, you'd know my name, you see. So then you can just be all excited and interested and wanting to get an opportunity of speaking to me. You won't get one of course—they'll see to that. That's your line, I think. Have you got it? You don't recognize me, but you know my name and you get quite excited about it. My line's a bit different. I don't know you, and I don't connect you with the girl in the lane even after I've heard your name, because, you see, I'm supposed to think Cissie is you."

Loveday began to laugh under her breath. Then all at once she stopped and pinched him very hard.

Someone was coming along the shrubbery path—a light footfall and a voice that hummed a light and pleasant air, a shadow in a black cloak. It was Hélène de Lara, and as she passed them by, she sang softly:

"New hope may bloom, and days may come,
Of brighter, purer beam;
But there's nothing half so sweet in life as
Love's young dream.
Oh, there's nothing half so sweet in life as
Love's young dream."

She ran up the steps and was gone.

Loveday pinched Hugo harder.

"Oh, she's gone in! Hugo, she's gone in! I'm locked out! What on earth am I going to do?"

They peered round the pyramid and saw the curtains part and fall again. There was no shaft of light any more. The door was certainly shut, and Loveday on the wrong side of it. She began to laugh again.

"I'll have to climb up the magnolia. If she goes into my room, I'm done. Oh, Hugo, what fun! Anyhow there's no hurry now, and we can talk."

"I say—I'm most awfully s-sorry."

"You needn't be—I'll get in somehow. I've always wanted to be a burglar. It'll be most frightfully amusing, but we'll have to let Hélène go to sleep first."

"Loveday—how on earth did you get here? I thought you were at Ledlington. You went there, didn't you?"

"I went there, but I didn't stay there. Emily was in an awful fuss because she was just starting off to go and see a tremendously old uncle who sends for her about six times a year, and if she doesn't come, he makes a new will and doesn't leave her anything—and she didn't think it proper to leave me with Andrew."

She gave a gurgle of delight. "Darling, if you could only see Andrew! He's so proper that if you were to cut him up small, there'd be enough properness in every little bit to last seven Mrs. Grundys for ever and ever. So I just *rocked*, and Emily was frightfully huffy and all stuffed up with the sermons she'd been getting ready to preach to me. It must be awful to be absolutely bunged up with sermons and not be able to get them off your chest because of having to go and stop your uncle from leaving you out of his will. I really did feel sorry for Emily. And right in the middle of all the fuss Hélène blew in and said would I come to her for the week-end?"

"How do you know her?" said Hugo.

"She's my cousin—and she's Emily's cousin too. My mother was Irish, you know, and Hélène's Irish, too. It's frightfully funny her calling herself Hélène, and de Lara; because of course she was just Ellen O'Brien, and she married a horrid little scallywag called Con Larrigan, and they went abroad and made some money somehow. And she came back de Lara, and she says Con's dead. And Emily says it's lucky for her he is. Emily's frightfully funny about the whole thing, and any other time I might have cried my eyes out and she wouldn't have let me go and stay with Hélène."

"How long is she going to be away?" said Hugo quickly.

"Why?"

"Because you oughtn't to be here—I don't like your being here."

"You said that just like James. James doesn't like my being here at all—James disapproves of Hélène very much. He did quite a lot of disapproving yesterday—he disapproved about me, and about Hélène, and about Emily going off to her uncle. James thought she ought to let Uncle Richard change his will and stay at home to chaperone me whilst he was being frightfully moral and high-minded and forgiving about my *escapade*—that's what he called it, you know *escapahd*. It sounds dreadfully snoopy that way. I felt quite sorry for James, because I know he'd planned a whole week-end of forgiving me and overlooking my *escapahd*, and it was simply snatched away from him. I think he meant to lecture me on Saturday and forgive me on Sunday and finish up with a nice magnanimous proposal after supper, when Andrew and Emily always go to sleep."

"Loveday, do stop talking nonsense! When does your cousin Emily come home?"

"Well, as a rule she gets wired for one day, and the next day Uncle Richard tells her he's dying every five minutes and wants someone to telephone for his solicitor about three times an hour, and the day after, he begins to get bored with Emily, and he says he doesn't think he's going to die this time. So I think she'll be back on Monday. She always comes back very cross, because Uncle Richard's housemaid gives her a lukewarm hot-water bottle and doesn't screw the top on tight."

"I don't like your being here," said Hugo gloomily.

"Fuss!" said Loveday. "I'm frightfully glad I'm here, and you ought to be frightfully glad too, because if I wasn't here, you couldn't—but perhaps you don't want to."

Hugo kissed her, but only once.

"I've got to get you into the house," he said.

"I don't want to go in a bit. You *are* like James, you know."

"You've got to go in. We shall have to see if we can open a window."

Loveday followed him meekly. She didn't in the least want to go in; she wanted to stay out in the moonlight, and be made love to, but when Hugo said "You've got to go in," she heaved a resigned sigh and followed him. She had a dreadful suspicion that Hugo would always make her do what he wanted.

They crossed the terrace and tried the sitting-room window very gently. The room was dark and the door bolted. Hugo began to be very seriously disturbed. If they couldn't get in—they *must* get in. They tried other windows, and found them all fastened.

"I shall have to go in with the milk," said Loveday in an almost soundless whisper that yet contrived to be gay. "I *am* glad I came out."

"What made you come?"

"I was looking out of my window, and I saw Hélène run down the steps—at least I thought it was Hélène. And I went to her room, and she wasn't there. And I went down to her little sitting-room, and the door was open, so I came out to look for her."

They had reached the back premises. A row of windows looked into a paved courtyard. Hugo fished out a pocket-knife and, standing in the shadow, managed to move the catch of one of them. He opened the window softly inch by inch and found himself looking in upon a scullery sink. Loveday had to climb over it.

She dropped lightly down and whisked round with a smothered laugh.

"I hope Hélène doesn't keep black beetles—I do hate them!"

It was not a romantic place for a lovers' parting; but as they leaned together across the sink and kissed, romance was there. Loveday clung to him.

"You haven't said you loved me—not once."

"That's because I do love you. You mustn't stop."

Loveday's clasp relaxed; she began to draw back. And then she was holding him tighter than ever.

"Hugo, I'm sure there are black beetles!"

"Nonsense!"

"I heard one—*rustle*. I'm sure I did."

"Nonsense!"

"It isn't. Hugo, it's so dark—and if I stepped on a black beetle and it squelched—"

Hugo detached her fingers—they were very cold. He heard a little sob in the dark.

"Darling, don't be a goose!"

"I do hate the dark and—and places where there isn't anyone, but you feel there might be."

"There won't be."

"There wouldn't be if it was you, but there might be when it's me. It's—it's a long way up to my room in the dark. Couldn't you—couldn't you just come part of the way?"

"No," said Hugo firmly, "I couldn't. You're being s-silly." He gave her a little shake, kissed her again, and pushed her away. "Shut the latch your side, and when you get up to your room open the curtains and look out. I'll wait till I see you."

The window shut between them. He heard her latch it and went cautiously back to the terrace. He had to keep close to the house now, for the moon was clear of the roof, and the path, the steps, and half the terrace were in moonlight. He waited a minute or two, and then ran for the steps and got behind one of the yew pyramids. From there he watched Loveday's window until the curtains moved. She looked out with the light behind her and kissed her hand.

Hugo took the path under the trees.

Chapter Twenty-Four

WHEN HE TURNED in at the gate of Meade House, it occurred to him for the first time that he was likely to find himself locked out too; but as he came round the turn of the drive, he saw the hall door standing wide and light streaming out from the hall. Even for Meade House this seemed odd and a trifle disconcerting.

He came across the gravel sweep, and saw Hacker in the doorway like a black shadow. There was a momentary effect of menace; then Hacker's voice:

"That you, Ross?"

It was Hacker's voice, but not quite his ordinary voice. Hugo had the impression that Hacker was trying very hard to be ordinary. He did not quite succeed.

Hugo said, "Yes—I'm l-late." And then, as he came up close, Hacker began to speak, to say something that never got farther than a single rough sound. With a sudden break he swung round and went striding across the hall and up the stairs.

Hugo waited to shut and bolt the door and put out the hall light. Then as he went up the stairs in the dark, the feeling of menace was there. He was conscious of it to the point of shocked expectancy. Something—some force of anger—something violent, horrible, malignant was there—waiting. If Hacker had sprung upon him with murderous intent, it would have been a sheer relief. The unseen menace was a subtler and more horrible thing.

The turn of the stair showed him Hacker's door with a line of light beneath it. He felt his way to his own room and lit a candle. Five minutes later he was calling himself a fool; but he locked the door and pushed a tin bath against it before he went to sleep.

He dreamt that he was dancing with Mme. de Lara in a fairy ring in the moonlight. The ring was a ring of scarlet toadstools, and Hélène de Lara wore silver slippers with scarlet heels. Someone was playing the flute, and away in the outer darkness he could hear Loveday crying. She was crying bitterly. But he couldn't go to her, because he couldn't get out of the fairy ring; the toadstools grew as tall as trees and burned with a red scorching fire; the wind blew over them and burnt him. But Hélène de Lara danced on. The heels of her shoes were scarlet flames, and her silvered hair was full of dancing fiery sparks.

He woke up hot and panting, and as he woke, he heard the handle of his door turn and the latch click. He called out at once, "Who's there?" and there was no answer, only a faint, faint sound of withdrawal. It was so very faint that he could not have said that he heard it, or that it was really a sound at all.

He jumped out of bed and went to the open window. The air of the house was heavy with menace. He did not sleep again that night.

Next day there was a comedy played at breakfast, the comedy of Hélène de Lara's invitation to dinner. There was a letter for Hacker and a letter for Hugo, sent over by hand.

Hugo opened his letter with a good deal of amusement. It smelt of violets, and began without a beginning:

"You are coming to me to-night, are you not? A quarter to eight. I rely on you. *Au revoir.*

H. DE L.

He looked up and saw Hacker's hand clenched on a torn envelope, Hacker's face forced to a dark indifference.

It was Minstrel who asked with a rasp, "What's Hélène writing about?"

"Asking me to dinner," said Hacker with a shrug.

Minstrel laughed.

"An olive branch! She hasn't asked me. You are favoured—or are you, I wonder? She hasn't the impudence to write to me, so she writes to you. Is that it?" He was tormenting Hacker, and knew that he was tormenting him.

He turned with a sneer to Hugo.

"You also have a *billet doux!* Are you also asked to dinner?"

"Yes, sir."

"Admirable! The lady is particularly charming and particularly hospitable, and particularly fond of novelty—ladies are, I'm told— this one has a passion for it—hence the olive branch. Hacker and I were out of favour, but as soon as you appear on the scenes we are forgiven—that is, Hacker is forgiven—she throws him a nice little bone—she invites him to dinner. He ought to show gratitude, but I doubt if he will—eh, Hacker? Gratitude's not much in your line—is it? I suppose you won't go?"

"Why not?"

Hacker got up scowling.

"Why not indeed? Why be proud? Why not crawl in behind Ross and lick the hand that throws the bone? I only wish she'd asked me too. I should have enjoyed myself—a most edifying spectacle."

The door banged behind Hacker. Minstrel pushed back his chair.

"Come and write letters! Hacker's got a damnable temper. Some day it'll get him into trouble. Come along and do a job of work. You won't earn your salary by going out to dinner. I suppose you think you oughtn't to work on Sunday—eh? Well, I can tell you this—my secretary works when I want him to work, if it's in the middle of the night, or forty-eight hours at a stretch. He's a machine, and he works when I want him to work—or he goes."

There was not, after all, very much work to do. Hacker came in presently and lounged in one of the big chairs with a novel and a cigarette. Minstrel dictated a couple of letters and began a third; but halfway through the first sentence he stopped.

Hugo looked round. He had got used to Minstrel's restless ways and quite expected to see him lost in a book or disappearing into his laboratory. What he saw was this—Minstrel looking at Hacker with an angry questioning stare, and Hacker—no, he was just too late to catch Hacker off his guard. When he looked, Hacker's eyes were on his book. But Hugo knew very well that they had not been there a second before; they had been looking at Minstrel, saying something to Minstrel. It was all over in a moment.

Minstrel swung round, pulling at his beard.

"I can't dictate. Finish the letter yourself, and keep out of my way, or I shall find myself sacking you."

"Do you want to s-sack me, sir?"

Minstrel swore at him.

"No, I don't. I shouldn't tell you to keep out of my way if I did. It's not you; it's those damned interfering busybodies who think that because they sit in a government office and fatten on red tape they can come down here and hustle me."

He picked a paper-weight off the table at Hugo's elbow, balanced it a moment, and sent it crashing into the book-case. It splintered the middle panel and fell with a heavy thud. He went striding up the room and stood staring at the damage. Then he laughed his rasping laugh and came swinging back.

"They rouse me. It's folly—but they rouse me. I'd like to smash them—like that!"

He turned on Hugo.

"Did you know we were having company tomorrow?"

"No, sir."

"Oh, you didn't? You don't know very much—do you? D'you still think I've been inventing a submarine?"

"Haven't you, sir?"

Minstrel pursed up his mouth and echoed him in a sort of snarling whine. "Haven't you, sir? Haven't you, sir? How discreet! How secretarial! No, sir, I haven't. And what's more you know very well that I haven't, unless you're even more of a fool than I ever took you for. A submarine!" He ran his hands through his hair and left it wild. "Does one correspond with the Air Ministry about a submarine? Does the Air Ministry send down its experts to haggle with me about a submarine? How much of a fool are you? Why, I believe—" He paused, caught Hugo by the shoulder and pushed him back, looking down at him with a hot, unwinking stare. "Are you fool enough to believe what you see in print? Why, upon my soul, I believe you are—I believe you are!"

Hugo felt his colour rise.

Minstrel went on looking at him for a moment, and then burst out laughing.

"My submarine *flies*, Master Ross! Put that in your pipe and smoke it!" he said and turned on his heel. The laboratory door banged on him, and the key turned harshly.

Hacker shrugged his shoulders.

"Sometimes I think he's mad," he said.

Hugo spent the rest of the morning wondering what method there was in Minstrel's madness. That the outburst had been calculated, he was sure. He thought it was to Hacker's order; and he thought that Hacker, for some reason, wished him to know, first, that Minstrel's invention was of the nature of an aeroplane, and next, that there was to be an official visit in connection with it on the following day.

Chapter Twenty-Five

HUGO WALKED over to Torring House with Hacker that evening. He found it rather a strange walk. Hacker did not speak once, and the menace which had been present in the night was with them in the dark woods. It seemed to fill them. It seemed as if Hacker was always on the edge of speech, always just about to say something, to do something. There was a sense of violence just controlled.

They came into the hall at Torring House, and all at once Hugo began to feel elated. The feeling puzzled him because, in the ordinary way, a dinner-party reduced him to a state of stammering alarm. Now he felt elated. He followed Hacker with a sense of pleased expectancy.

They came into the little room where he had talked with Mme. de Lara, and saw her standing under the tall lamp with the pale blue shade. The light gave her an elfin look, with her flaxen silver curls and a dress of moonlight blue.

Hugo's eyes went past her to Loveday. He looked at her because he couldn't help it. They had met in a dark lane, in a dark room, on a dark roof, and in a dark garden. He had seen her by the light of a street lamp, pale, ruffled, and dusty. He couldn't keep his eyes from her now. There was colour in her cheeks, and she wore a pink frock. She looked very young. She made his heart beat terribly, and under the eyes of Hacker and Hélène de Lara he felt himself blushing.

With a desperate effort he transferred his gaze and his blush to Mme. de Lara. If he had met Loveday's gaze, the disaster might have been complete. But Loveday was not looking at him at all. She said something to Hélène and she laughed quite naturally. And then Hélène de Lara had her hand on his arm.

"Well, my friend, you have come. Shall I tell you how pleased I am to see you?"

She kept her hand on his arm and just touched Hacker.

"James, you haven't met my cousin. *Chérie*, this is Mr. James Hacker, who is a very dangerous person for you to know, because he invents explosives and things like that, and our dear Emily would not approve of him at all. And this—" She drew Hugo forward and paused. "This, my dear—" She paused again, and Loveday turned and looked at Hugo.

Hugo admired her very much; she did it ever so much better than he; her eyes were as innocently unaware as a kitten's. She saw a pleasant boy, who was a stranger, and she waited for Hélène to introduce him. She could not have done it better.

Hélène introduced Mr. Hugo Ross.

Mr. Hugo Ross said "How do you do?" and Miss Loveday Leigh, who had not been given any name except *Chérie*, looked at him with an air of startled interest and said "Oh" in a very natural girlish manner.

"Oh—is your name Ross?" said Loveday. Then she said "Oh" again, with the effect of being a little out of breath. It was very well done.

Quite suddenly Hugo wanted to laugh. He and Loveday playing at being solemnly introduced! He turned to Mme. de Lara and said, stammering a good deal, that it was a fine night.

"Is it?"

Hélène de Lara still had her hand upon his sleeve. She withdrew it now, rather slowly.

"Perhaps there'll b-be a f-fog later."

Hugo didn't want to laugh any more. He was making an ass of himself, and his cheeks burned.

They went in to dinner, Loveday with Hacker and Hugo with Hélène, and from the time that they were seated Mme. de Lara kept up a soft, unceasing flow of talk—about music—about flying—about jazz—about the Schneider Cup—about all the cities in Europe—about the world's record flights. Her talk rippled like any stream that runs down an easy slope to an untroubled sea.

The little dinner was perfect in every way. Even Hacker's gloom lifted, and by the time coffee was served he had vouchsafed at least one observation. Loveday was plainly enjoying herself. Emily never gave parties like this. Emily only had people to tea. It was thrilling to wear a pink dress for Hugo to see, and to eat the most amusing things with names that kept you guessing.

Hélène stopped talking about record flights. As the servants left the room, she lit a cigarette, looked through the faint veil of smoke at Hacker, and asked,

"Now why didn't you bring Ambrose?"

"You didn't ask him," said Hacker rudely.

"Didn't I?" She laughed. "Did he expect that I would? He's like royalty—he says he will come, or he says he won't come—one doesn't ask him—especially when he is inventing something. What is it now?"

Hacker leaned back in his chair.

"Don't you read the papers?"

"Never. Why should I? They contain all the things which are not true, or which one knows already. When they are indiscreet, they lie—and when they tell the truth, they are as dull as ditch-water."

"How picturesque!" said Hacker with a sneer.

She turned to Hugo.

"He is rude because he is afraid of me. He is afraid that I shall ask him to be indiscreet. He is in the sulks, so I shall ask you instead. Tell me about Ambrose's invention."

"I don't know anything to tell," said Hugo.

"And do you think that I believe that?"

"It's t-true."

She waved away the smoke that hung between them and made an odd little monkey face.

"Then I shall tell you—and you shall tell me whether I'm telling true or not." She kept her eyes on him; dark, sad, malicious eyes. "I'll tell you this, but I won't tell you how I know—Ambrose has invented something that is going to sweep all the other flying things out of the air and leave it bare for him. Now isn't that true?"

"I don't know," said Hugo.

"Isn't it true, James?"

"Ask Minstrel."

"I don't need to—it's true. And I'll tell you what I heard, and that's this—they sent experts down from London to see a test, and he showed them a little model that they laughed at for a child's toy, and home-made at that—for it's true, isn't it, that he and you and Leonard made the parts?"

"Some of them," said Hacker.

Loveday was listening with all her ears and looking with all her eyes. Hélène laughed at her.

"Look at this child! Her eyes will fall out. She's admiring you, James, and thinking how clever you are. And she's wondering how your great clumsy fingers can make anything so fine and delicate as the sort of toy that Ambrose plays with."

Hacker looked at his hands with a certain complacency. Hélène blew him a mocking kiss.

"How nice to be so pleased with oneself! Perhaps, now that you are pleased, you will tell me if what I have heard is true. I have heard that the experts laughed until they saw what the little toy could do, and that then they didn't laugh any more. I have heard that they came away with long, grave faces. I have heard—"

Hacker frowned again.

"What have you heard?"

"What I have heard comes straight out of a fairy-tale. But that is just what inventors are doing, is it not? They are stealing all the things out of the old wonder-tales and making them come real. One day we say it's impossible, and the next day we are buying the magic over the counter and taking it all as a matter of course." She put her elbows on the table and leaned forward whispering, "James—is it true that it rises up quite straight without a run? Ah now, tell me!"

Hacker laughed.

"That's nothing!"

"Isn't it now? Listen to him, *Chérie!* Ah, James, be indiscreet and tell us about it! What can it do?"

Hacker pushed back his chair and stood up.

"What can't it do?"

"Tell us." She was whispering again.

"Not a word." He went to the door and opened it. "If you want to know anything, you'll have to ask Minstrel yourself."

"But we've quarrelled."

"Make it up." There was contempt in his tone; and all at once there was offence in hers—offence and dignity.

"I think we will go into the next room. Mr. Ross, has Ambrose ever shown you his collection of Chinese snuff bottles? He hasn't? Well, they're worth seeing—and if you can catch him in a really good temper, he likes showing them. But of course that's only when the sun shines in the middle of the night. You wouldn't expect him to have artistic tastes—would you?"

"I don't know," said Hugo.

She laughed.

"What a lot of things you don't know!" Then, on the threshold of her little room, she patted Loveday on the shoulder. "Go and talk to James. I am offended with him. Talk, or play the piano, or show him photographs—whichever he likes least. I wish to punish him."

"Thank you," said Loveday. She dropped a little curtsey, made a schoolgirl grimace, and went over to where Mr. Hacker frowned savagely at an innocent water-colour.

"Hélène says I am to show you photographs," she said, and forthwith picked up a little book of snapshots.

Hélène sat down on the sofa by the fire.

"I want more cushions. Yes, that blue one—and the one with the silver roses. Thank you. And now come and sit down and tell me why you blushed when you came in?"

Hugo did it again.

"Did I b-blush?"

She looked at him with an air of mournful reproach.

"Did you? Is that what you're asking me?"

Hugo went on doing it. The mournful look lifted; something sparkled and glanced.

"You might tell me why. Everybody tells me things except that sulky, obstinate James. Isn't he detestable? Do tell me why you blushed."

"It was very stupid."

"Was it? Why did you?"

"I s-saw you—"

"And you blushed for me?"

"It was very s-stupid."

Hugo hoped earnestly that she would believe him and talk about something else. He hoped earnestly that she really thought him a singularly stupid young man. If only he hadn't been ass enough to look at Loveday! He was aware of her now out of the tail of his eye, sitting up primly and turning the leaves of an album which Hacker made hardly a pretence of looking at. He wanted to punch Hacker's head; he wanted to throw the furniture about; he wanted to smash something and shout.

Mme. de Lara hadn't done with him.

"You *might* tell me," she said, and her eyes teased and promised.

"I had a m-most awfully f-funny dream last night," said Hugo.

"So bad that you had to blush for it?"

Hugo would have given about ten years of his life to have boxed her ears. He supposed she thought she was being attractive. He controlled himself sufficiently to look as if he thought so too.

He said, "Oh—no," and found a hand upon his arm. It clung there for a moment with a delicate pressure.

"Did you dream about me?"

"Yes, I d-did."

"Tell me! Ah now, do tell me! If I was in it, it's my dream as well as yours. What did we do in our dream?"

"We d-danced," said Hugo. He was looking down at the big diamond with its circle of tiny emeralds; it shone most amazingly bright. She had a little skinny hand. He thought how much nicer the ring would have looked on Loveday's finger. And then quite suddenly he hated the idea of Loveday wearing the ring, and he hated the ring.

"We danced—" echoed Hélène de Lara. Her voice sank and was sad; her hand fell from his arm. "We danced...Go on."

"We just d-danced."

He had a vision of the fiery toad-stools and of Mme. de Lara's burning heels and the sparks that flew from her hair. The wild dream and his own banal phrase shook him with inward laughter.

"Where were we?"

"It was a f-funny sort of place."

"Ah, tell me now! You're not telling me."

Hugo looked blank.

"We just d-d-danced."

Chapter Twenty-Six

"DO YOU LIKE looking at photographs, Mr. Hacker?" said Loveday.

"Not especially."

"I thought you didn't." She shut the album with a snap. "I think it's one of the most boring things in the world—so now we needn't do it any more. Why don't you go and talk to Hélène and let Mr. Ross come and talk to me?"

"I didn't know you knew him," said Hacker.

"I didn't say I knew him. He looks nice." She began to get up. "Let's go over to the fire."

Hacker pulled himself together. It was his business to keep Loveday from talking to Hugo. He said,

"I believe you do know Ross all the same. Where did you meet him?"

Loveday hesitated.

"Well—I don't know. I didn't say I *had* met him."

"But you *have*."

"Oh—well—"

"Is it a secret?"

"Yes, it is. No, I don't mean that. I can't think why you should think I know him."

"Well, you jumped when he was introduced to you."

"Did I?" Her eyes opened very wide.

"Yes, you certainly did."

"How clever of you to notice! It was only—only—well, I did know his name."

"Did you? I say, this is getting exciting!"

Loveday pursed up her lips.

"It isn't really."

"You knew his name, but you didn't know him by sight."

Her eyes opened still wider.

"How frightfully clever of you! How *did* you know?"

"Well, I was looking at you, and you didn't jump until you heard his name."

"How *frightfully* clever! Why were you looking at me?"

"Because you're rather nice to look at." He said it with the ease born of considerable practice.

Loveday's finger-tips pricked and tingled. It was not only Hugo who wished to box the ears of the person he was talking to. Her colour rose.

"I'm not the only person who's told you that, I'm sure," continued Mr. Hacker.

Loveday got up and walked over to the fire. The orange cat lay curled up on the hottest part of the hearth-rug. She knelt down and began to pull its whiskers. The cat woke up and sneezed. Hugo turned round to look, and Loveday addressed him.

"His name is Pif-paf-pouf. Isn't he beautiful?"

Mr. Hacker had apparently ceased to exist.

It was at this moment that the butler came in. He approached Mme. de Lara and said in a low voice,

"Miss Dumaresq is on the telephone."

"Ask her to give you a message."

He hesitated.

"Miss Dumaresq hoped you would be able to come for a moment."

Mme. de Lara jumped up.

"Why does one have a telephone?" she said, and ran out of the room.

Mr. Hacker strolled across to the fire. He frowned absently for a moment at Loveday on her knees beside the orange cat. Then, with the air of a man who has suddenly remembered something, he went quickly out of the room and shut the door. Hugo and Loveday were left alone, and Loveday opened her mouth to speak.

It was a most horrible moment, because Hugo was quite sure that they were not really alone; he was quite sure that they would never have been left alone; the telephone message and Hacker's departure were according to plan; they were being watched and tested.

Hugo did not think these things one after another; there was a sort of mental flash, and he just saw them. The flash did not take up an instant of time. He saw Loveday opening her lips to speak, and he knew that if she said so much as a single word, if she even said "Hugo," he would have failed, utterly and miserably. He could not warn her; she was going to speak—she was speaking.

She said, "Isn't Pif-paf-pouf a nice name?"

"V-v-very nice," said Hugo.

"Are you Mr. Minstrel's secretary?" said Loveday.

"Yes, I am."

"Do you like it?"

"V-v-very much."

Loveday looked down because she was afraid she would laugh if she went on looking at Hugo; he looked so embarrassed, and he sat on the edge of Hélène's comfortable sofa as if it had been a hard wooden bench. It was very funny. She wondered how long they would have to make silly remarks to each other, and she thought how awful it would be if she got the giggles. She tickled Pif-paf-pouf under the chin and said in a fluttered voice,

"Do you *really* like it?"

"Yes, v-very much."

Loveday said "Oh!" and took a plunge: "Oh, Mr. Ross—there's something I want to say."

"Is there?"

"Yes—I think I ought to—but I don't know—perhaps—" She hesitated, and before she could say another word the door opened and Mme. de Lara came in a little out of breath.

"I knew it wouldn't be anything," she said in a vexed voice. "Marie Dumaresq is the limit, and every time she makes a mystery and drags me to the telephone I swear I'll not be taken in again. Would you believe what she wanted? An address that I've given her one dozen times already! She tires me!" She gave the cushion with the silver roses an angry pat. "Where's James? Still sulking?"

Mr. Hacker appeared as if this had been his cue—perhaps it was. He came over to the group by the fire, and seemed to have recovered his temper.

Mme. de Lara looked at him teasingly.

"Have you thought of something to say? It's half an hour since you said anything, I believe."

"As bad as that? How dull of me! I've really got rather a lot on my mind just now, if that's any excuse. I shall be glad when Minstrel's got rid of this job." He laughed a little. "You think I'm bad-tempered—but you should see *him*. The fact is, after innumerable delays the Ministry have pinned him down, and he's sworn to hand over the plans and specifications tomorrow. They're sending a man down, and Minstrel's like a volcano in consequence—he does hate parting. You'd think he'd be glad to be rid of the whole thing—I know I shall be. It's a most infernal responsibility having the plans of a thing like that knocking about. He's so dashed careless too—as often as not he forgets to lock the safe, and when he does lock it, he leaves the keys lying about."

Hélène laughed airily.

"Well, it's safe enough. No one's going to steal his old plans."

Hacker frowned.

"Aren't they? Do you realize that they're worth fifty thousand pounds? *Fifty?*" He laughed. "They're worth a hundred or a thousand times that if you work it out in terms of cities. What's the City of London worth?" He laughed again.

Hélène lifted her eyebrows.

"What are you talking about, my friend?"

"L.S.D.," said Hacker—"and Minstrel's infernal carelessness. I shall sleep a good deal better when the Ministry has got those plans in their own official safe, and that's a fact."

Hugo found this very interesting. He began by wondering why Hacker's tongue had suddenly loosened; and then he decided that this also was according to plan. If it were to appear that Hugo Ross had sold the plans, it might be useful to be able to prove that Hugo Ross had knowledge of certain things—as that the plans were carelessly kept, and that they were due to be handed over to-morrow. He wondered when he was going to be afforded an opportunity of becoming a criminal.

He continued to sit on the edge of the sofa and to look very shy.

Chapter Twenty-Seven

HACKER MADE an early move, for which Hugo was sufficiently thankful. He shook hands with Mme. de Lara and felt her fingers cling to his for a moment whilst her lashes swept up and down again over darkly mournful eyes. They seemed to say, "Ah! If we were alone—"

Hugo turned to Loveday sitting on the rug beside the orange cat. He touched her hand, and she said, "You must say good-bye to Pif-paf-pouf—he is a very important person. Just feel how lovely and soft he is."

He stroked the orange fur, and as he did so, Loveday's hand slipped up to his and pushed a scrap of paper under his stroking fingers. Pif-paf-pouf gave a little sleepy growl as Hugo's hand closed. He rolled over and stretched himself. Hugo got up with a beating heart. He slipped the scrap of paper into his pocket and went out with Hacker.

The night was dark, cloudy, and mild; a gusty wind blew overhead in the tree-tops. They were hardly clear of the house before Hacker began to talk with a curious suppressed energy that showed itself every now and then in a word suddenly jerked out or over-loud.

"I wish I could be sure—" he began and then broke off. "Sure—you can't ever be sure of Minstrel. He's supposed to be handing over those plans to-morrow. Well, I'll bet anything you like that he'll play something up and go back on it. He loathes parting, and he won't part as long as he can invent an excuse—but he's never been as bad as this. It's getting on my nerves."

"Does it m-matter?" said Hugo. He wondered why he was being confided in.

Hacker gave a jerky laugh.

"Matter? That's good!"

"But why?"

"You heard what I said up there. The plans are too dashed valuable, and he leaves them lying about."

"Well, I don't s-see"—Hugo spoke in a slow, puzzled way—"I m-mean supposing the Ministry have the plans to start making the—the aeroplanes or whatever they are—well, you can't keep things like that very s-secret. I don't see it's really worth anyone's while to steal the plans."

"Don't you?" Hacker's tone was one of open contempt.

"No, I d-don't."

Hacker laughed.

"They're worth fifty thousand—the two secret processes alone—" He stopped with the air of pulling himself up.

"S-secret processes?"

"Well, you'd better forget that—I oughtn't to have said it—and yet I don't know that it matters. The thing's on my mind. D'you know what it is to have a thing so much on your mind that you can't help talking about it? No—I don't suppose you do." He walked for half a dozen yards in silence, and then said, low and abruptly, "It's the two secret processes that are worth the money. They're worth double—treble—but they'd *fetch* fifty thousand." He laughed harshly. "They'd fetch more in the open market—they'd fetch anything you like to ask. I can't tell you about them, but they're going to revolutionize flying. I tell you there's not as much difference between a toy balloon and the best modern plane as there will be between that plane and Minstrel's. There!"

The last word was fired at Hugo like a shot. He said, "Oh, I s-say!" and waited for more.

There was no more.

On the step of the house Hacker shook himself and said gruffly, "Don't talk about it." Then he went across the hall and up the stairs at a run.

Hugo followed slowly. He found his room with the blinds up, and he pulled them down carefully before he took out the scrap of paper which Loveday had pushed into his hand. It was a little uneven piece torn from the margin of a book; a letter or two of print showed at the edge. Across it in a faint pencil scrawl he read:

"Come to the scullery window."

That was all. He stared at it, angry and perplexed. Loveday had taken a frightful risk, and she was asking him to take a worse risk still. If the slip of paper had been seen, the game would have been up. It was a frightful risk to take. Only the most urgent necessity could justify it. Was there any urgent necessity? They oughtn't to risk a meeting unless a meeting was absolutely essential. Suppose Loveday only wanted to see him. What could have happened that could possibly justify their taking such a risk? He couldn't think of anything. But there might be something. It was most difficult to decide what to do. He wanted to see Loveday so badly that he was afraid of doing what he wanted to do; and he was afraid of going in the opposite direction and staying away, just because he wanted so badly to go.

He put out his light and opened the door of his room. There was still a light under Hacker's door. Then, as he looked at it, the door opened and the light went out.

Hugo stepped back and stood still, listening. He heard Hacker cross the landing and go down the stair, he heard him cross the hall below. He came out on the landing and stood at the head of the stairs looking over. There was the flash of a torch in the hall, and then the sound of the front door being opened softly. Hacker went out, and the door closed behind him.

Hugo went out too, by the back door. He put the key in his pocket and walked back to Torring House. He wondered a good deal whether Hacker was going there. It was lighter than it had been, because the moon had risen and the cloudy heavens showed faintly luminous above the black mass of woodland that surrounded the house. The wind went sighing overhead, and every now and then a gust bent the branches and set up a creaking and a straining.

Hugo came along the path which led from the drive to the foot of the terrace steps. The house was just a blur in the dark; the only light came from the veiled, dim sky. He skirted the house cautiously, and crossed the paved yard at the back of it. His outstretched hands touched the wall and he groped along it. Here was a door, and here a window. The scullery window should come next. He reached it and heard the sound, the only just audible sound of a gasp; then Loveday's voice, faint and shaky:

"Who—who is it?"

"M-m-me," said Hugo.

This time the gasp was louder.

"You've been years and years and years! I thought you weren't coming. And there are black beetles—one ran over my foot. This is an awful place. I'm coming out."

"No—I'll come in. It's safer."

He was considering that inside they would hear a step soon enough for him to get away. He climbed in, and found Loveday in his arms, cold and shaking. She had on a coat with a fur collar over her thin dress and the fur tickled his chin.

"Why didn't you come before? A scullery in the middle of the night is a most dreadfully frightening place."

"I couldn't. I couldn't read your message till I got back. I can't stop—it's frightfully dangerous. What's up?"

Loveday rubbed a cold, soft cheek against his.

"Aren't you pleased to see me? Aren't you glad you came?"

Hugo frowned in the dark.

"What's up? Why did you write that message?"

She gave a little whispering laugh.

"I tore a piece out of a revolting French novel of Hélène's. Ooh! *Such* a nasty book!"

"You shouldn't have read it."

"I didn't. I tore a corner off, and I went behind the piano and wrote on it."

"But why?"

"Because I wanted to see you. Don't you want to see me?"

Hugo frowned again, quite ferociously this time.

"Do you mean to say—"

She drew back an inch or two.

"How ferocious you sound! Are you going to be ferocious? Because if you are, I shall go away. I'm feeling frightfully weak after being trodden on by a black beetle and having to talk to your awful Hacker all the evening."

"I'm not being ferocious. But it's too dangerous."

"Don't you like dangerous things? I do. I was just smothering with dullness—a little more Hacker, and I should have been asphyxiated. Isn't it funny his name being James too? Isn't it awful to know two Jameses who are both simply smotheringly dull? I think the Hacker one's the worst though—because the other one does propose to me, and there's a sort of faint gleam of human interest about being proposed to, even by *James*."

"Loveday, d-do be serious."

"I *am*—I'm frightfully serious. It's a frightfully serious thing, because if I see much of Mr. Hacker, I might get to feel that I quite loved James. And if I got to feel that, I might say 'Yes' next time he asked me to marry him. He *is* better than Hacker."

"Loveday, stop talking nonsense! I mustn't stop—it's much too dangerous. If you haven't got anything to tell me, I must go."

"I've got millions of things to tell you."

"Not that sort of thing."

"How d'you know what sort of thing I mean?" She pulled away from him a little.

"I must go," said Hugo.

"All right—go!"

"Loveday!"

"I wish you would go. You're making me feel quite fond of James. *He* never wants to go away when he's talking to me."

"Loveday!"

"*Dear* James!" said Loveday.

Hugo shook her.

"Darling, do stop being such an ass!"

"I'm not!" She disengaged herself and receded somewhere into the darkness. "Why don't you go?"

Hugo was very angry. He put a hand on the wall and a knee on the sink. Loveday could just see him blocking the window.

"Are you going?" The whisper was a little fluttered.

Hugo made no answer. Loveday's voice reached him, defiant but shaky:

"You don't want to hear the really frightfully important thing I've got to tell you?"

He spoke over his shoulder.

"Is there something important—really?"

"Yes, there is." Her voice went off into a faint scream. "Hugo, I've trod on a beetle! It crunched!"

Hugo came back slowly.

"Where are you?"

"Here. Ooh! Hugo, don't go away!" She was holding tightly to his sleeve. "I shall really scream if you go—and I *have* got something to tell you."

"What is it?"

He put his arm round her, but he was still angry. Loveday snuggled up to him.

"I *do* hate you! But black beetles are worse." Then, as he jerked impatiently, "I can't tell you anything unless you keep still—and I *have* got something to tell you."

"What is it?"

She murmured, "I do hate you!" and then went on quickly, "I can't tell you anything while you fidget—and it *is* important. Oh, very well—I am telling you, only you don't *let* me."

"Loveday!"

"Pouf!" said Loveday. "Cross-patch!" Then she put her lips against his ear. "It's rather a frightening thing. That's why I don't want to begin—it frightens me."

Hugo patted her.

"Tell me."

"I came down—and it was all dark—and the black beetle trod on me like I told you—and I heard more of them. And when you didn't come, I thought you weren't coming, and I began to go back to my room."

"Yes?"

"I came out of the baize door that shuts off the kitchen part of the house, and I was standing in the back of the hall listening, and not sure whether it would be most frightening to go up the front stairs or up the back. I was afraid the back stairs would creak because of not having any carpet on them."

"Yes?"

Loveday pressed close to him.

"Someone came down the front stairs," she whispered.

"Who was it?"

"It was Hélène—but I didn't know it was Hélène then. I sat down on the floor, because my knees went like jelly. It was *horrid!*"

"What happened?"

"Hélène came straight down the hall towards me, and I thought I was going to scream, because I didn't know it was Hélène, and it might have been—anything. Ooh!"

He felt her shiver.

"Go on—you're not telling me."

"I *am*." She shivered again. "She came down, and just when I thought she was going to tread on me, like the black beetle, she opened the door of the study, and there was a light there—that's when I saw it was Hélène—and she spoke to someone—and it was a man."

"Hacker?"

"No, it wasn't. She said, 'Come along—he'll be here in a minute,' and a horrid man like a weasel with red hair came out of the room. And she said, 'Put out the light—I'll guide you,' and the light went out with a snap, and the man said—" She stopped.

She did not shiver, but pressed close to him, rigid.

"Go on."

"He said, 'Well? How did it go? How is our young Dreyfus?' And Hélène said, 'Poor Hugo!' in the weepy way she's got when she doesn't mean anything; and then they went into her sitting-room and put on the light."

"Go on!"

"I hate it!" said Loveday breathlessly. "I hate it frightfully. They went in, and she pushed the door, but it didn't quite shut, and I was so frightened I nearly died. And when I'm as frightened as that, I just have to do something, because sitting still's worse—so I crawled along till I got near the door. And Hélène said, 'He's coming!' And that frightened me worst of all, because I thought she meant you."

"Who did she mean?"

"She meant that awful Hacker, because she went to the door—the outside one—and she opened it, and someone came in, and she said, 'Well, James—he's here!' And Mr. Hacker said, 'Hullo, Miller!'"

"*Miller!*"

"That's what he said—'Hullo, Miller'"

"Good Lord!" said Hugo.

"And Hélène said, 'Ssh! The door's open.' And she ran and shut it, so I didn't hear any more. And I thought perhaps you'd had to wait till Mr. Hacker was out of the way, so I came back to the scullery—and then you came."

She began to tremble very much.

"Loveday—don't. What's the matter?"

"I'm frightened. Why am I so frightened? What does it *mean?* Why did that horrid little red-haired weasel say that? Why did he call you a young Dreyfus? Who was Dreyfus? Do you know?"

"Yes," said Hugo—"my uncle had a book about him." He spoke slowly, reluctantly.

"I knew I'd heard the name before. Who was he? Why does it frighten me? Hugo—tell me—*please.*"

Hugo spoke in a quiet, dry voice:

"He was a French Jew who was sent to penal servitude for selling French military secrets." He felt Loveday give a little gasp. He went on, "He didn't do it, you know. It was a put-up job. He was quite innocent, but he was sent to Devil's Island, and I think he was there about four years. And then there was a most frightfully famous case and the whole thing came out. It was a put-up job, and all sorts of highly placed people were in it."

Loveday clutched him.

"I knew I wouldn't have been so frightened if it hadn't been something horrid. It *is* horrid. And it's something to do with you, because that red-haired weasel person meant you when he said 'our young Dreyfus.' Hugo, I'm frightened—I'm frightened. It does *mean* something horrid. What are they going to do to you? Don't let them!" The words came pouring out helter-skelter; they were like little terrified things that were running away."

"Loveday—don't. It's all right."

He had stopped being angry; he was trying to comfort her.

"It isn't all right—I know it isn't. You say they sent that man to prison. Are they going to try and send you to prison?"

Hugo kissed her.

"It's all right—it really is."

"It *isn't*. They're trying to do something to you—I know they are. It's those plans—isn't it? I *know* it is. They're going to steal them themselves, and make out it was you, and send you to prison! Hugo—*Hugo!*"

The words had stopped tumbling over each other; they came slower and slower and at last stood still. It was as if they were afraid of being heard. Suddenly Loveday burst into tears.

"Hugo—don't let them! Go away! Why do you stay here for them to do dreadful things to you? Promise me you'll go right away at once."

She pulled his face down to hers, and he felt it wet and quivering.

"Darling, don't cry—p-p-please don't cry. I c-can't run away."

"Why can't you? What's the use of your staying here?"

"I want to save the plans—I might be able to, you know."

"What does it matter about the wretched old plans? I can't bear it if they hurt you—I *can't*."

Hugo hugged her.

"I won't let them hurt me. And it does matter. I can't tell you about it, but it matters frightfully. It—it matters so much that it would be worth going to prison for if I could save them. But you needn't worry, because I'm not going to prison. You see, I'm well up on them, because they think I'm just an innocent mug who hasn't got a suspicion in the world. I s-say, darling, you were topping this evening—you really were. You did it most awfully well—much better than I did."

Loveday sniffed and began to look for her handkerchief.

"I didn't feel topping—I felt like a melting jelly." She dabbed her eyes and gave the ghost of a laugh. "You *blushed*."

"That's my modest disposition."

"Why did you? Hélène thought it was because you were struck all of a heap by her. She said so when you'd gone—she made me frightfully angry. Why *did* you?"

"Never mind."

"But I want to know. Was it because of Hélène or—was it because of me?"

"Never m-mind."

She put her cheek against his.

"It might cheer me up a little if you told me. Was it because of me?"

"Yes, it was."

"Did you like my pink dress? Did you think I looked nice? You hadn't ever seen me properly before. Did—you—like me?" She ended on a little sob.

Hugo held her tight and said nothing. She felt his heart beat. They kissed rather breathlessly.

"I must go," said Hugo. He hoped she wouldn't cry again. It was dreadfully difficult to go away and leave her unhappy.

She drew away with a sigh.

"You won't let them hurt you?"

"Of course I won't."

"You're much cleverer than they are—that's one comfort."

Hugo felt immensely fortified.

"It's frightening—but it's exciting too," said Loveday in the dark. "It's—oh, Hugo, please, *please* don't let them hurt you."

She flung her arms round his neck, gave him two quick kisses, and was gone. He heard her feeling for the door.

"Loveday—you've got to shut the window after me."

There was no answer.

He turned resolutely and climbed out.

After a moment he heard the window shut.

Inside the little dark, close room Loveday groped her way to the door and leaned against it, blind and dizzy with tears.

"Don't—*don't* let them hurt him!" she said.

Chapter Twenty-Eight

FOR ABOUT ten minutes Loveday cried as if her heart would break. Hugo was going to be sent to prison—he was going to be led into some horrible trap and sent to prison for years and years and years—and they would never see each other any more. Perhaps Hugo wouldn't come out of prison until he was quite old; and then she, Loveday, would be quite old too, and they would both have grey hair. It was a frightful thought.

Loveday tried to make a picture of herself with grey hair. She had once gone to a fancy dress party with her hair powdered, and everyone had said how becoming it was. Perhaps Hugo would like her, even if her hair had got as grey as Cousin Catherine's before he came out of prison.

At this point she stopped crying. She began to try to think what Hugo would look like. It was frightfully difficult to think of Hugo looking old; she simply couldn't imagine him any different from what he was. And then, all of a sudden, she knew that she couldn't imagine him in prison, and she began to feel much better. Prison receded to an immense distance. Why should Hugo go to prison? He wouldn't. "And oh, good gracious me, suppose Hélène goes into my room and finds I'm not there! I must *fly!*"

She opened the door and crept through the kitchen and along a dark passage to the baize door which opened on the hall. Here she stopped to listen, pushed the door half an inch, and stopped to listen again. She was just going to open the door wide, when two things happened so quickly that she had no time to think or move.

There was the sound of an opening door; and, very nearly at the same moment, a vertical streak of light hung in the darkness before her. It was so unexpected that she almost cried out before she realized that Hélène's sitting-room door had opened, and that someone had turned on the hall light.

Her heart thumped, and she let the baize door swing back until the line of light was only a thread. She could hear Hélène's voice, and Mr. Miller's voice—and they were coming towards her—they were coming nearer. She gripped the handle so hard that afterwards her fingers were stiff. But she could not have moved to save her life. Through the tiny crack that remained she saw Mr. Miller's face—just the blur of a face in shadow, with red hair sticking up against the light. Mr. Miller made her feel quite sick.

He and Hélène went into the study, and after a moment they came out again. Mr. Miller was carrying a bag. They went back to Hélène's sitting-room.

As they went away, Loveday made her crack a little wider by pushing the door. Mr. Miller was going away; he had fetched his bag, and he was going away. Loveday felt unreasonably glad about this. She didn't like Mr. Miller at all, and she thought the house would feel much nicer when he wasn't in it. She hoped Mr. Hacker had gone too, because then Hélène would go up to her room and the coast would be clear. Of course, she could go up the back stairs. But she didn't want to go up the back stairs; for one thing they creaked, and for another, she just didn't like them; there was a black-beetley feeling about them. She thought she would wait here until Hélène went up; and she hoped very much that Hélène wouldn't be long, because she was beginning to feel most dreadfully sleepy—you do when you've been crying a lot. She yawned once or twice, and the darkness began to feel heavy and warm.

Hélène didn't come.

Loveday found herself waking with a start. She hadn't been asleep—she was sure she hadn't been asleep; but all the same she waked up with a jerk and pushed the door half open. The sound of a man's voice reached her. Mr. Hacker hadn't gone. He was there, in Hélène's sitting-room, talking to Hélène. And the sitting-room door was ajar; the hall was dark again, but she could just see the line of light where the door had fallen ajar. She remembered that Hélène had complained about the catch and had said she must have it seen to. She ought to have had it seen to before she had secret conversations with people in the middle of the night.

Before Loveday knew what she was going to do, she found herself halfway across the hall with her eyes on the chink of light and her ears straining to catch what Mr. Hacker was saying. She stopped with caught breath a yard from the door. If he and Hélène were talking about themselves, she would go away at once; but if they were talking about Hugo, she was going to listen. She didn't care how dreadful it was to listen at doors; she was going to do it—if they were talking about Hugo.

She listened, and she heard Mr. Hacker say in a tone of suppressed fury, "If you're going to risk spoiling everything at the last moment—"

Loveday hesitated, waited where she was, and heard Hélène say mournfully, "I think I'd be a good friend to you if I did."

Were they talking about Hugo? She wasn't sure. It was dreadful to listen if they weren't.

Mr. Hacker spoke again:

"Good heavens! Can't you be reasonable?"

And Hélène, with the ghost of a laugh: "I don't feel reasonable."

Then Hacker, roughly:

"You needn't have told me that. Look here, Hélène, business is business. If you're using this young ass to make me jealous, it's a fool's trick. You can play any trick you like when we're not up to our necks in a business deal. It's your way to play tricks, and I've put up with a damned sight more of them than most men would.

But I won't have a business deal spoilt because you take a fancy to see if you can't make me lose my temper—I'm not taking any, and the sooner you understand that the better. This is business and don't you forget it. If the thing goes well, you'll get two thousand. And if anything goes wrong, you'll be likely to find yourself in Queer Street."

"Someone will hear you if you speak so loud," said Mme. de Lara sweetly.

Mr. Hacker swore.

"Someday you'll get yourself murdered," he said; and Loveday shivered.

She wanted to go away, and she wanted to stay. She wanted to go to sleep and forget all about people like Mr. Hacker and Mr. Miller and Hélène; they made her feel very tired.

Then she heard Hélène laugh gently, and Mr. Hacker said,

"Are you going to be reasonable?"

"Are *you* reasonable? You see, it all depends on the point of view. To you it seems reasonable to ruin the poor boy; but to me it does not seem reasonable at all. I ask myself and I ask you—why should not Miller simply take the papers from him? I believe he can pick a pocket very well—he certainly looks as if he could. Let him then pick Hugo's pocket, and there we are—he has the plans, we have the money, Ambrose preserves his reputation, and all that anyone can say about our poor Hugo is that he was stupid enough and innocent enough to fall among thieves. To me this seems a perfectly reasonable plan."

Hacker swore again.

"How many times are we to go over the same ground? I tell you Miller won't steal the plans—that is to say he won't take them unless there's someone else to take the blame. His position is quite simple. He is acting as an agent in a perfectly *bona fide* transaction—he is buying from Minstrel through Minstrel's secretary. Minstrel's position is quite simple too. He is selling to Government, and his secretary is taking the plans up to hand them over. With Miller and Minstrel both so careful about their reputations, I'm afraid there's nothing for it but to sacrifice your poor Hugo. Minstrel won't sell to Miller openly, and Miller won't put himself on the wrong side of the law—so I'm afraid your poor Hugo must go to the wall."

"He isn't my poor Hugo," said Hélène sadly.

"You'd like him to be."

"Would I? Ah well, perhaps I would. Perhaps I'm tired of tricks and byways, and all the old stale things that I've hated for years. Perhaps I'd like to be young again. Do you know what that boy was playing on his flute when I went up through the woods?"

"Chuck it!" said Mr. Hacker succinctly.

"He was playing *Love's Young Dream*," said Hélène with a whispering thrill in her voice. She sang the words over softly as if to herself:

"New hope may bloom, and days may come,
Of brighter, purer beam;
But there's nothing half so sweet in life as
Love's young dream."

"Perhaps I've a fancy to go back into the dream again."

"Come off it!" said Mr. Hacker.

Hélène made a little sound of protest.

"I tell you, he touched my heart—yes, more than a little, with his youth and his music and his blush. Did you see how he blushed when he came in this evening? Poor boy I Ah, James—to be as young as that again! I tell you there were tears in my heart when he blushed." All at once her voice changed. "If you go on sneering at me like that, I shall tell him everything," she said.

Loveday remained standing a yard from the door. She heard Mr. Hacker make an explosive sound of rage, and she heard Hélène give a little gasp as if she were being shaken. Loveday rather hoped she was being shaken. Hélène's championship of Hugo infuriated her.

Hélène cried out, and Mr. Hacker said in a hard matter-of-fact way,

"Do you want that two thousand pounds?"

"You hurt me!" said Hélène.

"You want hurting when you talk like that. Besides, what's the good of it with me? You ought to know by now just how much ice all that rotten sentimentality cuts. You can amuse yourself with it as much as you please—but keep it out of business. Do you want the money—or don't you?"

"What a stupid question!"

Mr. Hacker laughed.

"In other words, you want it. Well, you'll get it if you're good."

Hélène yawned.

"I'm so sleepy. You must go."

"In a minute. Remember—to-morrow afternoon, and don't be late. And don't play the fool, or you'll be sorry for it."

Loveday shivered with cold. She ought to get away, because if they came into the hall, she'd be caught. She began to feel her way towards the stairs and, groping, touched the great bronze gong which stood a little to the right of where they began. She drew back her hand, quick and frightened, and the gong swung and struck against the wall. The dull booming note which it gave out seemed to Loveday to be the loudest and most dreadful sound that she had ever heard.

She was halfway up the stair before she knew that she had begun to run, and she had reached the turn before the door of the sitting-room was flung open. The light streamed out into the hall. She caught at the balustrade and stood there leaning over. She couldn't run any more, because she couldn't breathe. She felt as if she wouldn't ever be able to move again. They would put on the light in the hall. They would find her. And then...She couldn't look past being found. That was what made it so horrible. She would be found and—there wasn't anything more. It was a grey, dreadful blank.

She stared at the light and she heard voices—Hélène's voice, and Hacker's voice—and she saw Hélène's hand go up to the switch of the hall light. Hélène was standing in the doorway, and she put up her hand to find the switch.

Mr. Hacker said, "The door was ajar," and Hélène said "Oh!" and put her hand to the light.

Loveday winced as if someone were going to strike her. And then all of a sudden Pif-paf-pouf emerged from behind the gong. He gave a loud and joyful mew and walked into the light with his beautiful orange tail held high. He mewed again and rubbed his head against Hélène's ankle. Loveday heard her laugh.

"It was only Pif-paf-pouf!" she said.

Her hand dropped from the switch. They went back into the room and shut the door.

Chapter Twenty-Nine

HUGO TOOK his way back to Meade House for the second time that night. The light still showed through a chink in the curtains as he looked back at Mme. de Lara's sitting-room window. He stood for a moment on the terrace and watched the gleam. Hacker, Hélène de Lara, and—Miller—they were in there together, and he would have given a good deal to know just what they were talking about.

He went on his way with a certain impatience. Waiting for things to happen was the hardest job in the world. Ever since he had come to Meade House he had been waiting for *something* to happen. If it would only begin, it would be so much easier. He walked quickly, because he had the feeling that Hacker might be behind him; but when he came to the Meade House drive he stepped aside into the shrubbery that bordered it and groped his way to an oak that rose above the other trees. About six feet from the ground there was a hole in the trunk. From this hole Hugo took out the envelope which Daisy had given him.

He entered the house, as he had left it, by the back door, and reached his room without incident. He locked the door, sat down on the bed, and took out the contents of the envelope. He looked at them, frowning. Sheets of tracing paper; diagrams; formulæ that reminded him of his schooldays and rags in the "lab"—why did one always rag the "Stinks" master?

He could not make head or tail of the papers, so he put them away again and went to sleep with the envelope pinned inside the pocket of his pyjamas. He woke once, clutching them; and between waking and sleeping he thought he heard the door shut. He did not sleep again until the hour before the dawn. He lay awake and revolved endless plans which led nowhere. In the end he had no plan; and having decided not to have a plan at all, but to wait and see what turned up he fell asleep.

He woke an hour later with a most extraordinary sense of expectancy. It really was an extraordinary sense; he couldn't remember anything like it since the glamour had passed from waking up on his birthday and on Christmas Day. This feeling took him back to dark, bright wakings that seemed to be about a hundred years ago. It puzzled him very much.

He dressed, went down, and met the postman with a sheaf of letters. They were nearly all for Minstrel—nearly all but not all. At the bottom of the pile there was one for Hugo Ross, Esq. He went into the study, put Minstrel's letters down, and opened his own. It was from his uncle's solicitor, and it was quite short. It said:

"DEAR MR. ROSS,

"I am pleased to be able to inform you that our further search for your uncle's will has been successful. The will has been found. You are the sole legatee and executor. I suggest that you should come down without delay, as you will naturally wish to obtain probate as soon as possible."

Hugo read the letter through twice. After the second time he drew a long breath and looked about him. A change seemed to have passed upon everything. He could not have defined the nature of this change, but he was acutely conscious of it. Everything seemed to be a long way off and to have nothing to do with him at all. He wasn't Minstrel's secretary; he was Ross of Treneath. He folded the letter up and put it away.

Nobody else was down. He went out into the garden and began to walk up and down under the bare trees. He knew now why he hadn't been able to make a plan. It was because he needn't make one. He needn't stay here another minute; he had only to go to Minstrel and show this letter; he could be off by the midday train to town and catch the afternoon express. He felt a great flood of affection for Uncle Richard, who hadn't forgotten him after all. Uncle Richard hadn't forgotten, and Treneath was his. And Loveday was his. The heavy grey sky and the bare apple-trees looked a good deal like the Garden of Eden.

And then, with a crash like sudden thunder, the gate of the garden slammed in Hugo's face. He couldn't go in. He couldn't take Loveday by the hand and go into the garden and live happily ever after. He couldn't stop being Minstrel's secretary and catch the midday train and be off to Treneath. He had got to follow the Adventure to the bitter end. And all the savour had gone out of the Adventure; there was no romance in it any more; it was a horrid sordid business with a police-court at the latter end of it—a dirty, drab affair that was going to come between him and Loveday, and between him and Treneath. The letter in his pocket was his last chance. If he took it, everything was easy. If he didn't take it, he would never take an easy, pleasant road again. On the other hand—

Here he pulled himself up with a jerk. What was the good of arguing? He had certainly got to stay, because he had certainly got to save the plans, if there was any possible way of saving them. He turned his back quite resolutely on Treneath and went in.

Ambrose Minstrel was in the worst of tempers. He made a horrible breakfast of cold underdone mutton and cocoa, and swore at Hugo for an effete young pup because he refused to join him. After breakfast he kept looking at his watch and inveighing against the sloth, dilatoriness, and general incompetence of government departments.

At ten o'clock he told Hugo to ring up the Air Ministry. As soon as the call came through, he took over the telephone.

"I want to speak to Mr. Green," he began in his most disagreeable voice. "Oh—*is* he? Well, my time happens to be of value...No, I don't choose to give my name... No, certainly not...My good fellow, if you think I've the slightest intention of dancing attendance on a stall-fed, comatose, government flunkey, I can only assure you that you'd better think again....No, I can*not* wait. But you can tell your Mr. Green from me that it's waste of time for anyone to come down to Meade to-day, because the plans are not ready. I've decided to make certain alterations...Yes, I did say alterations. If you can't hear me, say so and send someone to the telephone who isn't deaf... Are you there?...Tell Mr. Green it's no use anyone coming down to-day...*Are you there?*...Oh, it's you, is it, Green? Have you had my message?...Yes—Minstrel speaking from Meade. It's no use your sending down to-day, because the plans aren't ready. I'm making an alteration...What's the matter with your line?...Oh, you *did* hear. I said I wasn't ready. When I *am* ready, I'll send Hacker up with the plans. I won't have people down here. D'you hear? I'm busy...Yes, I know it's difficult for you to grasp that. We're not all government officials—some of us work. Have you got that?...When? I *told* you when. *When I'm ready.*" The last words were almost shouted.

He thrust the receiver back upon the hook and turned on Hugo.

"That's the way to treat 'em. Treat 'em rough—treat 'em rough—treat 'em like dirt. Mud-brained asses, who think because they sit in a government office that they can dictate to me—*me! I'll* show them!"

He went off into the laboratory.

Hacker looked up from his table.

"What does he want to put their backs up for? He makes me wild."

"I expect they know him," said Hugo.

"They ought to. But he's getting worse. Of course he's a genius—but even so, there are limits to what they'll stand."

He yawned, stretched, and got up.

"Hanged if I'm going to work to-day! You can tell him I said so if you like—and if he blows up, let him blow up."

He went out of the room whistling and left Hugo wondering what was going to happen next.

The morning dragged. He had to stop himself thinking about Treneath, and he had to stop himself thinking about Loveday. Loveday wasn't an inspiration any more; she was a most frightful temptation. Loveday and Treneath—just to take Loveday's hand and go into his kingdom and shut the door and live happy ever after was so frightfully easy—and it was impossible—he couldn't do it. The bit of him that wanted to do it came very near hating the bit that couldn't do it.

The morning dragged interminably. At about two o'clock Minstrel stalked out of the laboratory and into the bleak fireless dining-room, where he partook of tinned salmon, *pâté de foie gras*—slabs of it on hunks of bread with the salmon—and a really fearful looking cup of cocoa which had grown cold with waiting. He scowled as he ate, and did not speak until he had finished, when he got up with a jerk that sent his chair sprawling.

He called back over his shoulder to Hugo as he left the room:

"Hurry up—I want you to take a telegram."

In the study Hugo asked tentatively, "Am I to telephone it?"

He had his head snapped off for his pains.

"I said take—T-A-K-E—*take*. You don't understand the English language, I suppose!" He strode to the study door and slammed it. "The trouble about you, Ross, is not so much that you haven't *got* a brain, as that occasionally some impulse from the great Inane prompts you to act as if you had some kind of thinking apparatus. Get a telegraph form and a pencil! Take this down! 'Green, Air Ministry.' That is the address. This is the telegram—'Am sending assistant with plans this afternoon. Do not send anyone down here. My time is valuable. Minstrel.' Have you got that? Read it over to me!"

Hugo read it over. He stammered a little over the word assistant. Was Hacker to take the plans? Hacker hadn't come in. He had gone out whistling more than three hours ago, and he hadn't come in. Hugo didn't think that Hacker meant to come in, and he didn't think that Hacker was meant to take the plans. His heart began to beat rather fast, and he coloured under Minstrel's contemptuous stare.

"You will now take that telegram to the post office and send it off. The word 'take' in this connection means 'convey'—it doesn't mean 'telephone.' Oh, by the way, there's a second telegram.

You needn't write it down if it doesn't stretch that—er—thinking apparatus of yours too much to remember three words—or, to be quite accurate, four."

"Yes, sir?"

What was coming? And why wasn't he to write the second telegram down?

"The name is Miller," said Minstrel. "Can you remember that? M-I-double L-E-R—Miller. And as the address is the one at which I understand you stayed when you were in town, perhaps you can remember that."

"Yes, sir."

Hugo thought that he might allow himself to look modestly surprised. He was in fact surprised into a condition of tingling expectancy. Miller—he was to wire to Miller, and he wasn't to write the telegram down. That is to say he was to walk into the village post office and write the telegram there as if it came from himself. He felt a natural impatience to know what he was going to wire to Miller.

He looked round at Minstrel and said,

"M-M-Miller? What am I to s-say?"

"I won't tax your memory. The message consists of three words—'Five o'clock to-day.' Kindly repeat it."

Hugo repeated the words. He felt sure that Hacker wouldn't return. It was he, Hugo, who would be given the plans to take to town. And somewhere on the way—at five o'clock to be accurate—the obliging Mr. Miller would contrive to relieve him of them. A subsequent inquiry at the post office would establish the fact that Hugo had met Mr. Miller by appointment, and that the appointment had been made as soon as he knew when the plans were to go to the Air Ministry.

He looked again at Minstrel, and found him dragging at his beard.

"Any s-signature?"

"No—it's not necessary. May I inquire whether this is what you call thinking?—because if it is, desist. Now get along!"

Hugo got along. What was he going to do about the telegram to Miller? He could send it, and send it unsigned, and pile up another damning bit of evidence against himself. Or he could send it signed with Minstrel's name, in which case Minstrel would merely repudiate the signature, as he undoubtedly meant to repudiate the message. Or he could omit to send the telegram. All the way to the post office he considered this alternative, only to reject it in the end as too dangerous. Supposing he altered the telegram, or didn't send it, or added a signature, and Minstrel rang up the post office. It was just the sort of thing that Minstrel might do—if he had the smallest lurking doubt of Hugo, it was what he was almost certain to do.

Hugo decided that it would be too dangerous to depart by a hair's breadth from the strictest path of muggishness. A single spark of intelligence would be fatal to his being entrusted with the plans. What was one more bit of evidence, however damning, if he could only leave Meade with the plans in his pocket?

The post office was also a general shop. It was kept by Mrs. Parford's brother, whose name was Alfred Dibbin. There were a good many people in the shop when Hugo entered it. Mr. Dibbin wore a worried air, and his hair was standing on end.

"No, we haven't any," he was saying. "I'm sorry, Mrs. Marsh, we don't stock it—No, sir, I'm sorry I can't change a five-pound note, not this afternoon—Now, Bobby, you just run along 'ome and ask your mother what sort of stamps she wants—and don't you go and forget the answer this time." He looked back over his shoulder, raised his voice, and called, "Chrissie!" and then began to weigh out fruit-drops with a slightly distracted air. After a moment he called, "Chrissie" again.

Hugo stood back to wait his turn. There were now three village women and a little girl waiting to be served. Mr. Dibbin went to the door at the back of the shop, opened it, and again called to the absent Chrissie. He came back, leaving the door open. It was just at Hugo's elbow. He wondered vaguely what Chrissie was doing; and as he wondered, he heard a giggle and the sound of hurrying footsteps.

Miss Chrissie came in rather flushed, patting her hair. She was a pretty girl with a bold rolling eye and a fine pair of rosy cheeks. She pushed the door with her foot, but before it shut Hugo heard something that he had not expected to hear. It brought him up with a round turn, and it settled the matter of the telegrams. He sent them both off and walked briskly back to the house.

The adventure was certainly afoot. He had done well not to take any chances over the telegrams, for what he had heard through the open door was the sound of a man whistling idly. The air that he whistled was the air that Hacker had been whistling when he walked out of the study. Hugo had heard him whistle it half a dozen times in half a dozen days, and he felt perfectly certain that he had just heard him whistle it again. He whistled flat, and always took a wrong note in the same place.

Hugo was very glad that he hadn't taken any chances over the telegrams.

Chapter Thirty

MINSTREL WAS in the hall.

"Where's Hacker? Yes, I said 'Where's Hacker?' Get a move on and find him! Out? How do you mean out? Why should he be out?"

"I d-don't know, sir."

"You don't know! No—you *wouldn't*. When did he go out?"

"Oh, hours ago."

"Hours ago—and not back? What does he mean by it? What does he think I pay him for?"

Hugo suppressed the temptation to say that he expected that Hacker was paid to keep out of the way when he wasn't wanted. He said nothing, and was sworn at for a tongue-tied booby.

"Did he say when he was coming back?"

"N-no, sir." He added innocently. "I d-don't think he m-meant to come back till late."

Minstrel stared at him. It was a cold, resentful stare.

"You don't *think!* I don't ask you to think—I don't pay you to think—I pay you to do as you're told. You'll have to take the plans to town instead of Hacker. I'm not going to keep them back just because he's out playing the fool, and have those cursed interfering busy-bodies at the Ministry come down here shoving their noses into what doesn't concern them and interrupting my work just because Hacker's played me a fool's trick."

So he was to go in Hacker's place. He was expecting it; but all the same there was a sort of shock. He asked,

"W-when?"

Minstrel took him up with a snort.

"When? Now—at once. Leonard'll drive you. You're to go straight to the Air Ministry and give the plans yourself to that ass Green."

"I'm not to go by train?"

"No, you're *not*—you're to go by car—*my* car. And you're going as soon as Leonard can bring the car round, so get a move on!"

Hugo got a move on. As he ran upstairs, he heard Minstrel's rasping voice at the house-telephone calling Leonard. He came down in a minute or two; and there was Minstrel in the hall again, walking up and down with long impatient strides. He tugged at an old-fashioned gold watch-chain and jerked from a waist-coat pocket a large chronometer with a mass of dangling pencils and seals attached to it.

"Come along—come along!" he said. "Leonard's bringing the car round. Go and see if he's there."

It was a physical impossibility in the time; but Hugo opened the door and looked out. Then, turning, he approached Minstrel with diffidence.

"W-would there be any objection—"

"*What?*" snapped Minstrel. "Speak out, can't you!"

"W-would you m-mind—"

Minstrel made a violent exclamation.

"Would I mind what? Haven't you got a voice—haven't you got a tongue? Can't you say what you want and have done with it instead of following me round like a puppy-dog and blushing like a girl—only a girl don't blush nowadays. I suggest that you join some young ladies' academy and learn how not to do it." He laughed a short raucous laugh. "Well, what is it? What d'you want?"

"I w-wanted to know if—that is I m-mean w-would there be any objection to my going to a s-shop—after I had been to the Ministry of course?"

"Buy up the whole town if you like!" said Minstrel contemptuously. "What sort of s-shop do you want to go to?"

He mimicked the stammer in a way that made Hugo see red. Rage nerved him to a supreme act of self-sacrifice. He drew his flute from his pocket.

"My f-flute wants m-mending."

Minstrel burst into a roar of laughter.

"Great Jupiter! He plays the flute! That finishes it! To a select academy for young ladies you must go! We'll advertise for one— 'Genteel surroundings. A refined atmosphere. All the comforts of a home. Music a speciality!'" His voice changed suddenly to one of sharp command. "There's the car. Get along!"

Hugo stood his ground.

"The p-plans, sir."

"I'll get them: Go and get in!"

Hugo went out on to the steps. It was colder; there was a little tingling breeze. He was glad of it. He got into the car with a word to Leonard and sat there leaning from the window, his eyes on the hall door.

In a moment Minstrel came out with a long envelope in his hand. Hugo's heart jumped when he saw it. The envelope was like the one which had been sent him by Ananias. He had been afraid that it would be sealed. But it wasn't sealed; the flap had been carelessly stuck down, and the gum was still wet. The papers had been just crammed in anyhow. They bulged, and the gum on the flap was wet and soft; it stuck to Hugo's thumb as he took the envelope from Minstrel's hand.

"*Personally to Green,*" said Minstrel, still in that sharp voice of command. "And you're to get a receipt from him, mind. And then"—he slipped into a drawl—"you can go and sack the City if you like."

He stepped back and stood in the open door.

"Right, Leonard!"

They started down the drive. Hugo looked back through the little window in the rear of the limousine and saw Minstrel standing on the doorstep, tall, gaunt, and untidy, with one hand at his beard. The wind blew in his ragged hair. He was watching the car with hot, unquiet eyes.

As they turned out of the gates, Hugo settled himself and drew up the rug. The envelope which Minstrel had given him lay on his knees. He drew the rug across it and folded back the fringed end so that it made a loose, untidy heap. Then he sat back and looked through the partition at Leonard's square shoulders and his neck with the black bristling hair growing rather low down.

Hugo had taken the right-hand corner; he was immediately behind Leonard. He stretched out his legs and leaned back. He was wondering whether Leonard could see him in the windscreen. It would depend upon the light—it had not been a bright day, and it was drawing towards dusk. He looked at his wrist-watch and saw that it was just on a quarter to four. He went on wondering about the wind-screen.

Presently he made a slight change in his position and drew the rug well up about him. Then he leaned back and shut his eyes.

It was nearly four o'clock. About five o'clock something was due to happen. He had plenty of time. But he wasn't going to bank on having plenty of time; and he wasn't going to bank on Leonard not being able to see him. Reflections were odd, chancy things; and he didn't mean to take any chances.

Under cover of the rug he was opening the envelope that Minstrel had given him. The flap came up easily enough. He got the papers out and slid them gently down on to the seat beside him. Then, under cover of getting out his handkerchief, he extracted from an inside pocket the envelope sent him by Ananias. It took him about five minutes to get the papers out of this envelope and into the empty one, because he could only move his fingers and he had to be very careful not to jerk the rug.

When it was done, he changed his position a little and threw the envelope out on the seat beside him. It didn't matter about Leonard seeing it; in fact it was quite a good plan that he should. He got the empty envelope back into his pocket, and came to the most difficult part of the whole job. He had to get out his flute and get Minstrel's plans inside it, rolled up tight. It took a long time, and it was surprisingly hard work. He would never have believed what hard work it was to roll up a number of sheets of paper without moving anything except your fingers. He was as hot when he had finished as if he had run a mile, and the rug was insupportable.

As soon as the flute was safely back in his pocket, he threw the rug off and leaned out of the window. It was dark now. They passed through a straggly village street and began to climb a stiffish hill. At the top Leonard slowed down, and after running at a crawl for a few hundred yards stopped dead and came round to the window.

"She's running very hot," he said in a worried voice. "I'll let her cool off a bit if you don't mind, sir."

"Is anything the matter?" said Hugo. "I don't want to be late, you know. We're running it pretty fine as it is. I don't suppose anyone stays in a government office after six—do they?"

"I don't know, sir. I'll just let her cool down a bit."

If this was a breakdown, Leonard was being a little previous.

"I don't want to run a bearing, sir."

"No, of course not. But Mr. M-M-Minstrel won't like it if we're late—he'll be awfully f-fed up."

Instead of answering, Leonard went forward and raised the bonnet. Five minutes later he got back into his seat and started again.

They ran over the brow of the hill and dipped down into a belt of woodland. The smell of damp leaves came up from it, cold and chill.

Hugo stopped feeling hot. For the first time he wondered, a little breathlessly, whether robbery with violence was to be the order of the day. The lonely wood had the air of having been especially designed as a setting for a little quiet highway business. Out of the recesses of his mind there poured a veritable mob of tales, in all of which valuables, a lonely traveller, and a dark forest played an uncheering part. In most of them the traveller was never seen again.

At this moment the car stopped and Leonard once more approached the window. Hugo experienced a number of sensations in rapid succession, the first of which was a most horrible stab of fear. He suppressed the impulse to shout for help, reflecting that if Leonard wanted to do him in, he had every chance of succeeding, as he could certainly give him three stone, and—this as Leonard put his hand on the door—he suddenly stopped being afraid and began, instead, to feel a sort of tingling excitement.

"What's the matter, Leonard?" he said.

"Well, I don't know, sir. I wish I did. She's running red hot and very lumpy. I'd like to get her into a garage where I can have a look at her."

"But there isn't a g-garage," said Hugo innocently.

"Well, sir, there's one about half a mile farther on. There's an inn there, 'The Wheatsheaf,'—a biggish place with a good garage, and if we pass it, there's nothing for ten miles. I don't like to risk going on like this—there's something wrong with the lubrication and we might run a bearing any moment."

"I don't want to be l-late."

"Perhaps you could ring up from the hotel."

"Well—I c-could."

"Yes, sir," said Leonard.

He climbed back, started the car, and proceeded to crawl between the lines of black shadowing trees.

Hugo sat up and did some thinking. It was just on five o'clock. The Wheatsheaf was Miller's rendezvous. Hugo was to go into the hotel to telephone, and there he would meet, or be met by, the red-haired Mr. Miller with the accent which Mrs. Miles considered to be Russian. He felt a very lively interest in what was going to happen after he and Miller met. Up to this point everything had been very well arranged. If he were really the unsuspicious fool they thought him, it would be the most natural thing in the world to go into the inn and ring up the Air Ministry to explain that he had been delayed upon the road.

He felt very curious to know what was going to happen at The Wheatsheaf, and he had to consider whether it was still necessary for him to play the mug. He thought that it was. He thought that it was not only necessary, but essential.

Minstrel—he had no proof that Minstrel wasn't on the straight. Strong suspicion and moral certainty are not proof. He couldn't disobey Minstrel's instructions on suspicion. He had got to go on in Minstrel's car and deliver his papers to Mr. Green. He thought the sooner he allowed himself to be robbed the better. He hadn't the least idea how Miller meant to get hold of the papers; but once he'd got them, he'd have no further use for Hugo—his idea would be to get across the Channel as quickly as possible.

Hugo rather thought it was up to him to smooth the ingenious Mr. Miller's path. Let Miller steal the wrong papers and get away with them as quick as possible. Hugo, with a clear coast and clear conscience, could then take any way he liked to town with his flute; whereas, if he dodged Miller here, he would certainly have to continue to dodge him all the way to town.

They emerged from the trees and saw the inn as a black blur set with little lighted windows. It had the look of a toy at that distance and against the sweep of lonely open country. There was not another light to be seen; only a formless landscape under a formless sky. The cloudy dark smothered everything except those little twinkling windows.

"Well—we've g-got here," said Hugo as the car drew up.

"Yes, sir," said Leonard. He didn't say anything more.

Hugo poked him a little—just to see.

"How l-long do you think you'll be?"

"I couldn't say, sir." He raised his voice a little as the hotel door opened. "How long will you be, sir?"

"I'll j-just put that call through."

The hall-porter must have heard both question and answer, for he met Hugo with, "You wish to telephone, sir?" And then, without waiting for an answer, "This way, sir. Mind the step. Allow me, sir."

Half a dozen feet of dark passage-way, rather stuffy; a step that was a real trap; a glimpse of himself in a huge old-fashioned mirror with a frame of tarnished gilt; and the porter was opening a door and standing aside to let Hugo pass him. He took two steps into the room and heard the door close behind him.

Chapter Thirty-One

HE WAS LOOKING for Mr. Miller, but he did not see him. He saw walls covered with old sporting prints, a clutter of outrageously incompatible furniture—an old warming pan, a fine tallboy, a staring Brussels carpet, a suite upholstered in crimson plush, white lace antimacassars, and—Mme. de Lara.

It was Hélène de Lara who gave the last touch of incongruity. She had an air of exquisite aloofness, a mournful elfin air, as she sat on the edge of one of the vast crimson armchairs pouring out coffee.

She looked up, exclaimed in a soft fluttered way, and almost dropped the heavy and much discoloured coffee-pot.

"You! Oh, my dear, how *nice!*"

Hugo crossed the room warily. He was still looking for Mr. Miller. Hélène de Lara's little cold fingers clung to his for a moment.

"To see a friend in this desolate spot! Isn't that just the very nicest thing that ever happened? I was so cold and so vexed, because I have been to town, and I should have been back at Torring House by now. Actually I have someone coming to dinner—an old friend—so I was feeling—oh, all at sixes and sevens, and wishing I had gone up by train—because trains don't ever have anything wrong with their engines—do they? And then, just when I was so cross—to see you! How nice!"

She had a way of looking out of those big dark eyes that suggested a great many things. Hugo, for instance, had to resist the pleasant suggestion that he was the one person in the world Hélène de Lara wished to meet, and that this was very natural because he was without doubt the most delightful, attractive, and charming young man of her acquaintance. Such suggestions, even if resisted, are not altogether without some effect on the atmosphere.

Hugo blushed.

"I want to put a c-call through," he said.

"Ah now, and I've just asked for one! And I'm afraid it may take some time—but they promised to tell me as soon as ever it comes through. Are you in a terrible hurry? Or are you waiting for your car like me?"

"W-well—I am."

"Ah! How nice it is to have a companion in misfortune! Does it console you a little to feel that you are consoling me—a great deal? And you'll have a cup of coffee now—won't you?" She was pouring one out as she spoke.

It was the second cup on the tray that made Hugo's gaze continue to travel round the room in search of Mr. Miller. The grinning mask of a fox set on the wall immediately above a case of dilapidated stuffed birds was the nearest approach to the redheaded gentleman with the Russian accent.

Mme. de Lara was holding out a coffee-cup.

"Black?" she said.

Hugo put some milk into it and took two lumps of sugar. He was wondering about the coffee. Mme. de Lara was drinking hers. He put the cup to his lips and pretended to sip from it. After that he stopped wondering. The coffee was certainly drugged. He had a very keen sense of smell, and this sense informed him that there was something in the cup besides milk, sugar, coffee and—possibly—chicory.

He began to wander round the room looking at the old prints and still pretending to sip the coffee.

Hélène de Lara never took her eyes off him.

"You like these queer old pictures?"

"V-very much."

He came to a standstill under the grinning fox. There was a rose-wood table on his right; a magazine or two had been thrown down on it; there were two metal ashtrays, a bright blue jar containing soiled calico daffodils; and a plant, which might also have been artificial, spreading stiff striped green and white leaves above a furiously shiny yellow pot.

Hugo gazed lovingly at the pot. As a receptacle for drugged coffee which one didn't want to drink, it was quite perfect. If Hélène would only look away for a second.

"Do you think that t-tallboy is really old?" he said.

Mme. de Lara did not look at the tallboy; she continued to look at Hugo. Her unwavering gaze said how clever it was of him to know that it was a tallboy and that it was old. He felt a schoolboy desire to pick up the case of stuffed birds and heave it at the lady. He repressed this desire; but his finger-tips tingled.

"That one over there," he said, pointing.

She did turn her head for a moment then; but only for a moment.

"I expect so," she said languidly.

Hugo had been very quick indeed; the stripy plant had received a lethal dose, and the empty cup was at his mouth. He tilted it, felt the last drugged drop against his lips, and then, with a half-suppressed yawn, he came across and put the cup down on the tray.

"It's w-warm in here."

He thought he had better go to sleep and let them get away with the papers—it would save a lot of trouble.

"Are you too warm? Why don't you take your coat off and be comfortable?"

"Well, I've got some p-papers of Mr. M-Minstrel's that I oughtn't to leave about—but I can put them in another p-pocket."

He took off his overcoat, hauled out the envelope, and put it into his jacket pocket. He didn't want Miller pawing him all over. If they were going to have the papers, they might just as well know where to look for them. He folded the overcoat, and for a moment the flute showed.

Hélène exclaimed, "You take your flute when you go to see other people, but you wouldn't bring it when you came to see me."

"I'm only taking it up to be m-mended." He yawned again. "I b-beg your pardon."

"You *do* look tired," said Hélène. "Why don't you have a little sleep? I'm sure Ambrose works you quite cruelly—he is cruel, you know. I told you we were friends once; but cruelty is the thing I can't bear." She put both hands to her breast. The diamond in her ring shone like a wonderful tear. "He *is* cruel—and I can't bear cruelty. There is something here that weeps when I see anyone being cruel. But men are all cruel, I think. I have had to weep so often." She put her hand across her eyes for an instant, then smiled sadly. "I don't think you're cruel, you know—not yet, Hugo."

In spite of everything, the thrill in her voice when she said his name did move him. It stirred the springs of his imagination, as acting has the power to stir them even when we know that we are being played upon. Hugo knew, and was stirred. He was glad when the door opened.

The porter stood there.

"Just a moment, sir, if you please."

As he went to the door, Hugo wondered what was coming.

"About your call, sir—the lady has one first—they say at the exchange that it may take time. Perhaps she wouldn't object to yours being put through first."

Hugo hesitated, then suddenly decided not to ring the Air Ministry, but to shed Leonard and take the plans to Mr. Smith. The embargo on a visit might now be considered to be off. Mr. Smith would know where Mr. Green was to be found after office hours.

He said, "No—it's all right—it doesn't matter—it's too late to catch the p-people I wanted to."

He hoped he had done the right thing. The whole affair was like a game of devil-in-the-dark. He and Susan used to play it with the Carnabys—a frightful breath-catching game in which you crept about shoeless, noiseless, in a dark room waiting to be pounced upon by the unseen "He."

He went slowly back to the red plush sofa where his coat was lying. He yawned again, said "I b-beg your pardon," and sat down. He thought the time had come when he might stare vaguely before him and desist from conversation. He was aware of a most sympathetic glance.

"My dear boy, you look dead tired. Do have a little nap. I'll wake you at once if your car comes round."

Hugo mumbled something and allowed his eyes to close. This was really a great relief, because he found it very embarrassing to have Mme. de Lara looking at him in that intense sort of way. He shut his eyes, let his head give a drowsy jerk, and was aware of a cushion where no cushion had been a moment before. Through his lashes he caught a glimpse of Mme. de Lara bending over him. The glimpse puzzled him; she was still looking at him as if—as if...There was a murmur of "Poor boy!" and something touched his cheek. He burrowed furiously into the cushion and threw out one hand.

Hélène de Lara stepped back with a caught breath that sounded like a sob. Then she went and sat down again on the edge of the big armchair.

Hugo began to breathe as if he were very fast asleep. The cushion hid most of his face. It was horribly soft and hot and feathery, and the feathers smelt of mould; but it was certainly useful.

The moments passed into minutes. There was a heavy stillness in the room, broken only by Hugo's own breathing and the sound of a clock ticking somewhere out of sight; he thought it must be in the passage. It ticked with a heavy irregular tick—dot *dash*—dot *dash*—dot *dash*. Hugo began to count the ticks, and then stopped because he was afraid of sending himself to sleep. He wished to goodness that something would happen. And as the thought passed through his mind, Hélène de Lara gave a little sigh and got up.

She came round the back of the sofa, leaned on it, and put a soft fluttering touch on Hugo's hair. It was most frightfully difficult not to move, but he kept still and went on taking those long deep breaths. At last his face was hidden—or nearly hidden. She stroked his hair two or three times, and then bent down and kissed him.

It was really the most frightful moment of the whole adventure, because he felt the blood rush to his face.

But Hélène had turned away with another of those sobbing breaths. She went to the door and opened it. After a moment he heard it close again. There was someone else in the room.

He heard Hélène say in her low mournful voice, "He is fast asleep. I touched him just now and he did not wake. The papers are in his pocket."

"How do you know?"

This was Mr. Miller. Hugo wondered again if the accent was really Russian.

"I saw him put them there. They are in a long envelope. He is very ingenuous of course—he showed them to me and told me what they were."

"Which pocket?"

They were quite close to him now; Hélène's dress brushed his knee; he felt her hand touch him lightly.

"Here—this is it."

The envelope came out easily. If he had been really asleep, the light touch would never have waked him. There was the faint sound of paper being folded; Mr. Miller was putting the envelope away. Then he spoke:

"You had better get away—as quick as possible. I congratulate you, madame."

"Don't!" said Hélène. "I—poor boy—I could wake him—now."

"You'd better not," said Mr. Miller. "You wouldn't like what you'd get for doing that." He laughed a little and said, very slowly and distinctly, "Two—thousand—pounds. That is much better—eh?"

"Don't!" said Hélène de Lara.

She turned and went out of the room. Mr. Miller followed her. They left the door ajar. The ticking of the clock was much louder now.

Hugo stayed just where he was for what seemed like a very long time. He heard a car go off in the direction from which he had come. That would be Mme. de Lara going down to Torring House to keep her dinner engagement. A minute later another car went off towards London. Mr. Miller was also on his way.

He got up, stretched himself, and rang the bell.

"Ask if my car's ready," he said.

As soon as the man was gone, he allowed himself to laugh. The car would be ready now—unless Mr. Miller was afraid of being followed. It would be rather interesting to see whether the transfer of the plans had cured the odd something which Leonard found amiss with the lubrication.

He picked up his overcoat and put it on. Just for one moment he had a sense of something wrong, something missing. And then he knew what the something was. He thrust a cold hand into an empty pocket.

The flute was gone.

Chapter Thirty-Two

HE STOOD there with his hand in his pocket. He didn't move it, because he couldn't move it. For a moment he could only stand there. He couldn't move; and, as certainly, he couldn't think. The flute was gone. This presented itself, not as a thought, but as a horrible concrete fact which he had suddenly run up against, and which had knocked all the thinking out of him. He felt very much as if he had run into a brick wall and been stunned.

The moment passed. He withdrew his hand slowly, and slowly he began to think again. The flute might have fallen out of his pocket.

He looked on the sofa and on the floor; but even as he looked, he knew that he wouldn't find it. It hadn't fallen out; it had been taken out. The only question was, who had taken it? Miller had gone to London, and Mme. de Lara to Meade. One of them had taken the flute and the plans that were inside the flute—the *real* plans. There wasn't any question that one of them had taken it. But which of them? Good heavens! Which—which—*which?*

Hugo began to steady from the shock. It wasn't Miller who had taken the flute—Miller couldn't have taken it. For one thing, he didn't know it was there—and Hélène de Lara did. For another, Hélène de Lara had had the opportunity of taking it whilst he was speaking to the porter, and Miller couldn't have taken it without his knowledge, because the coat was behind him and half under him all the time he was pretending to be asleep. Hélène had taken it.

Then, quick and sharp, "What a fool you are! If she took it, that's not to say she kept it. She'd give the plans to Miller—wouldn't she, you fool?"

The fool hesitated, and wasn't sure. It was of his folly that he had a doubt. She must have given them to Miller. She wouldn't take them back to Meade. Why, that was the plot—to give Miller the plans and to let it seem that it was Hugo who had given them away. It would certainly seem like that now. It could be shown that he had met Miller by appointment, and that Miller had gone away with the plans in his pocket. *Had he?* The fool wasn't sure—remained obstinate and immovable in not being sure. Suppose—Hugo opened the door and went into the hall.

The porter told him what he knew already. The lady had gone, and the red-headed gentleman had gone. They had gone in different directions. Then a surprise—"The lady left a note for you, sir."

The most ardent lover could not have snatched a love-letter more eagerly. The note was on the hotel note-paper, and it was very short. It began:

"MY DEAR,

"If you want your flute, come and get it. And if you want help, well—perhaps—I'm going home."

The signature was, "Hélène."

Hugo ran out of the front door and round to the garage. He found the car, and he found Leonard; they were at opposite ends of the rather ramshackle place.

Leonard didn't turn a hair. He said respectfully, "I think she's all right now, sir. I was just coming in to tell you." And that was that. What was the good of giving him the lie? Nothing mattered except to get back to Meade and to get there quickly. But would Leonard take him back to Meade?

He put this to the touch.

"Look here, I've got to get back."

"Back, sir!"

"Back to M-Meade. I've had my papers stolen."

"Stolen, sir!"

Leonard wasn't really a very good actor. He was too stolid.

"Yes, I must get back as quick as p-possible."

"Very good, sir."

There seemed to be an interminable delay before they got off. This was, of course, to be expected—Miller was to get as good a start as possible. Well, Miller had got his start. But had he got the real plans? Or had Mme. de Lara got them? Hélène de Lara had the flute. But did she know that the plans were in the flute? Or had she just taken it to tease him and to bring him to Torring House again? For the life of him Hugo could not be sure; and for the life of him he could not help remembering that Hélène de Lara had kissed him. How could she have known that the papers were in the flute? Perhaps she didn't know. Perhaps—

They started. The long interminable road stretched between him and Torring House. His thoughts pursued Hélène de Lara with an ardent intensity which might, or might not, have pleased her. Even if she had not known that the papers were in the flute, she would find them in a moment if she began to fiddle with it. Women never could keep their fingers off things. She might be finding the plans at this very moment.

They passed through the dark wood. But now it was most unromantically void of glamour; it was just another stage on the long, interminable road. If Hélène found the plans, what would she do with them? Would she try to catch Miller? Or would she take them back to Minstrel? Or would she try to drive with them some private bargain of her own? He stared into the darkness for the lights of any car that might hold Hélène de Lara and the plans.

Leonard drove slowly; it was half-past seven before they passed Meade Station. In another five minutes they were turning in at the gates of Meade House. Hugo tapped on the glass.

"You needn't drive up to the house. I'll get out here, and you can go straight to the garage."

Leonard nodded. He brought the car to a standstill, and Hugo got out. Then he drove slowly on, keeping straight ahead instead of turning to the right to take the gravel sweep. Huge saw the red light going away and, turning, ran back down the drive and out into the road.

He had burnt his boats.

Chapter Thirty-Three

LOVEDAY LOOKED UP from a book.

"What ages you've been, Hélène!"

"Have you been bored?" said Hélène de Lara.

She stood in the doorway of her sitting-room and looked at Loveday curled up in a big chair with Pif-paf-pouf on her lap.

"Oh no—it takes a lot to bore me. Did you do your shopping? What did you buy?"

Hélène slipped out of her fur coat and let it fall on the arm of the sofa.

"I did not buy anything," she said. There was something elusive in her voice. She came slowly over to the fire and held out her hands towards it.

"Oh, I am cold and tired!"

"What a waste of time and petrol to go all that way and not buy anything!"

Hélène gave a faint laugh.

"One doesn't always have to buy things—sometimes one has them given to one."

Loveday went back to her book. If Hélène wanted her to ask questions, she just wasn't going to do it.

Mme. de Lara went on speaking softly to the fire:

"Yes, sometimes one has things given to one. That is better than buying—isn't it? Anyone can buy; but a gift may mean—Ah, well, who can tell how much a gift may mean?"

Loveday continued to read.

Hélène sighed.

"He's so young, poor boy!" She hummed just above her breath:

"'Oh, there's nothing half so sweet in life as

Love's young dream!'

"You are too young, *Chérie*, to know what that means."

Loveday's shoulder jerked.

"I do wish to goodness, Hélène, that you would call me by my proper name instead of that ridiculous French *Chérie!*"

Mme. de Lara laughed.

"Oh, la-la!" she said.

Loveday fixed a bright angry gaze upon her. "Every time you do it I shall call you Ellen."

"Ssh!"

"Well, it's your own proper name. I can't see why anyone wants to be French."

"Ah well," said Hélène, "you are very young, Loveday. And I wish—oh, I wish I were as young as you, because, you see—*he* is young!"

"I don't know what you're talking about," said Loveday.

She turned a page and became, apparently, immersed in her book again.

"I was talking about Hugo," said Hélène sweetly. "Hugo Ross—poor boy!"

Loveday looked up.

"Why is he poor?"

"Well, he hasn't any money—has he?"

"That's not what you meant."

Hélène blew her a kiss.

"Are you interested? He would be flattered. But take care, *Chérie*—he is mine."

"Is he—Ellen?"

Hélène's eyebrows went up; her mournful eyes looked angry for a moment. Then she decided to laugh again.

"That was just a little rude. It is not attractive to be *gauche*—men do not like it. You will discover that, my dear, when you are no longer the schoolgirl." She made a little malicious grimace and added, "You are—interested in Hugo Ross?"

"Why shouldn't I be?"

"Why should you, when you have only seen him once?"

"Perhaps I fell in love with him at first sight," said Loveday with the grave stare of a child.

"If you did, you are wasting your time."

"Because he is yours?" said Loveday.

Hélène nodded. She walked across to the sofa, picked up her fur coat, and took out of the pocket the two halves of Hugo's flute.

"Is not this an original *gage d'amour?*" she said. Her eyes dwelt on Loveday. "*You* will not understand me when I say that it is more to me than diamonds. Any man without a soul can buy diamonds; but this"—she held out the two halves of the flute—"this is the boy's treasure—the thing he pours his dreams into—his romance. And he gives it to me to keep for him—until he comes." Her voice sank to a low murmur on the last words.

Loveday's heart thumped hard. She didn't believe for an instant that Hugo had given the flute to Hélène—Hélène was just swanking—she had taken the flute. But why had she taken it? What had been happening? And what was going to happen?

She got as far as this, and then—The hand that was holding her book closed hard on a sharp corner; the corner made a deep dint in her palm, but Loveday didn't feel it. Hélène was holding out the two halves of the flute; the open ends were towards Loveday; and she could see in each the edges of a tight-rolled paper whirl.

She gripped the book, and she didn't cry out. Her heart gave another thump. She laughed and said,

"I can't think why on earth you didn't go on the stage. You've got a simply lovely voice for it. You made me feel *gruely* all down my spine when you said that—'until he comes.' No—I can't do it—but you'd have made a simply wonderful actress."

Hélène lifted the flute to her cheek for a moment and held it there, smiling wistfully. Then she laid it on a table sacred to flowers and one or two rare and cherished bits of china.

"Perhaps," she said, "perhaps I wanted the larger stage, and a part in the great unwritten play."

Loveday bent down and kissed Pif-paf-pouf on the top of his orange head. Then she gave a gurgle of laughter.

"I suppose you know what you mean! Anyhow you made it sound lovely. I wish I could do things with my voice like that. Oh, by the way, Emily rang up."

"*Emily?*"

"Yes, Emily. She's back—and I can go home to-morrow. Aren't you pleased?"

"Ah now, I have loved having you—I think you know that, my dear."

Loveday didn't know it at all; she didn't think Hélène would love having anyone who poked fun at her and called her Ellen. But she admired the beautiful thrill in Hélène's voice and the mournful affection in her eyes.

"You seem to want me more than Emily does," she said. "Emily was just having a sense of duty about me. She said I could come back to-night if I liked, but she'd much rather I stayed till to-morrow—if you can put up with me till then."

"Oh," said Hélène, "but if she *wants* you—"

"She doesn't."

A fleeting gleam of annoyance just showed in Mme. de Lara's eyes.

"Ah now, Loveday, you must not be so cynical! At your age—" She sketched a little gesture of recoil. "Dear Emily! She has no children—you fill the empty place in her home. I think perhaps I am selfish to keep you here to-night. She will miss your welcome."

Loveday giggled.

"She didn't *say* she would."

"She is reserved and sensitive. I don't think you understand Emily, my dear." Hélène's tone was grave and reproachful.

"Perhaps I don't."

Loveday gazed at Hélène because she was so dreadfully afraid of looking at the flute. If only Hélène would go out of the room. She had an inspiration.

"Why don't you ring Emily up? Then *you* could give her the welcome and find out whether she's really raging and craving to have me back to-night. Because if she is, I know you'd be beautifully unselfish about it—wouldn't you? I mean you'd give me up—wouldn't you?"

"Of course," said Hélène. She went to the door, opened it, and turned on the threshold. "I don't think you really appreciate Emily," she said, and went out.

"She's simply dying to get rid of me," said Loveday to herself. "She's dying to get rid of me because she's expecting Hugo."

She jumped up with a little angry thrill running all through her. Pif-paf-pouf said "Grr!" and stretched a sleepy curled-up paw as she put him down in the seat of the chair with a pat. Next moment she was at the table and one of the halves of the flute was in her hand.

The plans had been rolled up very tight. She couldn't move them. How long would it take Hélène to make Emily have her back to-night? She undid her brooch, and with the help of the pin she got the tight roll to move. The paper tore, and a shred or two fell. A little more, and she could catch hold of it and pull. Out it came, and went down inside her jumper. Now the second roll. It came out more easily.

She got back into her chair, gathered up Pif-paf-pouf, and balanced the book she had been reading on top of him. Pif-paf-pouf stretched and sank into lazy slumber.

Loveday could hear Hélène at the telephone. Her voice was a great deal higher than usual. Emily was probably being firm. What on earth was she to do with the plans?

She rolled them the wrong way to straighten them. But they were awful things to hide—they crackled. If she pushed them down inside her jumper, they would crackle every time she moved. Horrible things! What on earth *was* she to do with them?

Hélène's voice stopped.

In a panic Loveday folded the papers across and shut them between the pages of her book. She pushed the book down between her and the chair.

Hélène found her kissing the top of Pif-paf-pouf's head. She smiled indulgently.

"Emily does want you, my dear. What did I tell you? I knew that she must be longing to have you back. Poor Emily! I have ordered the car for you at once. I knew she would want you to be there for dinner. And you must come back and see me another time."

Loveday kissed Pif-paf-pouf again, slid him gently on to the hearth-rug, and got up clasping her book. She was now as anxious to get away as Hélène could possibly be to see her go.

"I shall just have to throw my things in," she said. "Are you sure you wouldn't like me to stop and keep you company?"

Hélène smiled wistfully.

"Ah now, that's sweet of you! But—well, perhaps you guess. Do you?"

"That you want to get rid of me?"

Hélène exclaimed laughingly, "How terrible that sounds! And yet perhaps it is just a little true. And you must not be angry, Loveday, because one day you will understand and—and be very happy yourself when someone whom you care for comes to tell you that he cares too."

Loveday could have slapped her. She stood in the doorway with her hands behind her holding the book.

"I suppose you mean Mr. Ross is coming."

"Perhaps," said Hélène. "Ah, *Chérie*, love is a very wonderful thing. And some day it will come to you—some day a man will put his heart into your hands and—"

"Good gracious!" said Loveday. "You really *ought* to have been on the stage, Hélène. Well, I must pack. You can do the rest of that lovely piece another time—you do it most awfully well. But if I've got to dine with Emily, I can't stop and hear any more of it now. Emily's cook turns puce with rage if anyone's late for dinner." She ran upstairs.

"In another minute I'd have pitched the book at her head, plans and all," she said to herself as she jerked out her suitcase and threw the book into the bottom of it.

Emily would not have approved of the packing that followed; it was rapid and sketchy in the extreme—shoes, frocks, and a damp sponge-bag, all pushed in anyhow. It had the one merit of being swift. In six minutes Loveday was descending the stairs ready for the road. The suitcase was put into the car, an umbrella retrieved from the stand in the hall.

Hélène came out with a beautiful parting embrace. Loveday was enfolded, kissed on both cheeks, and murmured over.

"Come back, soon, *Chérie*," said Mme. de Lara.

"Thanks awfully, Ellen," said Loveday in a clear ringing voice.

Chapter Thirty-Four

IT WAS NEARLY half an hour later that Mme. de Lara's sad-faced foreign butler opened the door of her little room and announced Mr. Ross.

Mr. Ross came in in a hurry, heard the door close behind him, and beheld Hélène all in misty grey. She was bending over a great bowl of Parma violets; the attitude was one of extreme grace. For a moment she did not move, then turned slowly with half a dozen violets in her hand.

She said, "So you have come," and her voice was low and sweet.

Hugo found himself stammering her name.

"M-M-Madame de Lara!"

"Yes—Hugo?"

Hugo held out her note.

"You asked me to c-c-come."

"Yes—Hugo."

It was a boiling fury that was making him stammer. He had been quite cool until he came into the scented room and saw her; then suddenly he was angry with an anger that shook him, all of him—his speech, his thought, his self-control. He looked away from her and saw the flute.

It was lying on a little polished table guarded by a pair of Chinese dogs, fierce in white china which had withstood the changes and chances of four hundred years. A frail jar full of carnations made a delicately coloured background.

Hugo saw the flute, and the fury went out of him, leaving him cold and quiet. If she had the papers, she had them. He would soon know. He said,

"You told me to come for my flute. Why did you take it, Mme. de Lara?"

She sighed and touched her lips with the violets.

"Perhaps I wanted to see you—Hugo." Then after a little pause, "Are you angry?"

Hugo said "No" quite truthfully. He wasn't angry any more.

"I should not like you to be angry with me. People get angry so easily and for such little things. They do not always know how much even a foolish anger may hurt. I—Hugo, I have been hurt so often. I should not like to think that you would ever hurt me." Her voice dwelt on the "you" with the same sound that it had when she said his name; there was a sort of softening of her whole aspect, as if she grew younger, simpler.

Hugo walked to the table and picked up the two halves of his flute. Had she taken it for his sake, or for the sake of the plans? Everything turned on that. If the plans were there, if the plans were safe—

He turned the flute in his hand. The plans were gone.

He laid the flute back on the table and walked across to where Hélène was standing watching him.

"I came here because I wanted to ask you a question."

"Yes, Hugo." She spoke like a girl who is shy of her lover.

"I came to ask you where my papers are."

Hélène de Lara gave a cry of surprise.

"Your papers! Ah now, what do you mean—Hugo?"

"You know what I mean."

"*I—know?*"

"Yes, Mme. de Lara."

"But I know nothing. What papers?"

"Mr. Minstrel's plans. I was taking them to town. I missed them at The Wheatsheaf. Where are they?"

A look of horrified distress crossed her face.

"Hugo—you do not mean it! It is not true!"

"I missed them at The Wheatsheaf."

Mme. de Lara caught him by the arm. The few sweet violets she had been holding fell to the floor.

"Hugo—my poor boy! If it is true, it is—what is it for you? Oh, it cannot be true!"

"I missed them at The Wheatsheaf. Where are they?"

"My poor boy! Hugo, it is dreadful! Those plans—gone! It is ruin—disgrace. Oh, my poor boy!"

Hugo pulled his arm away.

"You were at The Wheatsheaf when I got there. I drank coffee with you. I went to sleep. After that the plans were gone."

His very bright blue eyes were fixed on her face. They read agitation, pity, sweet concern.

"Oh, my poor boy! Then it was my fault. What can I do? You looked so tired. And how was I to know?" Her hands were clasped at her breast, her eyes were full of tears. "How was I to know? You were so tired—I had not the heart to wake you. And I was not out of the room for more than three or four minutes. If the plans were taken, it must have been then, when I was out of the room."

Hugo smiled. She found an irony that startled her in his eyes.

She said "Oh!" and as the little sound left her lips, the door opened.

"Mr. Minstrel—Mr. Hacker," said the butler in his sad monotone.

The two men came in, and Hacker banged the door.

Hugo had turned. He saw Minstrel grimly furious, Hacker, the bully confessed, with an air of triumph, as who should say, "The rat's in the trap. Now for some sport!"

Minstrel opened his overcoat with twitching fingers, glared through a silent minute. Then with an abrupt and nervous gesture,

"Well, Ross—well?"

That he was in the wrong, and badly in the wrong, Hugo knew well enough. He had left Leonard to tell the tale he should have told himself. But there had been just the one faint chance of finding the flute unrifled. On that frail chance he had risked everything and lost. He looked steadily back at Minstrel and spoke quietly.

"Leonard has told you."

Ambrose Minstrel came out with a word which is not usually heard in drawing-rooms.

"Leonard!" he said. "Leonard has told me! Why is it left to Leonard to tell me, whilst you skulk here behind a woman? You've your lying story, no doubt, but you haven't the guts to stand up to me with it, you miserable, white-livered thief!"

"*Ambrose!*" said Hélène de Lara in a shuddering voice.

Hacker said "Sir—*sir!*" and put a hand on Minstrel's arm.

Minstrel turned on him snarling.

"Are you in with him? Are you going to take his part? If you are, I'll have no mercy on you—I warn you of that, Hacker. He'll rot in prison, and you can rot with him."

"I don't take his part—I don't take anyone's part—I want to get at the facts. You ought to hear what he's got to say."

"*Ambrose!*" said Hélène again.

"The plans are gone," said Ambrose Minstrel. His voice was like a cold east wind; the fury in it had frozen to a cutting edge. "My plans are gone."

He stared with his bloodshot eyes at Hugo.

"What have you got to say for yourself? My plans are gone."

"They were stolen," said Hugo.

He said this because he had to say something. He had to take his cue and play the part for which he had been cast. The play was set.

"Yes—stolen," said Minstrel with an oath. "Stolen by you and sold by you. D'you think you can humbug us? D'you think you can get away with it, you rabbit?" He laughed harshly and pushed Hacker forward. "Come on, Hacker! Tell him what you told me! Give him powder and shot and see how he stands up to it! How many shots does it take to kill a rabbit—or to make it squeal? Get on to him, Hacker, get on to him! And you, Hélène, come over here! Come along over here and see how he takes it! Now, Hacker! Now, Mr. Secretary rabbit!"

Hacker came forward. His air was sober, but his voice had the bully's note.

"You'd better make a clean breast of it," he said.

"It would be v-very convenient for you, Hacker—wouldn't it?"

Hugo had a fancy to re-write his part. He saw Hacker stare.

"Are you going to pretend you don't know? You're caught out. As it happens, I'd business at the post office, and the girl asked me about the telegram you sent—something about having overcharged you. Well, I thought it a very funny telegram, and I thought it my duty to take a copy of it for Mr. Minstrel."

"What telegram do you mean?"

"Are you going to pretend you don't know? It won't do, Ross. You wired to a fellow called Miller to meet you at five-thirty. As you didn't specify any place, it's obvious that this had already been arranged between you. You did meet Miller at The Wheatsheaf, on the London road about five miles this side of Frayling. You met him there, and you gave him the plans. You needn't trouble to lie, because Leonard's evidence can't be explained away."

Hugo looked at Minstrel.

"Are you going to say you didn't dictate that telegram to me?"

Minstrel swore again.

"You young pup! Is that your line? If it is, you'd better drop it." He laughed his rasping laugh. "So I told you to wire to Miller, did I? Perhaps I told you to sell the plans!" He laughed again. "Tell that to a jury and see if they'll believe you! Go on, Hacker!"

"It's not the first time I've come across this fellow Miller. He came nosing round here a few months back, and we sent him off with a flea in his ear. He's some sort of a Bolshevist agent and a thorough bad lot. When I went to your rooms in town and found Miller there, I thought it my duty to inform Mr. Minstrel. But he wouldn't listen to me—he said he knew when he could trust a man, and he damned me into heaps for interfering."

"That's true—I did." Minstrel was scowling, his hand at his beard. "I don't often say I'm sorry about anything, but I was a damned fool not to kick you out then and there. I was a fool, and I've got to pay for it."

"I don't think it would really have suited you to kick me out then, sir," said Hugo.

He had the satisfaction of seeing Minstrel explode.

"What d'you mean by that? What the blank, blank, blank d'you mean by that?"

"Something that may interest the jury," said Hugo.

He felt Hélène's hand on his arm.

"Don't—don't! Why will you irritate him? You are making it all so much worse. Ambrose—he doesn't know what he's saying."

Minstrel glared at her.

"Go on, Hacker," he said. "So I sent the telegram! Let's see if he'll say I wrote the letter you've got in your pocket."

"You'd better chuck it, Ross," said James Hacker. "The game's up. When Leonard came in with his story, we searched your room. This letter was found there."

He took out of his pocket a folded sheet, opened it, held it out.

"It's from a man called Rice, offering you five thousand pounds for the plans."

"I don't think he mentions plans," said Hugo. "The jury won't like it if you exaggerate, you know, Hacker. Did you find that letter to-night? Do you know, I thought you'd had it longer than that. And when did you add the noughts to Rice's fifty?"

Hacker was betrayed into bluster.

"Here—none of that! That won't go down."

"I'll keep it for the jury," said Hugo.

Minstrel caught Hacker by the arm.

"That's enough," he said—"that's enough and to spare. Let him talk to the police if he wants to talk—I've heard enough. Hélène, may we use your telephone?...Ring up Ledlington, Hacker—tell them what's happened and ask them to send someone along with a warrant. No, I'd better speak myself—I'll have to make the charge. And meanwhile—Here, Hélène, those shutters of yours lock, don't they?...I thought so. Lock 'em, Hacker, and then we can leave Mr. Ross to devise a few more ingenious fairy tales—he'll need 'em." He spoke with extraordinary energy and bitterness. His "Mr. Ross" cut more effectively than any term of abuse.

The fury had passed from his aspect; he was the wronged man, efficient in his appeal to the law. With a look of contempt he turned on his heel and opened the door for Hélène to pass out.

Hacker had drawn the white painted shutters across the garden door. He locked them now and came back with the key in his hand, speaking to Hélène.

"The other windows—what about them? Are the shutters locked?"

Hugo heard Hélène catch her breath.

"Always—at sundown," she said.

Then the three of them went out. The door closed, a key turned. Hugo was alone.

Chapter Thirty-Five

HE STOOD and looked at the door for a little while. He had plenty to think about. He wanted to sort his thinking and get it clear. Now that the thing had come, he felt quite quiet and cool. Nothing really mattered except the plans. Had they got them, or had they not got them? And then...when he said "they," which of them did he mean? There was Hélène de Lara—and there were Minstrel and Hacker. Hélène had had the flute—and the plans were in the flute—and the plans were gone. Hélène therefore had had the plans. But had she handed them on to Minstrel and Hacker, or had she got them still? Was she, in fact, playing Minstrel's game, or was she playing a game of her own—a game in which she beckoned Hugo as a partner? She had looked at him as she went from the room—a quick backward look unseen by the others; her eyes had said something—had promised and implored. Was it just play acting—an effective exit? Or was he in fact being beckoned to take a hand in Mme. de Lara's game? He didn't know.

After a minute he turned from the door and began to walk slowly up and down. It was when he turned for the third time that he saw the brooch. He was looking down, and as he moved, a point of light flashed at him from the floor with just the tiny rainbow flash that you get from a point of dew.

The brooch lay under the table where the Ming dogs grinned fiercely over his flute. He stooped and picked it up, a basket of silver tracery heaped with tiny jewelled flowers—Loveday's brooch.

Hugo stood with the brooch in his hand. He had seen it on the front of Loveday's pink dress yesterday evening; he knew it at once—a silver basket heaped with little pink roses and green jewelled leaves. It brought back the picture of Loveday standing here, under the lamp. That is what he thought of first—just Loveday, and how she had taken his breath away because it was the first time he had seen her properly.

He wondered how she had dropped the brooch, and whether she had gone back to Ledlington. He hoped she had gone back, because he didn't like her being in the sort of house where Miller and Hacker could come and go as they chose. He hoped she had gone back to safe, dull Emily Brown.

He turned the brooch over to look at the catch. The catch was all right, but the pin was so much bent that it fixed his attention. What on earth had she done with the pin to bend it like that? She couldn't have worn the brooch in that condition—the pin was all wrenched to one side and wouldn't meet the catch. What had she been doing to wrench it like that? And why had it dropped just here by the table where his flute was lying?

He looked from the table to the brooch, and back again to the table. Then he bent forward and picked up a tiny shred of paper from the carpet just at his feet. It was a scrap of tracing paper. He stared at the bit of paper, and then at the two halves of his flute. The brooch—the flute—the scrap of paper—Loveday. He had wedged the plans pretty hard into the flute. Someone must have had a job to get them out. They might have been prized out with a longish pin; but the pin would get badly bent, and the paper might be torn. An empty flute, a bent pin, a torn scrap of paper, and—Loveday. Hugo very nearly shouted her name aloud, because all at once he was joyfully, unreasoningly sure that it was Loveday who had taken the plans.

He put her brooch in his pocket and examined the table closely. There were one or two more shreds of paper. He picked up the flute and held the open ends to the light. *And the open ends were scratched*—they were most blessedly and indubitably scratched.

The relief was so immense that it set Hugo's spirits bubbling crazily. He flung the flute back on the table, caught up one of Mme. de Lara's violet cushions, whirled round the room with it in an abandoned dance, and finally kicked it from the hearth to the window. He wanted to laugh, and he wanted to shout. Nothing mattered if it was Loveday who had the plans.

But he must get away from here and go to her. The plans must be safe in the hands of Mr. Green of the Air Ministry before Miller discovered that he had been done. He hadn't the faintest idea how he was to get away; but neither had he the faintest doubt that he would be able to do so. He thought the adventure was going extremely well, and the only thing that bothered him was that he couldn't hug Loveday and tell her how clever she was.

A soft, undefined sound made him turn towards the hearth. On either side of the white marble mantelpiece there were hangings of old Spanish embroidery; they covered the wall with straight, pale folds, and showed tints of lemon, straw, dead rose, and ashen blue, wonderfully worked by the patient fingers of half-cloistered ladies.

The sound came again. The right-hand curtain moved, slid back, and discovered a door which Mme. de Lara was closing behind her. In a flash Hugo thought of the evening before, when he and Loveday had been left alone together, and he wondered whether it was Hacker or Hélène de Lara who had stood watching and listening behind those hangings there.

Hélène let the curtains fall and came forward with a finger at her lips. With her other hand she caught at his sleeve.

"Ssh!" And then, "Oh, Hugo!"

"What is it?"

"I want to help you—Hugo."

She breathed quickly, and she was pale; the hand on his arm trembled.

"How can you?"

She whispered close to his ear.

"I can help you to get away."

He drew back half a pace.

"And suppose I don't want to go?"

"You must—you must!"

"W-will you tell me why?"

"Because you *must* go."

This was what Hugo had said himself; but he felt curious to know why Mme. de Lara should say it. He didn't trust her the hundredth part of an inch, and he said,

"Why should I run away from a p-perfectly m-monstrous accusation?"

She was holding his arm now with both her hands.

"Hugo—I must make you see—I must make you understand. You're *ruined* if you stay. You are absolutely ruined, because they have such proofs." She shook him in what appeared to be an access of terror. "There's that letter offering you money. And Leonard says he saw you talking to a stranger in the lane one day, and he says he heard the man say you could fix your own price. And James Hacker says the girl at your rooms told him what friends you and Miller were, and that she'd heard Miller offering you any price you liked. No, Hugo—*listen!* You *must* listen. It—it's breaking my heart. I'm not blaming you—I only want to help you. I only want you to see what proofs they've got. There are other things too—James told you he knew about the telegram. Oh, can't you *see* that you haven't got a chance? And Ambrose is so vindictive. He's cruel—*cruel*. He hasn't any human feelings at all. He only cares for his inventions—and if one of them is touched, he hasn't any mercy. He will send you to prison. I tell you he and James don't know what pity means. Ambrose only cares for his inventions, and James is jealous because he thinks I care what becomes of you. And they've got the proofs. They'll send you to prison." It was a flurry of soft shaken words and soft trembling breath very close to him, while her hands implored him. "Hugo—I'll let you out. They don't know I've come. I can help you to get away. You must go abroad where they can't touch you—I have a friend who will help you. You're not safe in England—Ambrose means to send you to prison."

It wasn't very easy to think in the midst of all this; but something quite clear and definite came to Hugo even as a hot, bright tear fell on his sleeve and glistened there. It made him think of Love-day's brooch, and the way the little flashing stone had caught the light. And quick on that came the clear and definite conclusion. Mme. de Lara was lying when she said that Minstrel and Hacker didn't know that she was here. He felt quite sure that they knew, and he felt quite sure that she was here because they wanted him out of the way. Hélène was there to scare him, to get him to bolt. That was the plan—a much cleverer plan than he had guessed. They wouldn't risk a prosecution. They wouldn't need to risk anything if they could induce Hugo to give himself away by bolting. Hugo in the dock might be dangerous; but Hugo a fugitive in France would be the very convenient scapegoat which they needed. The whole thing stood out as sharp and clear as if a bright light had been turned on it.

Mme. de Lara's voice went on:

"Hugo—speak—say something! I'm not blaming you—I want to help you. And we must be quick—oh, we must be quick. There's no time to be lost."

This, at least, was true. He must get away, and get away quickly. And yet—if Loveday hadn't got the plans, he would be damning himself past hope. Not for the first time, the only thing to do was the thing that would damn him deepest if it didn't come off. It was hit or miss, but he had to chance it.

"Hugo—*say* something," said Hélène de Lara.

Hugo found himself stammering. "W-what do you w-w-want me to s-say?"

"Oh, so many things—only there is not time now. But one day we will meet, and you shall tell me all—all that is in your heart."

Hugo wondered if she would like it if he did. He imagined not. He said,

"W-what c-can I do?"

"Oh, you must go at once—it is your only chance. Have you any money?"

"Yes," said Hugo.

This was horrible. He wanted to be gone. The room was stiflingly hot. Hélène de Lara did not move him now. He came near to hating her. He stepped back and said,

"How c-can I go?"

And in a moment she was at the shuttered door unlocking it.

"This way—you must go this way—down the terrace steps and along the path." Her breath caught. "Oh—the little path! Do you remember? We came along it together. Oh, you must go!"

He asked no better. But she had not played her scene to the finish yet. As he opened the door and stepped out on to the gravel, she was beside him.

"Oh, why cannot I come too?" she breathed.

"*P-please* go in."

But when he had crossed the terrace she was still there, a faint grey ghost in the light which came from the open window.

"Hugo—wait! I have things—to say."

"G-good-bye!"

"No, not good-bye—not like that!" She pushed something down into his pocket. "There is the address I told you of—the friend who will help. You will need a passport, and you must get across quickly. He will help you if you show him what is in the packet. Oh, you must go!"

The last sentence did shake him a little; it had such a heart-broken sound. Was it all acting? He hoped with all his heart that it was—but he wasn't sure.

He had descended a couple of steps, when she called his name in an anguished whisper:

"Hugo—don't go!"

"I m-must."

He turned to say it, and felt her arms about his neck. She kissed him twice. Her face was wet. With a gasp she pushed him away.

"Oh, go—*go!*" she said; and without a word Hugo went.

He had never been so glad to say good-bye to anyone before.

Chapter Thirty-Six

HÉLÈNE DE LARA went back slowly to the house. Once she turned and stood as if she were listening. On the threshold of her room she waited for a long minute looking into the darkness.

Mr. Hacker spoke behind her from the lighted room.

"Hélène! What on earth are you doing? For Heaven's sake, come in and shut the door!"

She came in then, but slowly. The lighted, scented room looked strange; she felt as if it was far away from her. She was still out there on the dark stage of the terrace, a broken-hearted woman sending her young lover away, perhaps for ever. Her face was tear-stained and her eyes tragic.

Ambrose Minstrel, with his back to the fire, cocked an eyebrow and pulled his beard. James Hacker, sitting carelessly on the sofa end, swung his legs and tried to look indifferent.

"A most effective scene!" said Minstrel. "Effective and affecting! I was touched to the quick. My compliments, Hélène!"

Hacker's black eyebrows drew together.

"Well, he's gone," he said—"to the devil, I hope."

"France will do," said Ambrose Minstrel. "I hope he realizes what a vindictive person I am, and that the only way he can escape penal servitude is by putting the Channel between us without a moment's delay. I don't think he's got much brain, but he'd better not have time to use what he's got. I hope you bustled him, Hélène."

Hélène threw back her head.

"He is gone. Is that not enough for you?"

"Come off it!" said Hacker roughly.

She turned on him with a sob.

"Is it not enough that I have done what I said I would do? What do you care how much it has cost me to do it? What does any man care so long as he has what he wants? I tell you I am sick of men and their ways. Oh yes—sick at heart and tired—so tired that I should like to sleep until the world has grown a kinder place for women."

"Chuck it!" said Hacker. He put a hand on her shoulder. "Look here, Hélène, you make me sick when you gas like that. You've done your job—at least I hope you have. Is he going to France?"

Hélène nodded.

"Then that's all right. I told you he'd stampede if you pitched it good and strong. Well, he's off the map, and I think we'll give him twelve hours' start before we notify the police. We've left our telephone off the hook, so the respectable Green won't be able to get at us to-night. Now are you going to feed us?"

"No," said Hélène in a choked, passionate voice.

"I wish you would! I'm fed to the teeth with sardines and cocoa. Give us a decent meal for a change—just to celebrate the occasion."

"The poor boy's ruin and my broken heart—shall we celebrate that?" said Hélène de Lara.

The hand that was on her shoulder closed in a grip that made her cry out, and as the cry left her lips, the front door bell rang in a hurried violent peal which was immediately repeated.

Hacker's grasp tightened for a moment. Then he jumped down and made a stride towards the door.

"Hullo! What's that?"

"It seems to be the front door bell," observed Minstrel. He appeared to derive considerable amusement from the obviously disturbed condition of his assistant's mind. "Perhaps you would like to go and see who it is," he added.

"I have a butler," said Mme. de Lara.

Ambrose Minstrel laughed; and to the sound of his laughter the hall door opened, and at once there came voices, footsteps, the rattle of a handle, and the vehement entrance of Mr. Miller unannounced.

He banged the door behind him and stood up against it out of breath.

"Where is he? Where is he?"

"What is it?" said Ambrose Minstrel sharply.

Hacker was staring incredulously.

"What's up? Speak, can't you!"

Mr. Miller's face was pale and glistening, his red hair rumpled; he seemed half choked with rage and hurry.

"Where is he?" he said, and lapsed into another language. He appeared to be cursing very fluently.

Hacker caught him by the arm.

"Here, what's the good of that? What's happened?"

Miller pulled an envelope out of his coat pocket and flung it furiously on to the floor.

"See what the dash, dash, dash, dash blank has given me! See how he has us fooled!"

"*What?*" said Minstrel.

The one word carried so much violence that Mr. Miller with a gasp stopped swearing.

"He has us betrayed—bamboozled! He has the trick on us played, that cursed secretary of yours!"

"*What?*" said Minstrel again.

He glared first at Miller, and then at the crumpled envelope. Two of his great strides brought him to the door.

"What's this? What are you saying? Pick it up!" he said, and stirred the paper with his foot. "D'you hear what I say? Pick it up and give it to me properly! And don't come using your filthy foreign oaths to me! Do you hear? Pick it up and speak with respect, or out you go! You're not in your damned Leningrad now, Mr. Miller, and you'd do as well to remember it and mind your manners. Thank you—that's better."

He took the envelope with a certain lofty air, drew out the papers which it contained, unfolded them, glanced them rapidly over, and burst into savage laughter.

"He's right! By gum, he's right! Here, Hacker—here's for you!"

He rolled the papers into a rough ball and tossed it to Hacker.

"Read, mark, learn, and inwardly digest! It's the old moral— 'Despise not thine enemy.' We've been done, my dear Hacker— done brown by an innocent, lisping fool of a boy!"

Hacker was smoothing the papers out. He was darkly flushed, but his big hands were steady.

"What is it?" said Hélène de Lara. "What has happened— James?"

Hacker held out the envelope.

"Is this what you took from him at the inn?"

"Yes—it is."

"Your envelope?" He addressed Minstrel.

"My envelope, Hacker—not my plans. Our young friend has most ingeniously extracted the plans. What you have there is rubbish."

"He must have had it ready." Hacker spoke in a dull, brooding voice. There was something alarming about his restraint. "How did he know?"

He took Hélène by the arm with violence.

"Did you tell him? Did you give us away? Because if you did—"

Hélène cried out, "I did not—oh, I did not! Ambrose—he is hurting me! James!"

"Let go of her!" said Minstrel contemptuously. He pulled his beard, frowning.

Miller looked from one to another. He was wiping his face with a dirty silk handkerchief.

"Where is he? And where are my plans?" he burst out. "I come here because at the hotel they tell me that he has gone away in your car, with your chauffeur. It was in that car he came—isn't it? And in that car he go—and what is that? Is it your car—or what is it? What makes this? Where is he? Am I played false with? Do you betray me too? Do you give, and take away? It is your envelope, and not your plans—wasn't they? It is your secretary that gives them, and that goes away in your car—haven't he? And I ask, where are the plans and the young man? And you say—what do you say? I ask where is he—this cursed Ross? And where are my plans?"

"Dry up!" said Hacker.

He left Hélène and came to Minstrel's side.

"Why did he come back?" he said.

Minstrel nodded.

"You have some gleams of intelligence!" He rolled a red, baleful eye at Miller. "That chattering monkey appears to have run to tongue. Yes—you said; why did Ross come here? That's it—why did he?"

"He came here?—he came back?" said Miller excitedly. "And why did he do so—and where are my plans?"

"Hold your tongue!" said Minstrel. "You'd better." He dropped to a low confidential tone. "He changed the plans in the car—got the false ones off on Miller—and then he came back here. Great Jupiter! Why did he do that? Why didn't he get away with the plans? He could have given Leonard the slip easily enough."

He put out a gaunt, stained hand and beckoned Hélène.

"Come here! And mind you tell the truth. Stop acting if you can, and see if you can throw any light on this. Ross came here to you. Now tell the truth—why did he come?"

"Oh!" said Hélène. It was a sharp cry of protest.

"He followed you. Why did he follow you?"

An odd quivering smile broke the line of her lips.

"I think you'd better answer," said Minstrel.

Hélène flung out her hands.

"Oh, you men!" she said. She looked at him through her eyelashes. "Have you never followed a woman, Ambrose?"

Minstrel showed his teeth in an ugly grin.

"You *invited* him here?"

She laughed.

"How dreadfully obvious! If you want to know, I played a little trick on him—when he was asleep at the inn. I took his flute, and I left a note to tell him that if he wanted it—" She smiled and looked down; her small foot tapped the floor.

"I see. And he came—for—his—flute—"

He stared across her at the table where the flute lay between the grinning china dogs—stared, then went over and picked the two halves up, one in each hand. He came back as he had gone, slowly. Then all at once, with an indescribable ferocity of manner,

"He came for his flute, did he? Then why did he go away without it? You little play-acting liar!"

"Ambrose!" It was a frightened gasp.

"Hélène!" There was a frightful mockery in voice and manner.

She put her hands to her face and shivered.

"Ambrose—don't! James!" She took a step towards Hacker, but Minstrel's long arm came out and plucked her back; the bony fingers clamped her wrist.

"Ambrose—it is true. I would be afraid to tell you anything that was not true—*Ambrose*."

He gave his raucous laugh.

"Stick to that—you'll find it safer. So you took his flute. Why?"

She spoke from behind her hands in a sobbing whisper.

"I wanted—him—to come—and get it."

"A youthful idyll in fact! Strephon and Phyllis!" He pushed her to arm's length, pulled down her hands roughly enough, and laughed again. "Phyllis! Great Jupiter—*Phyllis!* Well, you took the flute, and he came for it. He—came here—for his flute—at a moment when everything—*everything* depended on his getting clear away. He came—back here—*for his flute*."

He had slipped the two halves into his left hand. He tossed them now into the air and saw them fall.

"I don't think he came back for your *beaux yeux*, Hélène. He came back for his flute because—the plans were in the flute."

"By gum!" said Hacker. The dark flush ran up to the roots of his hair. "By gum—you're right!"

He caught up one of the halves and shook it.

"It's empty—now," said Minstrel. "The plans were in the flute, and we left him alone with it and helped him to get away."

"What is this—what is this?" said Miller. "What is it that you say? What have he done?"

Hacker made a plunge at the door.

"He hasn't gone far. If he's made for the station, I'll catch him with the car."

"No!" said Hélène. "No, James—wait! You're wrong. Listen! No—really. Oh, you must listen to me! I was here when he came in. He went straight to the flute, and he picked it up. And when he turned it in his hand, I could see into the halves of it, and they were empty."

"You're not making this up? You'd better not." This was Minstrel with a rasp in his voice.

"No—it is true—really true. And besides—"

She hesitated.

"Besides? Go on!"

"Ambrose! How rough you are! I am telling you. Just before he came in, I was looking at the flute, you know. I put it together—I tried to play it. Then I took it apart again. There was nothing in it—*really*, except—"

"Except *what*?"

"A little shred of paper dropped out—on to the table—oh, the smallest piece. I heard him coming and—"

Minstrel and Hacker were at the table. They spoke low to each other. Hacker moved the china dogs, went down on his hands and knees, searched the carpet, and found what Hugo had dropped—a shred of tracing paper. He got up, holding it out on his palm.

"The plans were there—the plans are gone. Will you swear the flute was empty when you handled it?"

"Yes, it was empty. It was empty before Hugo came in."

"The plans were there. This is a piece of the paper. You brought the flute here, and then—what happened then?"

"I brought it in here. I put it on the table."

"What is all this?" said Mr. Miller. "I cannot understand what happens. And where is Ross? That is what I ask—haven't I? Where is that cursed Ross?"

Hacker went on without taking any notice.

"You put it on the table. Was anyone here?"

"Loveday! Oh!" said Hélène. She gave a little scream. "Oh!"

Minstrel and Hacker were close on either side of her. Miller made a sound, and then stopped because Minstrel jerked about and looked at him.

"*Loveday?*" said Hacker. Then quickly, "Did you leave her alone? Could she have got the papers out?"

"I went to the telephone," said Hélène.

"And left the flute?"

"Yes—I left it. How could I know?"

"Then she stole the plans."

"Great Jupiter!" said Minstrel quite softly.

Hacker broke in again.

"Where is she?"

"Gone home—gone back to Ledlington—to Emily Brown."

None of them had heard the door open. The sad-faced butler stood there looking apologetic.

"It is Mrs. Brown on the telephone, madame."

"Mrs. Brown!" Hélène's hand went to her throat.

"Yes, madame." He stood there bowing.

Minstrel nodded, and Hélène de Lara went out quickly.

They heard her cross the hall, and then the door closed behind Antoine. Miller began to say something, and stopped. Hacker stood with the two halves of the flute in his hand; he turned them this way and that awkwardly. Minstrel jerked an impatient shoulder and, walking to the fire, thrust at it with his foot. The log fell over flaring, and a shower of sparks went up. Miller looked from Hacker to Minstrel, met a hot resentful stare, and shifted his gaze. The dirty handkerchief came out again. No one spoke until, with the sound of running feet, Hélène came back, opening the door with a push and slamming it behind her. Her eyes were really frightened.

"She's gone!" she said.

"Gone?"

"Loveday—she's gone!"

"Pull yourself together."

"She's gone!" said Hélène in a shaken voice.

"Emily says—they found her suitcase in the porch—nobody has seen her—she's gone."

"Then she *did* take the plans!" said Hacker with an oath.

Chapter Thirty-Seven

THE CAR RAN smoothly down the dark road. Loveday watched the darkness flow past. She felt as if she were flying, as if the excitement which possessed her were bearing her up like wings, up and on to some place which she couldn't see. She had never felt so thrilled in her life.

The suitcase was on the seat beside her, and Hélène's book was in the suitcase, and the plans—Minstrel's plans—Hugo's plans—were in the book. She had carried them off under their very noses—yes, under Hélène's very own powdered nose; and she was getting away with them in Hélène's own car, specially provided because Hélène wanted to get rid of her before Hugo came. It was *frightfully* funny.

What was she going to do about the plans? Hugo must have hidden them in the flute—and he wouldn't have done that if they hadn't been simply frightfully important. She wanted terribly to know what had been happening. Hélène had gone off—to London— no, of course it wasn't London really—Hélène had gone off to the place that horrid Hacker had told her to go to when he had said she must be sure to be punctual. Well, anyway Hélène had gone—

and she had been away for hours—and when she came back she had Hugo's flute—and she was making pretty sure that Hugo would follow her—that was why she had sent Loveday away.

Loveday sat up quivering with impatience. At first she had only thought of getting away with the papers; now she began to think about Hugo arriving at Torring House—he might be getting there at this very minute—he might be there now. Every moment she and the plans were being carried farther away.

All the bubbling pleasure went out of her. If Hugo had had the papers and lost them, that horrid Hacker might be able to hurt him. She must give the papers back to him before anything dreadful happened—she simply must.

They had run about two miles, when the car slowed down and stopped. Loveday looked out. There was a red lamp ahead of them, and from away on the right came the chuffing sound of a train.

The chauffeur looked round.

"It's the level crossing, miss. The train's just coming in—we shan't be long."

Loveday sat back again. An idea had come into her mind like a flash of light. It wasn't there just before she saw the red lamp, but it was there quite bright and clear by the time Albert Green was saying "miss." She sat back and pulled the suitcase towards her. Thank goodness it was Albert who was driving, and not the thin, dark foreign chauffeur who had taken Hélène to London; he had sharp eyes that frightened her a little. But Albert was just a bun-faced Ledlington boy. Loveday wasn't the least bit afraid of Albert.

She felt for the book that held the plans, folded the papers up as tight as they would go, and pushed them well down inside the pocket of her coat. Then she turned the handle of the door on her left and waited.

The train puffed into the station and left the crossing clear. The gates began to move, and just as Albert let in the clutch, Loveday opened the door and slipped out into the road.

She watched the red tail-light get smaller and smaller as the car receded, and then, turning, began to run back along the road by which she had just come. When she had run a little way she walked, and when she had walked a little she ran again.

Two miles is a long way at night on a lightless road. Loveday didn't like the dark; the trees made rustling noises overhead, things creaked in the hedgerows, and the sound of her own feet frightened her. She stopped running because she felt as if everyone must hear the sound of her feet. And then she laughed, because there wasn't anyone to hear. There were empty woods, and empty fields, and an empty lonely road. She stopped laughing. It was very dark and very lonely, and she didn't like it.

She was panting a little when she came into the drive that led up to Torring House. It was even darker here than it had been on the road, because the trees hung over it and blotted out the moonless sky. She thought she heard a footstep, and stood still to listen. Then, in a panic, she ran on again. She could see the lights of the house, and she wanted to get closer to them.

Her heart was beating so fast when she stopped that she couldn't hear anything else, and the more she strained to listen, the less she could hear. From where she stood she could see the fanlight over the hall door. She looked at it, and all at once the door was opened wide.

Antoine had opened it. She could see him with the light shining down on him from the globe immediately over the door. He had opened the door to let someone in. Loveday saw a man's back, and then she very nearly called out, because just before Antoine shut the door the man turned and she saw his face. And it was Hugo. It was Hugo whose footsteps had frightened her. It was Hugo—and she had missed him.

Albert Green drove on from the level-crossing in a thoroughly pleasant and contented frame of mind. His home was in Ledlington, and as soon as he had dropped Miss Leigh he meant to go round and see his young lady, who lived in the same street. Her name was Maudie Tillett, and she was a very superior young lady. She worked in a milliner's shop, and it was only since Albert had become second chauffeur at Torring House that Miss Tillett had so far condescended as to accept from him a lady's dress ring set with pearls and turquoise.

Albert toyed with the idea of taking Maudie for a spin. Maudie hadn't seen him with the Bentley; and he had a feeling that he would like Maudie see him with the Bentley—Maudie was rather high in her notions. Pleasant thoughts of showing off before Maudie continued to occupy him until he drew up at the gate of Mr. Brown's villa on the outskirts of Ledlington.

He got down, opened the door, and received a severe shock. The rug was on the floor, and Miss Leigh's suitcase was on the seat; but Miss Leigh wasn't anywhere at all. He moved the rug and he moved the suitcase, he walked round the car and returned to the open door and the prospect of a seat occupied only by a suitcase.

When he told Maudie about it a little later, he said he was struck all of a heap. He pushed back his cap and scratched his head. He was not a quick thinker, but when put to it he could "do a bit of thinking." He told Maudie so. "I dunno where she gave me the slip, and I dunno how she gave me the slip, and if you ask me why she gave me the slip, well, you're asking me something I can't tell you. But I can do a bit of thinking if I like, and the longer I got thinking about it, the clearer I could see that I was going to get into trouble over it. And what I said to myself was, 'Now why should I get into trouble for the like of her? It's everyone for himself when it comes to a row, and I didn't *ask* her to give me the slip.' So I made up my mind what to do, and I done it, and I'm not telling anyone what I done—only you, Maudie, because I know you're safe, and it stands to reason you wouldn't want to get me into a row."

"That's right," said Miss Tillett.

When Albert had finished thinking, he picked up Miss Leigh's suitcase, tiptoed up the steps with it, and deposited it in the porch just outside the hall door. He then went back to the Bentley and drove away to see Maudie. As far as he was concerned, he had taken Miss Leigh to Laburnum Lodge and left her on the front door step. What had happened to her after that was no concern of his.

He took Maudie for a very pleasant spin.

Chapter Thirty-Eight

LOVEDAY WAS tired and cold. She was tired of the dark, and the damp that dripped from the trees, and she was tired of waiting all alone in the cold whilst Hugo was in a warm scented room with Hélène de Lara. Sometimes she walked up and down, and sometimes she stood still. The time dragged by in slow, dark minutes.

Minstrel and Hacker passed within a yard of her, walking fast—black figures going by without a word, black figures unknown but frightening. She held her breath until they were quite gone, then turned and stared at the door under the fanlight until it opened and the two black figures went in. She recognized Hacker, and guessed at his companion. The door shut again.

They were in there—and Hugo was in there—and she was outside in a horrible dark, cold drive without the least idea of what was happening or of what they were doing to Hugo—they might be doing simply anything. Loveday began to feel quite desperate. She felt she simply must find out what was going on. If she left the drive she risked missing Hugo. But she just had to risk it—she just had to find out what was going on.

She ran along the dark path that led through the shrubbery to the steps under the terrace. The window of Hélène's sitting-room was there just across the terrace, only a few yards away. It was there, but she couldn't see any light. She crossed the gravel and pressed close to the glass. It was all black, thick, opaque; she couldn't see anything. But she could hear. She could hear voices, but they were faint and muffled. That meant that the shutters were closed. She strained with all her might, but the voices were only a blurred murmur that told her nothing.

She could not have said how long she stood there. It seemed a very long time. Sometimes there was no sound at all, and sometimes the sound was so faint that she could hardly be sure of it. And then, all of sudden, there was a real sound, very sharp and clear and most terrifyingly close at hand. It was the click of a key. Someone was opening the shutter. Someone was going to open the door.

Loveday didn't know she was going to run, but she found herself on the other side of the terrace quite close to the steps, with all the breath gone out of her and her heart thumping like mad. The long French window had opened. Light came from it in a beam that died gradually into dusk.

Loveday ran down the steps.

There were two people coming across the terrace. She stepped off the path and took the old black yew-tree for shelter, just as Hugo had done on the night Hélène first brought him to Torring House. It was Hugo and Hélène coming now. She was sure of that even before she heard their voices. She held her breath. What did it mean? Hélène and Hugo! She held her breath. They were there, just at the top of the steps, and she heard Hugo say, "Good-bye," and heard him stammer over saying it.

Loveday felt something like a little fiery spark—she thought of it like that afterwards when she tried to understand what had happened. There was a little fiery spark. It went off with a flash somewhere in her mind, and everything in her caught fire. Hélène's murmuring voice was like a wind that fanned the flames—Hélène's whispering, heart-broken voice.

Loveday came forward a step. She didn't care now whether they saw her or not. She felt like a blazing fire that everyone could see.

Hugo was coming down. No—he had stopped. Against the lighted window she saw two dark figures that melted into one.

"Hugo—don't go!" Hélène—Hélène said that; and Hugo stammered, "I must." The two dark figures were one.

The fire in Loveday died with a dreadful suddenness at the sound of a kiss. It died, and she was cold—burnt out and cold.

"Oh, go—go!" said Hélène.

She pushed Hugo away.

Hugo came down the steps, and passed so close to her that she could have easily touched him. She didn't touch him. She stood still.

Hugo went away. He went away down the dark path, under the dark trees. She heard the sound of his feet—and she stopped hearing it—there wasn't any sound at all. Hugo had gone away.

Loveday came out on to the path and looked back at the house. She felt like Lot's wife; she felt like a frozen pillar of salt, frozen tears. She looked back at the house, and she saw Hélène standing on the step of her sitting-room with the light behind her.

Hélène stood there looking after Hugo. And all at once Mr. Hacker came up behind her, and she turned and went in. The door shut, the curtain fell. The house was dark. Loveday was all alone.

She put her hands before her face to shut the darkness out, and just as she did so, something moved close beside her. If her hands hadn't been over her face, she might have screamed before she could stop herself. As it was, her cold fingers pressed her lips and the scream was only a choking gasp.

Something moved, rustled, and scuttered away. A rat, or a rabbit—she didn't know what it was; but she began to run, and as soon as she began to run, panic came over her. She ran without knowing where she was going. Once her coat caught on something. She jerked it free so desperately that the strong stuff tore and the sound of the ripping cloth added to her terror. She bruised her shoulder and her knee before she reached the drive. She ran on not knowing where she was.

Hugo didn't run. He walked at a good brisk pace, because he had to get to Ledlington, find Loveday, and get away to town with the plans. When, he heard the sound of someone running behind him, he stopped to listen, and before he knew what was happening Loveday ran into him in the dark and nearly knocked him down. She was running blindly with her hands out before her. They struck his arm, and she came sobbing and choking against his shoulder.

He knew it was Loveday almost before he knew that it was going to be anyone at all; he heard her sob before she touched him. And then, in a second, she was in his arms and he was saying her name:

"Loveday! Loveday!"

Loveday's panic was so great that it could hardly be greater; yet when her groping hands touched a man's arm she came to the nightmare point where a dream *must* break because we can bear no more. Her dream broke when Hugo's voice said "Loveday!" and his arms tame round her close and safe. She dropped her head upon his shoulder and stayed there, neither breathing nor thinking.

"Loveday! What is it? Loveday—darling!"

Loveday drew breath again, but she did not lift her head.

"What is it? Have they hurt you?"

Loveday drew away.

"I've got the plans!" she said.

Chapter Thirty-Nine

They caught a train at Meade Halt—caught it by the skin of their teeth, running for it as they had run for Loveday's train on the night of their first meeting.

When the train left the station, Loveday sat back in her corner and shut her eyes. She didn't want to talk and she didn't want to think, and she didn't want Hugo to touch her. They hadn't really talked at all; because you can't talk when you're running. She had given Hugo the plans and said, now she would go back to Ledlington. And Hugo had said, how could she go back to Ledlington all by herself in the middle of the night?

Loveday was miserably aware that if she had had any proper pride she would have insisted on going back to Ledlington. Nine o'clock isn't the middle of the night really; and even if it were, a girl with any proper pride would rather walk seven miles by herself along a lonely country road than run away to London with someone who didn't love her, or he wouldn't have kissed other people.

Loveday despised herself dreadfully for not having any proper pride. She felt she would rather die than go along that dark road again with things rustling in the hedges and strange, crying sounds coming suddenly out of the dark cloudy air. She was passionately glad to be in a lighted railway carriage with Hugo; but she wouldn't speak to him, and she certainly wouldn't let him kiss her.

Hugo felt dreadfully damped, because he wanted very much to kiss Loveday and to tell her how clever she was, and all about Treneath and his uncle's will being found. And then he called himself a perfect beast, because of course she was most frightfully tired and it was much better for her to go to sleep—only he didn't see why she couldn't have gone to sleep with her head on his shoulder.

At the next station a fat man in a large overcoat got in, and did a cross-word puzzle all the way up to town.

The clock on Mr. Smith's mantelpiece struck eleven.

"Well," said Mr. Smith, "we shall see what we shall see." He addressed a stout, round, plump-faced gentleman, who gazed at him with some asperity and replied,

"That's all very well."

"We shall see what we shall see," repeated Mr. Smith. "To which I would add the cheering phrases, 'Don't be down-hearted,' and 'Never say die.'"

The short stout gentleman snorted. "That's all very well!"

"You repeat yourself, my dear Green," said Mr. Smith.

Mr. Green snorted again.

"If what you say is true, that man Minstrel's assurance is past belief."

"Nothing is past belief," said Mr. Smith placidly.

"I tell you," said the indignant Mr. Green, "I tell you, he browbeat me—he positively browbeat me. He said if we hadn't worried him out of his life, he'd never have sent the papers off by this young fellow-me-lad of a secretary—said it was my fault if they were lost—*my fault!* Personally, I believe the man's out of his mind. He raved up and down my room like—like a hyena, and he told me he'd driven at seventy miles an hour to get here. I tell you I think he's mad."

"There's a little method in his madness," said Mr. Smith dryly.

"He's a most unpleasant fellow to deal with— offensive—downright offensive. He seemed to think I was a policeman—a *policeman!* Seemed to think it was my job to go dashing round the country arresting his damned secretary! Told me in the most offensive terms that it was my job! Mad, I say! Anyhow the plans are gone!"

The door opened. Mr. Smith's confidential servant approached him.

"Someone to see you, sir."

He laid a strip of paper on the arm of his master's chair. Mr. Smith took it and got up.

"The dining-room, Walters." Then, as the man withdrew, "Will you wait a minute, Green? I think—no, I won't tell you what I think. Converse with Ananias until I return."

Ananias cocked a cold eye at the guest as Mr. Smith went out. When the door had closed, he sidled to the end of his perch, once more regarded Mr. Green with distaste, and then in a very ostentatious manner turned his back.

Mr. Smith went into the dining-room, and found two young people where he had only expected to find one. Mr. Hugo Ross was on one side of the room, and Miss Loveday Leigh on the other. Mr. Hugo Ross was flushed, and Miss Loveday Leigh was pale—Miss Loveday Leigh was very pale indeed. Hugo was the nearest to him.

He said, "I've got 'em, sir! I've g-g-g-got 'em!" And without more ado he thrust some badly crumpled papers upon Mr. Smith, who took them in an absent-minded manner and continued to look inquiringly at the pale girl on the other side of the room.

"L-Loveday got 'em!" said Hugo eagerly.

"Indeed?"

"I thought I'd absolutely mucked it up. You see, he sent me off to town with the p-plans, and they drugged my c-c-coffee—only of course I wasn't such a mug as to drink it. And I let them take the p-plans Ananias sent me, because I'd hidden the real ones in my f-flute—only they took the flute too, and I thought I'd absolutely m-mucked it up—only Loveday got them back. And we had to run like billy-oh to catch our train, and I thought we'd better come straight to you, because I haven't the l-least idea where to find Mr. Green at this time of night."

"How very lucid!" said Mr. Smith. "A—er—most masterly abstract." He glanced at the crumpled papers, then gazed at the pale young lady. "Miss—er—?"

"L-L-Leigh," said Hugo, and blushed.

Mr. Smith bowed.

"If Miss Leigh will excuse us, I should like you to repeat, and perhaps elaborate, that highly interesting statement of yours to my friend, Mr. Green—he happens to be in the next room. I feel sure that the flute episode will appeal to Green."

He led the way from the room. The door closed.

Loveday sat down on a chair by the fire. All the excitement was over. Everything was most terribly flat and dull. A horrid succession of flat, cold, dull, unprofitable days stretched out before her to the very end of her life. She would rather—oh, *so* much rather—be escaping in breathless terror hand in hand with Hugo. What was the use of saying what she would rather do? She would never run away hand in hand with Hugo any more. It was all over. Everything was quite safe, and dull, and cold.

She put her head down on the arm of Mr. Smith's shabby old leather chair and began to cry the dreadfully miserable tears of buoyant youth. She went on crying for a very long time.

She didn't know when she drifted into sleep, but she woke with a start to find Hugo's arms round her. Hugo was kissing her, and the dreadful thing was that before she quite knew what she was doing she had kissed him back. It was frightful.

She drew herself away with a sob.

"Don't! Oh don't!"

"Darling—it's all right—it's all *right*. Green's got the plans. We've brought it off! Aren't you glad? Aren't you happy? Darling— what's the matter—why mayn't I kiss you?"

Loveday strained away from him.

"You kissed *her!*"

"Loveday!"

"You kissed *her*—Hélène. Oh, I saw you!"

It was Hugo's turn to draw away.

"Loveday, you don't believe that!" He got up. "Loveday!"

Loveday got up too. It is easier to be proud when you are standing up.

"You *did* kiss her! I came back to find you, and I was at the bottom of the steps—and you said good-bye to her—and she kissed you—I *know* she did!"

Hugo didn't blush; he got white. A minute ago everything had been all right; and now everything was too rotten for words. He looked at Loveday, and Loveday looked at him.

"You don't love me," said Loveday. "Go away! Go to *Ellen!*"

"Thank you!" said Hugo.

He turned away. She had hurt him so frightfully that he didn't want her to see his face. He wanted a minute to pull himself together. Why had everything gone to bits like this? He turned away.

"Why did you kiss her?" said Loveday.

"I didn't."

Something had happened. Loveday believed him. She couldn't explain why she believed him, but she did. Whether it was something in his voice, or something in her own heart, she couldn't have said. But she believed him. She believed him, and she said in la laughing, crying voice,

"Ellen was always a most frightful snatch-cat. Emily always told me she was. I believe she tried to snatch Andrew. Oh, just fancy anyone wanting to snatch *Andrew!* Hugo—are you frightfully angry?"

"Yes, I am," said Hugo. He turned his head away.

Loveday had no proper pride. She flung her arms round his neck.

"Hugo—don't be! I'm frightfully miserable—at least I was frightfully miserable when I thought you didn't love me."

"Perhaps I don't," said Hugo; but he put his arms round her.

"You *do*—I know you do! You don't love Ellen a bit—you love me!" She put her face up to be kissed. "You haven't told me what's happened."

"You didn't seem to want to know."

"I didn't want to know—when I thought you didn't love me. But I want to know now. Tell me! Tell me what's happened!"

Hugo hugged her.

"Green's in there," he said—"and he's got, the plans. So that's all right. But I say—would you believe it?—he's had Minstrel and Hacker here already!"

"How could he?"

"They must have run the innards out of that old car. Don't you see? They wanted to get in first with their story."

"Hugo—he doesn't believe them!"

"I don't think he wants to have an official row with Minstrel. I think they'll patch the whole thing up and save Minstrel's face. I don't think they care so long as they've got the plans. They couldn't prove anything, you know."

"But *you*—" said Loveday. "Hugo—what happens to *you?*"

He laughed.

"It's not me-r-it's *us*," he said.

"Oh, tell me!"

"My uncle's will has turned up."

"Oh!" said Loveday.

"He's left me Treneath. I knew he meant to—but he really did it. Loveday, we can get married! We shan't have to wait. We can get married at once. You'll love Treneath. Oh, Loveday, you will—won't you?"

Mr. Smith opened the door gently. He had just let Mr. Green out and made some noise about it, but apparently neither Hugo nor Loveday had noticed anything. They did not notice that the door had opened, neither did they notice when it closed again.

Mr. Smith closed it and returned to his study. He took out his watch and glanced at it.

"I think I'll give them another five minutes, Ananias," he said.

THE END

Lightning Source UK Ltd.
Milton Keynes UK
UKOW06f1655170616

276538UK00022B/330/P